I0566125

CRIMSON
Footprints III

THE FINALE

SHEWANDA PUGH

Crimson Footprints III
Published by Razor's Edge
2nd Printing
Printed in the United States of America
All rights reserved worldwide

Copyright © 2017 Shewanda Pugh
Cover art and Interior Formatting by Cassy Roop of Pink Ink Designs
www.pinkinkdesigns.com

This is a work of fiction. Names, characters, places, and incidents are either the product of the author's imagination or used fictitiously. Any resemblance to actual events, locales, or persons, living or dead, is entirely coincidental.

This book, its contents, and its characters are the sole property of Shewanda Pugh. No part of this publication may be reproduced, stored in or introduced into a retrieval system, or transmitted in any form or by any means (electronic, mechanical, photocopying, recording, or otherwise) without written, express permission from the author. To do so without permission is punishable by law. Please purchase only authorized electronic editions, and do not participate in or encourage electronic piracy of copyrighted materials. Your support of the author's rights is appreciated.

CRIMSON
Footprints III
THE FINALE

CHAPTER
one

DYING WAS SUCH A NASTY BUSINESS. All coughs and withered limbs with promises laid bare. Deena Tanaka knew it well. Not in the silent march of anticipated demise; no, her recollections came from violent interruptions of life in its prime.

Her grandmother was dying. An old woman comprised solely of hope and sharp wit, love and biting judgment. She had emptied out her tank without refills to spare. Deena discovered that even when the very old died, it burned her with a righteous injustice better suited for the young.

The old woman cleared her throat. Rocks and sand paper on ash, Deena thought; that was what it sounded like. Her husband, Tak, set aside his sketch pad, unfolded long legs, and stood. Three strides brought him across the harsh lighting of Grandma Emma's hospital room and to her side without a word. He moved like music without melody, Deena realized, like song without sound. Silent, yet purposeful, graceful without pretention; he simply didn't have to try. Some things, like people, simply were.

Tak grabbed the rose water pitcher from a nearby stand and filled a paper cup with water. He adjusted Grandma Emma's seat, leaned forward, and brought the drink to her lips. She sputtered, choked, and finally recalled the rhythm of drinking—it was the same way each time. When she'd had her fill, Tak sat the cup aside, smoothed down her hair, and adjusted the incline of her bed until she lay parallel to the floor once more. Deena came over and slipped a hand into her husband's. Together, they watched and waited for her to close her eyes.

Grandma Emma snorted out a laugh.

"You two gonna hover over me in death, too?"

Tak grinned.

"Only if you'll do me the honor of your unparalleled company," he said.

She opened her eyes because she could always manage that for Tak.

"Old dog," she murmured. "Always too fresh at the mouth."

Tak sat on the bed's edge, pulling his wife by the hand that still held his. Despite the banter, despite the lightness in his tone, she saw the worry lines that cornered his eyes and the frown pulling down the edges of his mouth.

"I love you," Deena mouthed. Tak smiled faintly and returned the words.

Grandma Emma groaned, no doubt touched by a shade of pain.

"I've been waiting," she said, "on my boy to visit. All day and he ain't seen about his mama."

Tak and Deena exchanged a look. Her father was her grandmother's only son, murdered when Deena was eleven.

She moved to say as much, only to have the slight shake of her husband's head thwart her.

"I'm gonna die," Grandma Emma announced. "Soon."

She opened her eyes to see how the declaration sat with them. Deena stood, hand still looped with her husband's, arms limp at her sides, unsure of what to do with herself.

It was one thing for them to know it, to be told it by the doctors, and quite another for Emma to resign herself to it.

"You can't think like that," Deena said. "Don't let them have the final say—"

Her grandmother waved a hand and choked out a laugh. "God handed in his verdict. The coroner's waiting on me."

Deena blinked.

"What am I supposed to say? You're my grandmother. I don't want you to—"

"You've had me locked up in this sick folks' prison for months. It's time you let me out."

Her gaze swept the confines of the upper level hospital room, taking in the starched and well-tucked sheets, the narrowness of her bed, the endless units beeping and judging and handing down verdicts with each assessment of her body. Sharp white lines formed the walls, polished linoleum for the floor, and fluorescent lights bright enough to dilate the pupils reared down on them, as if warming a chicken to hatching. Just outside her window, the Atlantic Ocean stretched on, always beyond their view with her insistence that she keep the blinds closed.

"Grandma, you will be fine. You have the very best doctors in the city and—and—"

They could do nothing for her, of course. Had done nothing, but make her comfortable.

She looked to Tak for help.

"Out," Grandma Emma managed. "Out of here."

End stage Alzheimer's. A place where speech sometimes made no sense or was forgotten. Where food could be inhaled instead of eaten. Where privacy during bodily functions was a long forgotten privilege.

Her grandmother's gaze shifted from Deena to her husband.

"You," she said.

Tak leaned forward, already in the throes of some secret conversation, judging by the way his mouth turned up.

"Get me out of here," she said.

He released Deena's hand and took one of Grandma Emma's in both of his.

"Tell me where," he said.

Deena scoffed, earning only a flutter of lashes from him.

"Tak, we can't—"

"Tell me where," he said again, softer still. "Anywhere you say."

Her grandmother's smile spread wide as the grandest valley. Her body shook with the roughest of asthmatic laughs. It ended in great gasps.

"That how you get my granddaughter? You ol' swindler."

Tak leaned over and whispered in her ear, whispered with the corners of his mouth turned up. He set her laughing till she choked. Deena swatted him on the arm.

"What have I told you about that?" she said. "She shouldn't—you shouldn't—"

Except he said something else, and her grandmother roared anew, making her granddaughter wonder when she'd seen her so happy.

"She's delicate," Deena said. Except she wasn't and she never had been.

Deena rose and went to the corner, leaving them to their hushed talk.

It was their way. Even on death's doorstep, apparently.

She snatched back the curtains, took a seat in the corner, drew up her shawl, and looked out on night's landscape.

Cool air fogged the windows, blotting out the seamless expanse of ocean she expected. A rattle of window hinted at the howling winds that came next. For three days, winter had been near frigid in Miami. All this from a place that saw beach-time on Christmas Day and surfing on New Year's.

Deena glanced over at her grandmother and her husband.

They were plotting, having dropped all pretense of humor. The man she loved and the woman she loved, voices hushed as not to be overheard. But Deena didn't care. She'd veto whatever scheme the two had set their sights on. Rest, comfort, and medical care were what her grandmother needed. Nothing else would suffice.

Eventually, Deena began to drift. Long days at work, checking in on the kids, and bedside duty every night at the hospital meant that sleep came in snatches and whispers. For now, her grandmother's illness had shoved aside mounting worries about her oldest son, Tony, getting into the right colleges, thoughts of Mia picking up her grades, or the possibility of Noah calming down. For now, she could think of nothing but her grandmother and all their wasted moments, stolen by stubbornness and disagreements.

"Dee."

Deena woke with a start, scorched by the certainty that it had happened, that death had come on her watch. But Tak's wide-eyed look and shake of the head said no, they had a little longer.

"I need to talk to you," he said.

They sat in the shadows, all lights extinguished in her sleep so that only the one over the doorway remained. Tak's face floated, hollowed and shadowy, camp ghost-story style and divested of its body.

"I'm listening," Deena said.

He drew away with a bite of his lower lip and a pinched expression. Wrestling and weighing his words. Accepting and rejecting each one.

"I promised your grandmother we'd take her somewhere."

"Well, that's fine. But it wasn't in your power to promise."

Something flickered there, a wink of annoyance, a shadow of challenge. Just as quick as it appeared, it was gone, his expression smoothed out to earnestness.

"Hear me out," he said. "She hasn't been anywhere her whole life, Dee. Only where she was born in Eufaula, Alabama, and the one time we evacuated to California for the storm. We talked—"

"You talked?" Deena said doubtfully. Her grandmother hadn't been lucid enough to navigate the intricacies of a conversation for a while now. Their discussion, whatever it was, had to have been entirely one-sided, right?

"We talked," Tak repeated, firmer still. "And this is what she said. She had me take it down."

He stood, lean body unfolding in skimp lighting, and dug deep into the pocket of his jeans. Long-sleeved black thermal stretched over muscles flexing imperceptibly, flat against well-worn jeans and hard, narrow hips. Age had done him justice as superbly as his father. They said that black didn't crack. Hell, Deena thought, there wasn't a monopoly on that after all.

"She even signed it," Tak said. "After I read it to her."

Deena looked around. "How long have I been sleep again?"

It didn't seem long enough for a signed contract. Earlier that day, she couldn't get her grandmother to say if she wanted red Jell-O or green, but a pretty man could do wonders, it seemed.

Deena took the paper, which she read over and over again, before dropping it to the floor.

"Dee—"

"No. Hell no."

"Sweetheart, it's what she wants."

"She doesn't know what she wants!" Deena turned from him, an old familiar urge to scream bubbling to the surface. Any mention of her family, of her kin, had that sort of power.

"You can't possibly want this," she said. "Or think it's a remotely good idea."

Tak dropped down next to her. "I want her to have peace. And I love her enough to make that happen."

Deena looked up at him then looked away. She exhaled air she hadn't known she'd hoarded and looked down at the paper once again.

"It's not fair when you say it that way. I need choices, Tak. Control. You know that, don't you?"

"I know it. But that's not always an option."

She shot a look at a blackness devoid of stars, bereft of clouds and as emptied as she felt at the moment.

"All of them?" Deena said. "An open invitation to Hammonds and Tanakas?"

Tak had the decency to offer an apologetic smile. "Apparently, she wants nothing less."

CHAPTER
Two

WATER RUSHED FROM THE FAUCET IN A burst of
energy Tak couldn't hope to replicate. Both hands
in, he allowed the coolness to run into and over his hands,
before bending over enough to splash his face. Maybe sanity
would find him again.

He hadn't meant to overstep his wife's feelings or to
minimize them, even. Instead, he'd reached a junction where
he felt she was making the wrong choice. And like men were
hardwired to do, he snatched the wheel of the car, jumped
the curb, and ran them both into a proverbial sidewalk of
people.

Still, he wasn't convinced of his wrongness—only in the
hastiness of his decision. But this was the woman who raised
his wife and his brother's wife, for whatever that was worth.

Their happiness was indebted to her; their lives intertwined. Even if hers did stand at an end.

So, she wanted her family together. She wanted her granddaughters back: back and in the bosom of the family they'd understandably fled. After all, he'd been the one to convince Deena that her happiness wasn't tied to their approval, their affection, their understanding of who and what she was. And since she'd gotten that message, finally gotten it, she'd unfurled into a woman he'd only sensed, but already loved. Steely, heart beat-steady, and certain of her worth, she gave love with a fierceness that belied her upbringing. In spite of all that, he told himself, even as he rushed back for an encore.

Tak turned off the water and sighed.

Everything in him screamed to protect her from another whisper or hint, another moment of ache. Yet, he couldn't protect her from life, from family, for whatever truth waited for her.

And according to Grandma Emma, more truth was to be had.

THEIR TRAVEL AGENT had hell ahead of him without realizing it. A family reunion, he'd said. Wonderful. You're footing the bill? Even better. Yes, yes. I'd be more than happy to field all the arrangements, he'd told Tak again and again.

He thought the Tanakas were so generous for the bonus they'd given him, on top of the pre-established commission.

"No worries," Tak told him. "When it's done, you'll have earned this money."

So the fun began of gathering his family and hers on short notice. For Tak's brother, Kenji, the Major League Baseball season had just ended, freeing up his ability to travel. His wife, Deena's younger sister, Lizzie, while available, took far more cajoling and smooth talking than Tak had in his arsenal. In fact, Tak quickly discovered he had no weapons to oppose her with. She hated her family, all of them. No location could entice her; no pretty words would persuade her.

Deena, Lizzie, and their dead brother, Anthony, had been the unwanted additions to the Hammond family. At the heart of this rejection was a bottomless sort of bigotry, made unbearable when their white mother murdered their black father. They were thrust on his family not hers, and left to the mercy of their malice. Since Hammonds, by nature, were a boisterous bunch who took pride in speaking their mind, Deena, Lizzie, and Anthony found themselves as children on the receiving end of unfiltered contempt, made rancid by grief. Hammonds were responsible for a whole assortment of psychological scars, healed by time, stubbornness, and perseverance. Asking Deena and Lizzie to spend time with their family was the equivalent of asking them to cuddle the tiger that mauled them.

But they needed to do this. Tak couldn't say why, or for what purpose, only that he felt certain of its necessity. In the end, it was putting pressure on Lizzie's husband, his kid brother, that did the job. He had a way with her that Tak couldn't quite get, a way of slicing through caustic to the cream, a way of smoothing out razors into silk. "You owe me," was Kenji's response on convincing her, before following it with a dial tone. Something told Tak that his IOUs would mount in the coming days.

The others were easier. Hammonds came with the promise of a free trip, out the country as a bonus. With each phone call, Deena's apprehension about the indiscriminate nature of her grandmother's invitation sprung like a weed and grew, choking everything and everyone around them. She snapped, she snarked, she glared, she kept silent, and hoped above all that the Tanakas would, at least, reject the invitation. But they wouldn't. Not with Christmas on the horizon and their having made a tradition of meeting in California anyway. For them, it meant a shift in destination at someone else's expense, a chance for Aruba for the holidays.

So, in the end they were set.

Not a single rejection to their invitation. In fact, Tak's family was thrilled at the idea of meeting the rest of Deena's family at long last.

Deena's family.

Who they couldn't hope to understand.

CHAPTER *three*

THEY'D DECIDED TO HOLD THEIR impromptu reunion at their estate in Aruba over Christmas break. While Deena had hoped for resistance to any change of holiday tradition, somehow Aruba held more sway. With their travel agent needing only a few weeks to make sense of the particulars like birth certificates, passports and expedited services, Deena used that time to try and talk her husband out of the trip.

"You don't understand," she reminded him for the umpteenth time. "My family's not normal. Haven't you noticed? We prefer a mutually agreed upon distance."

Tak, who had taken over her home office for the planning of their trip, didn't even bother to look up from his scribbles.

"Well maybe, Dee, it's time for that to change."

Time for change, said the artist, said the man who spent

days mulling over life's intangibles and losing himself in them for days at a time. Time for change, said the man who set emotions to music, stretched heart and soul on canvas for all. How raw it must be, how rewarding, to dig deep and find beauty, to find light even in the shadows. But a week of Hammonds was what he wanted. She couldn't wait to see what he painted, what he sang, what he thought after that.

CHAPTER
four

Oɴ ᴀ Tᴜᴇsᴅᴀʏ ᴍᴏʀɴɪɴɢ, Dᴇᴇɴᴀ's immediate family prepared for departure. Tony, slim, long-bodied with shoulders hunched in that perpetual state of adolescent angst, gutted out the mailbox thoroughly, before dragging his suitcases out to the car. He made two phone calls by the trunk, the first undoubtedly to his best friend, Lizard, an Irish-Jewish skateboarder who lived next door with his mother, a feminist and sex therapist of notoriety who traversed the daytime talk show circuits whenever her new drivel released. His father, an archeologist, spent most of his days in places where people weren't, returning for endless over-the-hedge conversations about flint tools and plant life in the Paleolithic era. Deena figured he must have been a behemoth in bed, to hold the interest of a woman who sold sexual freedom for a living. God knows it couldn't have been the conversation she clung to.

Tony called Wendy next, one of his closest and oldest friend, held onto from his earliest days in Miami. Unlike with Lizard, there were no eye rolls and snorts on his end this time, no guffaws of laughter rupturing the air. He did, however, turn his back to Deena. That was something new.

Mia nearly toppled her mother on her fly out the door. A slam of her skateboard to pavement, a jump and jerk later, had her careening for the idling taxi van at high speed, one duffle bag in hand.

Mia, with her flannel in the summer and ripped jeans, whose hair was never quite tamed or washed clean. Mia, who knew Latin, Japanese, Spanish and more poetry than her mother could ever hope for, but also knew every horror icon from Nosferatu to Jigsaw. She took solitude over girl friends, her skate and surfboard over nail polish, and had an appetite both massive and bizarre: Iguana in Trinidad, brain curry in India, river eel in Japan. Mia lived for adventure; she was all Tak and no Deena.

Tony jammed the off button on his cell and scowled before shoving it into his pocket. While she'd heard nothing of his conversation with Wendy, Deena could imagine its gist. After all, he spent most days gnawing away his lips over what music school would undoubtedly have to reject him. He reasoned that he hadn't been introduced to the study of music until eleven—other kids saw it at three or four. He seemed to forget his sister Mia, who had begun piano lessons at three but was much more adept at managing an epic flip on that godforsaken skateboard than she was at conjuring up a decent version of 'London Bridge'.

Tony, on the other hand, had taken to music in

desperation. He had more than an ear for music, more even than his perfect pitch. Obsession made him think in notes and dream music. His early college admission applications, long sent to five of the best programs in the country, included *Fini*, a symphony he wrote himself. It also included a segment of him performing the fugue in Beethoven's *Sonata Opus 106* at a school recital the year before. It also included, by his mother's force of hand, an essay detailing how his symphony had been inspired by his life of homelessness and the search to find his family. Deena had to stand over him to make sure he included as much in what he mailed to every school. Take embarrassment, she'd told him, take weakness, and make it your strength. Sometimes, it's the only weapon available.

Music had started out as a parental hope to conjure discipline and expand their son's view of the world. It succeeded tenfold. It didn't need Tak's bribe of any car of Tony's choosing in exchange for the mastering of three instruments. Nonetheless, the Porsche sat in their garage, a bold bribe paid out in full. It was the Tanaka way, not the Hammonds'. Deena couldn't imagine what they'd give him for his high school graduation, his college one, or when he married one day.

Noah burst by, bubbling, humming and pausing only to thrust in time with his own rendition of the Batman theme song, before powering onward with his luggage. It seemed not to matter that he wore a green and massively obnoxious Incredible Hulk fist on one hand and the cape of Superman on his back.

Three children and she recognized not a one as being of

her own design, not even when the eldest was technically her brother's child.

Others would travel with them to Oranjestad: Mrs. Jimenez, their maid; Antonina, their au pair; and Mario Saunders, the resident chef, who busied himself daily with threats about finding work elsewhere, never mind his incomparable salary.

Finally, they were on their way. First, to pick up Deena's grandmother, then onward to Miami International where they would board an early evening flight, first class, to the island. No one in the car had much enthusiasm for the trip, as all of them, except Grandma Emma, had just summered there. Meanwhile, she was too busy with anticlimactic sleeping to bother with excitement.

On the flight the children busied themselves with iPads and groans of boredom, long past the enraptured face-to-window presses typical of majestic destinations. But Grandma Emma was a different story. Seated next to Tony with a blanket over her lap, she gazed out on open blue waters, eyes steady, gaze clear. Deena wondered what she thought, remembered, considered. She wondered what it must have felt like to face definitive lasts. Last vacations, last gazes of open water, last plane ride perhaps? Deena wondered if, when her time came, she would be as graceful and accommodating of death.

Aruba eventually came into view. A dot of honed-in green, nestled into shimmering blue waters, it burst into calypso colors and sharp-edged countryside as they grew near.

Oh, did it stand alive, ushering Deena back to sweltering

nights, sweat, and soca skin-to-skin on the dance floor. There'd been no children then. Only Tak and Deena and all the touches they could stand. She could drown with that, Deena realized. She could drown, content, so long as his fingers touched her body and her arms wrapped him in the end.

Once landed and with luggage in hand, they were driven from the airport to their chateau on Malmok Beach. They weaved away from the city along LG Smith, straddling the sea as delicate raindrops fell. A tiny island was all Aruba was, no bigger than DC, though pulsing with flavor.

In a few minutes' time, they arrived at their summer home.

Two floors of pretentious estate stretched to the ocean's edge in unhurried grandeur. It was the sort of pompous residence celebrities bought to assert their wealth. Two dozen bedrooms, ten bathrooms, in addition to indoor and outdoor pools. There was more, of course, much more. And all of it was Deena's.

It never got old for her: wealth, deference, power. She'd shattered the glass ceiling with her own two fists. Wealthiest architect under fifty. No preludes, no preamble. While she was far from the iconic figure that Tak's father was, hers was a name worth knowing and knowing well.

Deena stood in the entrance hall of her vacation home, one of three they owned. Her chef pushed past her muttering, while the au pair struggled with an armful of bags, each donned with surfer waves.

"Really, Mia," Tak snapped as Antonina dropped a fistful

of bags. "Think you could trouble yourself with more than a skateboard for once? She's not your valet, you know."

Mia's gray eyes flitted up to her father, painted with what her mouth wouldn't say, before snatching two suitcases from the floor and barging up the stairs.

Tak sighed. "Is it time for this already?"

"She's thirteen, so yeah," Deena said.

"Well," Tony said and gave his parents a one-sided smile on entering. "This should be fun. Like a rollercoaster-with-no-brakes kind of fun." He picked up his guitar case, balanced his horn case atop it and grabbed the handle of his rolling luggage for the journey. "Tell Mario I'll find something in the fridge later." He too started off.

As soon as he'd left, a shout of outrage pierced the night.

"The satellite isn't working!" Mia cried. "No one can live like this. Call someone. Please."

Deena and Tak exchanged a look. In twenty-four hours, a handful of attitudes would transform into a hurricane of the same.

"You get your grandmother settled in. I'll take care of everyone else," he said and disappeared just as the driver helped Grandma Emma over the threshold.

CHAPTER
five

RAIN.
Despite the vast swaths of ocean enclosing Aruba, rain almost never happened. Twenty inches a year, they said. That made it ideal to visit, impractical to live in, yet gorgeous to look at.

From the moment Deena slipped into her hot tub, drink in hand, she faced the shoreline—unable to look away. What was it about that vast expanse of nothingness that drew her in irrevocably? Timeless was what those still waters were. Unconquerable, even.

People used to believe that monsters roamed the seas. And what were monsters but those things which people were unwilling or unable to understand? There'd been a philosophy teacher back at MIT, Dr. Grossman, who'd said that philosophy was but the questions science had yet to answer, a recognition of man's limitless ignorance.

Deena spent a semester in philosophy pondering how and why she believed everything she did and whether her beliefs could withstand philosophical inquiry. She didn't leave with a feeling of certainty, either. While she'd never been fool enough to embrace the stink of her grandfather's theological convictions, she nonetheless could smell their stench. Interracial marriage was unnatural, according to him, a slight against God, a sign of self-hate. Never mind the rabid, foaming-at-the-mouth vitriol he passed off as sermons of love. No, the world came to an end when folks forgot themselves and started mixing.

How lame. How positively weak in the face of reality. Of all the evils in the world, all the greed, hatred, starvation, oppression and genocide, her grandfather's lone issue had been over which adults other adults slept with.

Deena set aside her shimmering pink drink and dipped low in the hot tub. Once, that rancid old man's voice barked into her brain, hijacking her dreams, piercing her waking hours. She'd been so fearful of loving Tak because to love him wasn't the easiest choice. But if regrets were billion dollar bills, then she'd go to bed a pauper.

She could have laughed at her old self. Her grandfather, Edward Hammond, the man with all the answers. The man with one hate-filled daughter, another who flinched at his name, and a son who sold drugs until he was murdered. Of course, a man like that would have all the answers.

All the wrong answers.

Joy burst through her like rays of the sun, warm,

illuminating, stretching. She had love, loads of love, family, friends, security. Hell, she had a husband with a gorgeous face, the stamina of a racehorse, and a body made for snug fitting jeans. Life was so delicious; she could have sent word to the kitchen for seconds and thirds.

Life was too delicious, perhaps.

Too delicious to last, that is.

CHAPTER
six

THE MOON HUNG LIKE A SLIVER ON invisible thread, yellow-tinged and ominous in a starlit sky. Tak stood under the hooded covering of the back terrace, eyes fixated on his wife. He could watch her, he thought, with those thick rivulets of hair in every shade of brown, already saturated to dripping in the water. Even, creamy skin with a smattering of freckles across the cheeks and full lips that turned up with a pout. He had traced those lips with a thumb, with a tongue, with lips of his own. Most every inch of him knew what those sweet beauties felt like and most every inch of him wanted reacquainting. Their last few days had been so busy, their moments together too brief. He could watch her, he knew, or he could do more.

How he had gone without touching her, he couldn't know. How he had gone without tasting her, he couldn't know. Not when she stood before him, a lexicon of sweet curves, a blueprint for all others.

Two hints of wet white fabric cut low at cleavage and high at the hips. Deena filled them with supple softness. He knew those curves with his fingers and had memorized the feel of them under his lips. Somewhere in South Beach was a woman desperate to purchase the same full breasts and the same sleek hips and rounded backside, the same smooth, heat-inducing body. Enough for two kids and a few false alarms. Maybe enough for a third.

The kids were asleep. He'd put Noah down himself and checked in on the other two, plus Deena's grandmother. But it didn't mean that no one else was around.

Some part of him wondered if he cared. After all, he had that feeling. That superhero feeling that made him think he could tear through reinforced steel to get to her.

Deena's eyes closed and her head tipped back, arms resting on the edges of the hot tub with a pink cocktail in hand. In that moment, Tak envied the drink under her touch, firm against her hand.

He'd been a little tired…and consumed lately. Work, family responsibilities, and all the little things, had a way of wedging between husband and wife. It wasn't as if he didn't know all the ways he'd been unfair either. Unfair in that he made love to her in that tired way husbands love their wives—quick, cursory, with satisfaction as the primary goal. She'd known pleasure, yes, but only because pleasure was the inevitable outcome in a series of well-tried steps.

Tak thought of her legs wrapping him, her back arched for him. He wanted her pulling and tearing and insane with her want for him. No talk of meetings or colleges or Noah acting out in school. Just him, her, and sweat.

He crossed the terrace to the hot tub straddling the pool. He peeled off his shirt and jeans, leaving just the boxers, before splashing in and earning a yelp from Deena. He buried that with a kiss as his hands found employment lower, gliding down her back and dropping to her backside to explore.

They should have found calm waters there, having sailed these currents so often. They should have found the steadiness of familiarity, the evenness of rote memory. But it wasn't meant to be.

Maybe it was him. Maybe even the urgency of his touch. When he drew her near, she mewled for him, a soft sound of yearning he hadn't anticipated. Fingers ran up through his hair and clutched, entangled as their mouths grew urgent.

Moonlight fell like a spotlight on them, lighting them for whoever took notice. They counted the seconds in kisses, measured the moments in touches. They had pulling, grasping, fumbling fingers that shredded clothes, leaving them floating away.

He tasted desperation. Pressed body to body so that even water couldn't slip between, they rocked together, fitting and molding, mouth to mouth, soft to hard. Sweat fell from his brow, streaking his face, tainting their lips. Even it emboldened her, as her nails drew fire down his back, as she rocked against him with the ledge for support.

He pulled the string of her bikini top and let the fabric fall away. A possessive hand, then a mouth, found its way to a single hardened nipple. She groaned, back arched to overextension, hand rushing through and through his hair.

Heart halfway to hemorrhaging, he allowed himself a cautious look back and found no one.

He might have been gentle. He might have, if she hadn't wrapped into him so tight, if she hadn't said she needed him, if she hadn't let out that ragged, quaking moan the second he slipped into her.

With her leg still around him, Tak grabbed her by the waist and tilted, so that her hips went up, her back arched, leaving him with the sharpest of angles to explore. Tak reared back and slammed.

The sound from her throat was guttural, primitive, spastic. Her mouth hung open as if she might shout, before a mere gasp escaped it. He gathered her up while still planted deep, still throbbing, and trailed kisses down the pulse of her neck. Ever so slightly, she trembled.

Tak reared back, hesitated, and then slammed again, sloshing water from the tub to wet tiles. Deena bit down on her fist and stifled a cry, just as he ran a hand down her breast, over her hip, before settling on the curve of her ass.

"Tak—"

It was all he allowed before a shove took him as far as her body allowed, before hunger and greed found its way in.

He found a monstrous jackhammer of a pace, cramming her with violent, splashing thrusts—thrusts so powerful, so furious, that he could hardly find time to breathe. She pulled him in with every pound, digging into his backside with her heels, bidding him harder and deeper, wilder with every thrust. To see them would have been to believe that he had his way with her, that it was he who dominated that time.

But to feel her, to feel her as he did, was to know that he had no sense of control and that she had long since mastered him.

She let out a cry and shuddered. He could close his eyes and know what it looked like: lower lip trembling, hands gripping—gripping at him, at surface, at anything. Rolling through her in quakes, boiling water that waved to her core.

He snatched her to him, knowing that his finish would follow, and buried a grunt of satisfaction between her lips. That was all it took—all it ever took: a look, a touch, her body, and the whole world incinerated for him.

Tak withdrew himself and exhaled.

"I love you," he said and pressed his forehead to hers.

Sweat coalesced on their faces before they pressed lips and parted.

"You knocked over my drink," she said.

Tak lifted his head, still flushed and unfocused, before spying the upturned glass. Bright pink liquid pooled beneath it in a run to their tub. He grinned. He had no remorse for the drink. After all, he had been jealous of it.

"It got in my way," he said and tilted her chin, thoughts already with yet another kiss. A flicker of a smile passed over her, before being supplanted with a glance at a nearby deck table. On it, sat her purse.

Odd, Tak thought, to drag a purse around at your own house. But then she kissed him, melting his wonder with her touch.

CHAPTER
seven

Tony sat on one side of his bed, back arched, feet planted to the floor. Facing him and mounted to the wall was an army of autographed guitars. A sleek, white glossed bass one tipped in candy red had been autographed by soca legend Peppers Montane. Next to it was the shimmering electric blue instrument that once belonged to one-man-reggae machine Drew Jeffrey. Adjacent to that was a golden god of a guitar, complete with flawless sound. It had been autographed by a master of calypso, dead before his time. This wall, not unlike the one at home with memorabilia from two dozen American icons, held more flash than the much more substantial collage of autographed drumheads painting the wall above his headboard. He had living legends and dead ones in a collection that spanned three continents. Each bedroom he called his, whether in Miami, Aruba,

London, or Tokyo, paid homage to international legends. In a glass case back home, he had a shimmering white glove from The King himself, bedazzled in Swarovski crystal. His adoptive mother's eyes had crossed when Tak had it shipped in from an auction for him.

Tony dialed Wendy's number and gnawed on his lip when the phone rang. It was only sort of late, closing in on midnight, but if her parents happened to be around, there'd be no way she could answer.

The sound of her voice told him they were working third shift at the hospital.

"Dude," she blasted. "You were supposed to call hours ago."

A smile found its way to his lips.

"I had an emergency, Wend. The satellite's out. Even prison has cable."

He could imagine her rolling her eyes. Wendy never needed more than a channel willing to air reruns of M*A*S*H for happiness. All else was drivel.

"What did you get into tonight?" Tony said. "And don't say anything that starts with Gage Sawyers."

Gage Sawyers was the newest addition to Edinburgh Academy, the sort of school where status was measured not by designer brands—after all, everyone had those—but by a weird amalgamation of legacy status, familial prestige, and exoticism, for extra points. Tony, who had once been a pariah at the same school, had risen in standing alongside a rise in his parents' wealth and prestige—matters other students seemed better versed in than him. The Porsche in his drive had given him extra oomph; it was the best thing going and a strong frontrunner to the Audis, Infinitis, and Benzes that peppered student parking.

Gage Sawyers had none of that. A drop-in from a netherworld, he was the indifferent, angst-ridden boy who played basketball on scholarship and shirked all company. Well, all except for Wendy's. In the lunchroom at school, in the hallway, he had a lazy half smile on standby for her alone. The light in his eyes faded the second she left. It reminded Tony of his early days at school and how Wendy had been his first friend, his best friend, until Lizard came along. What Tony had taken to be some real connection between them seemed to be some variation of Wendy's pity. She gravitated to the new lonely boy, whoever that was, it turned out.

The thought filled him with a bitter sort of ache.

"We had pizza," Wendy said.

"Hope that was all he had," Tony bit, without knowing he would.

All he did know, in fact, was that Gage Sawyers made him want to thrash something, preferably the smile on his face.

"He's nice, Tony. If you'd only get to know him. You have so much in common—"

"Like what? Being black?"

"That's stupid," Wendy said. "I'm black too. Why would I say that?"

Tony squinted at the Peppers Montane guitar before him. Was that a smudge? Had Noah been here fingering things again? If he had—

"You're going to see her tonight, aren't you?" Wendy said.

Tony sighed.

"So, she doesn't even have a name anymore?"

Silence met him on the other end. He used it to switch the phone from his right ear to the left.

"I don't like her," Wendy said. "I wish you wouldn't... chase her so."

His breath came in subtle drafts, his rising annoyance battling with the fact that this was Wendy. Silly Wendy, as he sometimes called her. Whatever she said, however she said it, it was never meant for harm.

"You know it's not like that," Tony said. "There's chemistry between us. That's all."

He didn't know why he felt pressed to explain, but a glance at his watch said that it would have to wait.

A quarter after midnight and the house stood quiet. Everyone should have been asleep.

"I have to go," Tony said.

Wendy drew in a sharp intake of breath.

"Be careful," she said. "Don't carry all your credit cards or a big wad of cash. Leave your passport at home. Stay away from dark streets and strangers—"

"Wendy—"

"Make sure not to give out directions; I don't care how nice the people look. Stay away from locals and neighborhoods and if someone tries to mug you—"

"Wendy—"

"Give them whatever it is they want."

Tony sighed. He hadn't really been expecting to skate past Wendy's flood of paranoia; still, he'd managed to rush her through it. Leaving her to her monologue could have him watching the sun rise while waiting.

"Don't go anywhere with her," Wendy blurted. "She's a local."

"And you're being a snob. Talk later." Tony hung up.

He managed to get in a quick shower before slipping into a dark tee, ripped jeans, and Jordans, and riding the banister down to the first floor. A fifty dollar bill slipped from his hand to the driver they'd hired for the trip. Destination, Oranjestad. The driver already knew just where.

Tony sat back, fingers drumming out rhythm bass on his thigh. Coastline rushed by on one side, with ocean water lapping turf as they threaded the Boulevard. One road ran the length of the island, a single thoroughfare as the artery of the island.

The drumming of his fingers incited some never-heard whistle, something funky and shredding with flavor. Were he home, he would have filled out the sound's nether regions with a bit of flirting winds, an incision of mocking brass, before tearing it all down with a thunder of percussion. He could hear how it should be. He could always hear that.

Nestled between squat, square adobe fixtures in mango, pistachio, turquoise, and white, Tony's destination came into view. A nothing from the street was what it looked like by day, but at night, neon and drumming and liquor had it pulsating with life. Tony threw open the door as the driver pulled up, sprung free, and sprinted to Lila Dahl in the swallow of a breath. He snatched her up, high and by the waist, before burying the last of her squeals in a kiss.

When she pulled away from, her cheeks flushed from his affection.

She stood tall before him, nearing his six feet in heels,

with her brush of hazelnut skin and burst of cherry lips glistening under a flash of blue light. Her dark hair fell in loose curls to her waist. Lila Dahl smoldered in tank tops and burned hot in the simplest of tees with curves melting to slimness and narrowing into nothing of a waistline.

She kissed him again, in that way they always kissed. Never steady, never sure, but with just enough hunger to sate until an uncertain next time.

"I didn't think I'd see you so soon after summer," she said. "Ronnie, Tito, and Paul will be so excited to know you're back. Everyone will, really."

Tony pulled her in as snug as she could fit. She could save the guys for another day.

For the moment, he wanted him and Lila and a little touching, maybe even a splash or two of alcohol. After all, he was of legal drinking age in Aruba.

CHAPTER
eight

Marbles. That was the word that rolled in Tak's mind early the next day, glinting and changing direction as he squinted at the chrome wheels halting in the driveway.

When Tak was a boy visiting family in Denver, Uncle Yoshi would always buy sacks of marbles for the boys to play with. Three bags, with Tak, the guest, picking first. With the offering dangling, Tak would look from it to his older cousin, Mike, certain that whichever one he chose would be the one Mike had to have. And when Tak grabbed it, Mike would cry out and claw for the prize.

The size, color, or number of marbles in the bag never made any difference to Mike. Scuffed ones were desirable if Tak put a hand on them. Cracked ones even better, if that's what Tak wanted. Eventually, Tak and Mike's younger brother John made a game of it, eyeing out the least desirable sack and snatching at it greedily, only to trade it the second Mike opened his mouth and bawled.

Once, when the marbles came around, Tak got a different idea. He stood there, like usual, with the dangling three bags, gaze shifting from them to Mike. He wanted to see, just once, what Mike would have wanted for himself, if he ever deigned to have his own mind. They were two pre-pubescent cowboys waiting on the draw, neither giving the slightest of signals—until a flicker of doubt sliced Mike's features. The middle one came to Tak as a whisper. When he snatched for it, aqua boulders with lava red centers, Mike howled like a hyena. Grinning, Tak bolted with the bag, actually tearing the mesh away, and not realizing the extent of his damage until he hit the front door, where his marbles skated in a dozen different directions. Some off the stairs and some to the street, with a few into the dog house of his cousin's only sometimes pleasant German Shepherd. There were marbles that seemed to evaporate, too, lost to foliage and mean-spiritedness, Tak presumed.

That was the memory Tak held on to as the Tanakas ushered in.

His grandmother was the first to arrive, on the arm of Aunt June, who was Mike and John's mother. Their dad, Yoshi, who was the younger brother of Tak's father, trailed behind with luggage scraping his arms and scuffing the hardwood floor. He wouldn't waste honest earned dollars on money-begging tips for the driver: his words. Instead, he wrestled his way in then yelled for Tak and Tony to help.

An hour and a half later, Yoshi and June's daughter,

Lauren, arrived on a flight in from New Orleans. Still donning the raccoon shadows of a teen Goth era they'd hoped would pass, she was only a little rounder than the last time Tak had seen her. He accepted the one-armed, uncommitted hug she offered, only to have it followed by a demand to know which room she'd been stuffed in. At the news that she'd share it with Mia, she cursed and said something about vacationing in Maui with friends instead.

"It's never too late!" Tak called after her, before Deena squeezed his arm in warning.

"Lauren is Lauren," she said. "She's always been something of a lark."

Funny, he thought. A harsher word came to mind.

Tak's brother, Kenji, arrived with his burgeoning belly of a wife and two sons in tow: Brandon, who could have doubled as Noah's younger and slighter twin, plus Elijah, who looked more like his mom than anyone. No sooner did Tak sweep the boys into a hug than did the door slam shut behind his favorite cousin, John.

"Where's your wife?" Tak said, setting the little ones aside so they could tear off at freight train speed.

Color rose to John's cheeks, but he merely shook his head.

"Work," he explained. "She sends her apologies."

It turned out Tak had a few apologies for him too.

"Well, since you didn't bring her, chances are that you'll be bunking with your brother. Unless he decided to bring… what was her name again? Michelle."

John sighed. "We both know that Michelle deflates and rolls into his suitcase at night."

Indeed. Tak grinned before pulling his cousin into a mighty embrace, not because he didn't see him often—they were neighbors nowadays—but because he sensed heaviness about him.

"I'll drop in later, OK?"

Whatever the problem, Tak sensed that Allison's absence had less to do with work overload and much more with the smoldering brunette John had taken on as a secretary.

Mike burst in with a pile of luggage, and Michelle, no doubt, in the folds. He wore a smoke gray tee with four elements of the periodic table mashed on the front, so it read: 'Lithium, Carbon, Potassium, Me.'

Deena burst like an orangutan, red faced and guffawing, as Tak looked from her to the shirt. His older cousin, finally peaking at the hairline, beamed and stood up a little straighter. Too pleased, as far as Tak was concerned.

"Deena," Mike said, in that way that always curled Tak's hands into fists. "I knew you'd get it." He passed his cousin to embrace his cousin's wife, held her for a beat too long, and took off for the staircase.

Halfway down the hall, Mike realized he had no idea where he was going and turned, only to make a show of noticing Tak for the first time.

"Upstairs, third door on the right. With John," Tak said.

The clench in his jaw settled the second Mike disappeared. Deena, he knew, wasn't the only one who had to suffer through the presence of family.

"It was elements of the periodic table," she explained. "'L and i' for lithium, 'C' for carbon and 'k' for potassium. The shirt said 'lick me.'" She looked at him as if wondering about the quality of his education. "Jeez, honey. Didn't you pay attention at all in school?"

Tak rolled his eyes. "Only when they were passing out the paints."

The driver they'd hired for the duration of the stay ambled in, overstuffed bags hanging from his limbs.

"Which room did he go to?" The middle-aged man breathed, mouth parted with a need to pant. Tak looked from the driver to Mike and back again, before shouting up a string of rudeness after his cousin. He'd turned the man into a bellhop, and, like natural, expected Tak to tip.

Their reunion had officially begun.

Deena's family arrived like the rolling flood of a severed dam about a half hour later. Aunts and cousins once, twice, and three times removed, poured in, each clapping Tak on the back and squeezing him. Next to him, his wife took nods of acknowledgment and lukewarm hugs instead. It made him think of the days when they were young and dating, fearful that neither of their families would accept the other. Now Tak embraced every relative of his wife's, accepted kisses on the cheek from some, and navigated surly greetings as surely as if they'd come from his kin. But none of that overshadowed Deena's relationship with Tak's father, who thought of her as his own, nor her relationship with Mike, who wasn't beyond getting on one knee with a ring for her.

Still, the ice greeting between Deena and the Hammonds was more than the usual clipped hellos, prompting Tak to ask her what it all had been about.

His wife treated him to a polite, board meeting smile.

"They know this is your doing," she said, "and that I

wouldn't occupy the same room as them on purpose."

'Mutually preferred distance' was what she always called it. Though he sometimes wondered how mutual.

CHAPTER
nine

As a Buddhist, Tak had no business overseeing the stringing up of Christmas decorations in the ballroom. Time rushed like speed dial, bleeding the overseeing of banquet duties into the festive nostalgia of Christianity.

Housekeepers hoisted up on ladders, running blinking lights crosswise down the hall. For whatever reason, the left side stayed low no matter what he said, just like the Christians stayed busy no matter what he shouted after them. Deena, with her faux commitments: a phone call here, a text message there, only to scurry out when he spied her nibbling on strawberries.

Uncle Yoshi strode in next and made a line for the *yakitori*. Hovering over the elongated grill to the right of a gargantuan Santa, he paused only to rummage through the skewers for the fattiest pieces, before moving from chicken to beef tongues.

"*Oli—*"

"Tell me when your father's coming," he gruffed, then spun around in a circle. "What? No sake?" He waved a skewer in Tak's direction and cursed when a hunk of pork belly flopped onto the marble.

"If you'd give them a chance to finish setting the food out—" Tak began, before stopping as Lauren fluttered into the room, gliding in layers of black fabric. Since Tak had seen her last, she'd touched up the raccoon shadows and paired it with some lipstick that looked like a wound.

"Ugh, you're eating again," Lauren groaned and swept over to the food with a critical eye. "Soba, udon, sushi, rice, yadda, yadda, yes." She halted at a pan of braised barbecue brisket. "Good Lord, yes," she managed before going back for a plate.

"Listen," Tak said with an eye on more lopsided lights. "You guys should have a better eye for these Christmas decorations since—"

"I have to go," Lauren said and hoisted on the candied yams before departing.

Uncle Yoshi, who had followed her plate with his eyes, went in for the yams himself.

Tak opened his mouth to ask his uncle if he'd look over the remaining work since he seemed content with camping out in the ballroom anyway, but then he remembered a thorny and dehydrated Christmas tree from years past, decked with stringed popcorn and homemade yarn ornaments. Tak's mouth snapped shut on the request.

"You want to say something?" Yoshi said and shoved more *butabara*, or pork belly, into his mouth.

A dollop of dark tare sauce hit the front of his white polo. He didn't seem to notice.

Were it not for the features, Deena once told him, the subtle things that made a Tanaka a Tanaka, she would have never believed that Tak's father and this man were brothers. But it was all there for the seeing: smooth, rich golden skin, thick tresses that ran sleek as an oil slick, and dark almond eyes that always seemed softer on the second or third look. After there, the changes grew subtle, losing themselves to the particulars. Sharper chisels of the face for Tak and his father left them with definition and a touch of stubborn chin. Uncle Yoshi, on the other hand, buried all that in plumpness.

"I heard your son upstairs," Yoshi said. "On bass. Better than you, I think."

He gave a mutter of appreciation for the food and dropped another splat of sauce.

Say what you would about his family, Tak thought, they'd taken to Tony as sure and certainly as they had Mia or Noah. Predictably, a change of surname was all it took.

"He is better than me on bass," Tak said and reached for a wad of napkins from a nearby table. "Better than most, in fact." He retrieved a bottle of iced water, unscrewed it, and dampened the napkins for his uncle. "Now, I need you to stop making a mess," Tak said. "And don't eat so much. You'll spoil your appetite."

He swabbed at his uncle's stain, before his narrowed dark eyes concentrated on the vast sweep of the ballroom. It was the sort of room that glimmered in opulence, that pushed the boundaries of luxury. It made him think of old English country homes and bygone gentry, once content to spend their days entertaining.

"Stop that. You'll turn into your wife," Yoshi snapped and snatched the wad of napkins from Tak. The dabs he made bled the brown stains, smearing instead of controlling. "You're getting as bad as your father. Always on me to lose weight." Yoshi glanced down at his skewer. "But this kawa," he said and tore teeth into a stick of chicken skin. "Kawa and me cannot part."

Tak resigned himself to directing the staff as they decorated, speeding up the process as family began to file in. On sighting Tak's father, Uncle Yoshi slid down to the beverages, as if to make his gorging more innocuous. More lights went up, less red, no green, and briefly Tak entertained himself with the idea of mounting a Buddha in the center of the room. What was it that Grandma Emma said all those years ago, on discovering her evangelical granddaughter would marry a Buddhist?

Whoever heard of a fat Chinese man being the son of God?

Tak grinned. He swore; that one never got old.

Their first night turned into something of an impromptu party, once the decorations were up and Tony took to a lively string of Christmas hits on the grand Fazioli in one corner. Though Mario had gone to a great trouble in representing two divergent food cultures, no respect had been paid to that, judging by the plates made. Scallion rolls with black-eyed peas, *sukiyaki* alongside cheesy mac and cornbread. Mia was the most egregious of the lot, with her oysters and offal smashed in black-eyed peas and topped in soy sauce. And off in one corner was John, with a hodgepodge of uneaten food and a glass of red wine already tipping toward empty. Having a talk with his cousin shot up on Tak's to-do list.

CHAPTER
Ten

DEENA ROSE FOR THE SUNRISE, grabbed her pencils and pad, and took a glass of OJ to the terrace. Before the bustle of family made it impossible, she wanted to slip in a little work.

A "shameless swipe at immortality" was what her father-in-law now called her projects. The sleek keyhole of a skyscraper in Milan, the arcing half-circle hotel straddling the Indian Ocean in Bali, and the undulating wave of smooth grace embedded in the cliffs of Cabo San Lucas. All the work of ego, her father-in-law chided, with all the humility of a British king.

Her latest attempt was a recreation of Frank Lloyd Wright's Mile High dream. It was exactly as outrageous and consuming at it sounded, as reckless as it dared be in an age of terrorism: a skyscraper thrusting a mile in the air.

She had no buyers for such a thing, no investors willing to front for such a hemorrhaging project, but she had the inclination to obsess over it anyway. For now, Deena Tanaka stood as the preeminent female architect in a field dominated by men. The feminist in her wanted to smash at every consonant and vowel in that statement until only "preeminent" and "architect" remained. Top architect automatically meant top male, with a rush of testosterone fueling their war. Deena knew she wasn't the first girl to take a running smash at the field's proverbial glass ceiling; she would only be the first to shatter it so thoroughly.

When the sun made its presence known, Deena took breakfast in the ballroom with her family. Chef Mario, who complained nonstop about a night of labor while they slumbered, served eggs in every style, alongside biscuits, pancakes, French toast, sausage, bacon, and an assortment of other delights. Guests were left to serve themselves.

As Deena piled her plate, her gaze fell on Tak's aunt, Asami. If perfection had a walking synonym it would be her. Skin smooth and firm and vehemently denying her age, her hair flowed and tapered as if combed purposefully by the wind. Beauty found its way in subtle details, resting in the bow and arch of her lips, in the slightness of curves on a slender body. Never had Deena seen Asami outside of makeup or tasteful wear. That morning she donned a crisp, asymmetrical summer dress that had to be tailor-made and paired it with simple string of pearls. Across from her, her husband Ken wore slacks and a white button up, sleeves rolled up as he sipped coffee. They could have been a million other places in the exact same wear: a business office, an office party, a night out on the town. It could have been a romantic evening for two. No matter the time or place, they were two fixtures of perfection without fail.

Arms slipped around Deena's waist and lips pressed to her neck.

"They're not as flawless as you think," Tak said. "Some are just better with their masks than others."

Masks. As if they needed any. In her husband's family, the biggest scandal involved missing a mortgage payment. In hers, it was the murder of her father.

Tak released Deena just as his gaze fell on John. The entire time he'd been standing there, John had busied himself by shoveling eggs back and forth across his plate. Tak elbowed his way through throngs of wild children in every shade, barely avoiding Noah mid-backflip, scolded him, and finally dropped across the table from John.

"Where's Allison?" Tak asked, eyes on his cousin's berries and mandarin slices artfully arranged into a frown.

"Don't know," John said and stabbed at his eggs.

"You don't know," Tak echoed, weighing out each word.

John tossed his fork and glared at him.

"She left me. OK? The day she disappeared, I got divorce papers. I thought you, of all people, would have figured it out."

Figured it out? There had been fights, yes. Screaming, hysterical brawls with furniture broken and accusations hurled like slime on a wall. Still, Tanakas didn't file for divorce. Ever.

"You…let her go?"

It was the wrong thing to say, he knew. As he considered

how to amend this blunder, Tak's thoughts drifted to his father and the xenophobia he once had. Back then, he wanted Japanese spouses for his family and saw anyone else as a threat to tradition, a promise for unwanted change. Was this the omen portended? Tanakas getting divorced? The idea felt otherworldly, abhorrent. Giving up on someone was for before marriage. It had no place after vows.

"We were unhappy, Tak. I thought time would see us through. I was wrong."

"John, you can't just—"

His cousin shoved aside his plate, hard enough to unseat the eggs and scramble the frown, before excusing himself from the table.

"John!" Tak called, feeling the inward cringe. "John, wait!" Though he knew he'd already lost him.

CHAPTER
eleven

TONY'S BREAKFAST SHOT FROM BELLY to toilet fast as the favored horse in this year's Kentucky Derby. Their au pair—who, in his opinion, needed to concentrate her efforts on Noah alone—stood outside the door tsk-tsking.

A shower and change of clothes later had still left him reeking of alcohol.

"Antony?" she called through the slab of wood in her slaughtered Russian English, robbing his first name of its critical blend. "Antony, I called the physician. He will take good care. I verified credentials."

Tony retched wildly into the toilet, spewing with a jerk of his body what he hoped was the last of his Jägerbombs.

"I'm OK," he managed and flushed down the filth. The second he did, he vomited again. "I'm OK," Tony repeated, with less fervor.

A night with Lila ended like this, with Tony groping for memories and spewing up foreign substances. Beer, rum, tequila, he'd even tried ecstasy once, though he'd take third world prison conditions over admitting to any of his friends or family. Anyway, once had been more than enough, as doing the stuff had blurred his vision and doused him in paranoia.

His girl, the Caribbean Amerindian who cursed in Dutch, was as turbulent and majestic as a summer storm, and as prone to jamming a flower in her hair as she was to drowning in vodka and tearing off her shirt. Lila Dahl wasn't the sort of girl a guy made plans to hold on to; she was the girl you chased without hope of ever catching.

For now, that was plenty enough.

He was her soft spot, she always said. The boy who sped her pulse and slowed her heart, the one who made her feel and think. Sure, he was a teenage boy with all the hormone-induced hang-ups of one, but he hadn't let that consume them. He was different in that way, she said.

They met last summer in Oranjestad, on a vacation that had been uneventful before then. Like usual, Tony had resented the insistence on summering that people with money tended to have. A sullen evening of souring over the absence of Lizard and Wendy sent him out into the city, looking for who knew what where. Lila had been waitressing at the restaurant he wandered into and asked him if he wanted a beer. Him, at seventeen? A beer? Unable to resist the offer, he agreed, only to choke on the first swig. Lila laughed—laughed this sultry, booming sound that weaved through him and upturned the corners of his lips.

Tony went from not caring that a girl was laughing at him, to wanting her laughter even more.

He'd asked her out with his hands wringing under the table and his gaze flitting as if to flee. She accepted on condition that he ask again, but that time while looking at her.

He took her to all the wrong places when she got off work, places where cash reigned and the walls glinted like gold. Her yawns sliced like foreboding through his nervous chatter on music and musicians: he was on the fast track to friendship land, for sure.

But then she asked him out the next night, that time to Loose, their eventual favorite club. Pulsating reggae and calypso, strobe lights and grinding made the possibility of him and her skyrocket to a promise. They went out again the next night, and by the third, they were making out on the dance floor.

"Antony!" His au pair rattled the door, yanking him from the reverie. "Antony, talk to me. Tell me if you are conscious."

What kind of eighteen-year-old had a nanny? He could drink in Aruba, smoke cigarettes and vote in America, yet according to his adoptive mother, he needed milk and a nap. 'College' was the word he used to rouse him from annoyance. A few months more and he'd be away from the fretting and hand wringing of his mom and babysitter.

"Go away," Tony said in a voice like granite. "I'm an adult. Go find a child to look after."

He journeyed to the sink to freshen up, knowing she'd be there when he opened the door.

CHAPTER
Twelve

TAK HEADED UPSTAIRS JUST AS people began to drift from the ballroom. He sought out his oldest son, sent the au pair on her way, and waited for the hurl fest to cease.

When Tony opened the door, he froze at the sight of his father.

"I—I've got a bug, I think. Probably ate something wrong at the airport," Tony said.

Tak sniffed.

"Drank something wrong is more like it," he murmured.

Tony shook his head in protest, only to wince at what had to be scissoring pain.

"Grab a V-8, take another shower, and come spend time with your family. I really don't care what your head feels like. Next time you show up smelling like a wine cellar, I'll put the au pair on night shift."

Tak gave his son's shoulder a squeeze, looked him over discreetly, and then headed downstairs.

He could have handled that differently. He could have screamed and raged and reminded Tony of what they expected from him. But Anthony Tanaka was no longer the terrified eleven-year-old Anthony Hammond. Soon, he'd be leaving for college, where alcohol and worse abounded. So, Tak practiced trusting his son and reminded himself to have faith in the job he'd done—even if there hadn't been time enough to do it.

Tak made it downstairs and immediately wished he hadn't.

"Sexuality can hardly be defined by the neat categories presupposed for us," Lauren said. "It's mass brainwashing and socialization that forces the choice between boy and girl, man and woman. Heterosexuality and homosexuality are prisons of the same design."

Jesus Christ.

Lauren sat across from Deena's aunt, Rhonda, her wife Mary Ann, and a blank-faced male cousin of Deena's. Everyone stared back at her, wide-eyed.

"So...you're...bisexual?" the guy ventured.

"My God. You're imprisoned by labels! Enslaved by propaganda. Society is polluted by the insistence on categorizing only so they can marginalize. You have to reject these norms outright." Lauren nibbled on some toast.

"What's happening?" Deena said, appearing at Tak's side with coffee in hand.

"Lauren's happening. Lauren Tanaka."

"If you insist on a label," his cousin continued, as if such a thing were a sign of limited intelligence, "then pangender works fine."

Rhonda and Mary Ann exchanged a look. Deena's cousin leaned forward.

"Does that mean that you're...with both parts?"

"It means that I refuse your labels. Although I do have a vagina, since you're doing inspections."

Deena choked on her coffee. Tak mulled over the best way to shut Lauren up. He considered tackling her, but dismissed it.

"Mia's room," Deena gasped. "She's in it."

"Not anymore," Tak said.

Mike showed up with a broad smile, on special reserve for Tak's wife.

"Regular little freak show isn't she?" He took a massive slurp of OJ. "Yesterday," Mike said, "she went on about how sex was an inherent good that should be practiced as frequently and with as many partners as possible." He shrugged. "Can't say I argue much with that. Though your grandmother looked pretty sickened by the discussion."

Deena buried her face in her hands.

CHAPTER
Thirteen

DEENA'S THOUGHTS WERE ON HER mile-high skyscraper again. While family drifted from the ballroom to the terrace and beyond, she stood stoic, hoping to make her presence known long enough that she wouldn't seem rude once disappearing. When all but a few stragglers remained, she went for her grandmother, parked in one corner, and offered to wheel her outdoors with the others.

"No," the old woman said, as if she'd be content to watch the help clean.

"Well, are you ready for a nap then?" Deena said.

Grandma Emma shook her head, yet kept silent.

Deena wasn't very good at this. In fact, she sucked at being a nurse. She hadn't the patience for the careful ministrations it required, or the ability to anticipate every need.

"Let me take you outside, OK? You can sit under a tree and—"

"I'll sit with you," she said.

Deena exhaled. Things would be fine. If her grandmother wanted to spend beautiful days, maybe even her last days, ball and chained indoors, so be it.

Her last days. Air seeped from Deena's balloon of annoyance with the realization, leaving only the quiet unease of reality. Her grandmother would be dead soon. For once, sketched dreams could wait.

Deena bounded around to Grandma Emma, crouched before her, and took both papery hands in hers. They would do whatever she wanted, however she wanted, as long as she could possibly stand it.

She opened her mouth to say so and was assaulted by a snore.

Of course.

With a sigh, she gathered up her grandmother, her drafts, and a copy of Frank Lloyd Wright's *A Testament*, and wheeled her into the study.

Outside, the sounds of family traveled muted, but near euphoric. Splashing, squeals and then the slicing in of up-tempo bass as the hired DJ went to work. In a crowd of thousands, Deena could make out the thrilled laughter of her son, Noah, always tinged with an air of mischief. A streak of self-appointed superiority set him apart, making him ringleader no matter the number of troublemakers. That was what she heard out there: the gratified cackle of a boy getting away with something, possibly even everything.

Deena stared at the steel sliver she'd committed to paper,

a design representative of heights man had yet to reach. Bold, sleek, empowered, sexy, she'd coined it The Stiletto, though it was an endearment she'd never admit to.

The Stiletto was a technical challenge, comprised of riddles about load bearing, oscillation, and cost. Each one pulsed Deena's temples and throbbed the bridge of her nose. If only—

"You got your whole life to draw," Grandma Emma said. "Spend some time with your family."

Deena looked up from her corner drafting table and tried to blink away wayward brown tendrils. When that didn't work, she swatted the hair from her face.

"One lifetime to design is hardly no time," she said.

Her grandmother's eyes snapped to attention.

"You know, your granddaddy—"

"Don't—"

Deena clamped down on her retort, twisting it till it buried belly deep. A measured exhale later had her back at her center of calmness.

"He was a hard man," Grandma Emma said. "Too hard on you, I suspect. But he loved you and he—"

Deena smashed her drafts so they sailed airborne. Then she stood and strode out the room.

She didn't talk about him, wouldn't talk about him, not to her grandmother of all people. The man her father called father. How much of her self-worth, her uncertainties, had been enslaved to what that man thought? What would it have taken for her grandmother to stand up to him even once? She pushed away the thought. Gone was the girl who feared truth in that man's message; in her place was a woman who knew better.

Deena went to the billiard room in search of a moment to exhale. She opened the door and froze at the sight of her mother-in-law behind the bar.

Tak's mother gulped Belvedere straight from the bottle. It ran rivers from the corners of her mouth, darkening her emerald blouse and pooling at her feet.

She dropped the bottle when their eyes finally met.

No. This couldn't be. Not after so much. Not after forgiveness had been given.

She went wild at the thought. Tak, her husband, had done what Deena never could. He'd swallowed past the pain of his mother's polluted love, never retching when it made him sick. Every day for more than a decade, his mother, this addict, walked out on her children anew. But she had cleaned up for him, gone sober on the day that her son nearly died.

"He loves you," Deena said. "When your husband called you a worthless common drunk, Tak stood by you. He defended you, though God knows you never earned his loyalty. You can't even figure out how to be conscious for him, let alone anything resembling a mother."

Hatsumi Tanaka stared, gray eyes glistening and watery, nostrils flared, lips hammered shut. Then her gaze dropped to the Belvedere and Deena's brain fractured. She snatched the bottle and hurled it at her mother-in-law's head.

Tak's mother ducked. A thousand shards and sprayed liquor burst against the wall like fireworks. Deena grabbed another bottle and another from the bar, hurling top shelf liquor, glass chunks, anything, at that same stretch of wall.

This woman didn't deserve Tak. She didn't deserve a son who could forgive neglect, indifference, and isolation, or a son who would protect a mother who had never protected him. She was a wound, a heartache, a nothing. Deena screamed it with all the fury suffocating pain could muster.

CHAPTER
fourteen

A STUMBLING STEP AWAY FROM TAK'S mother, and away from the reek of liquor, had her wading through molasses, stomach lurching, vision convoluted as she collapsed into the wrong someone.

"Deena?" Mike said. "Deena, what's happened?"

She heard voices, growing closer all too soon. Knowing what she looked like, what she smelled like, and the mess she'd left behind—

"Mike, the door. Don't let them see."

He scurried to the single exit, hit the lock, and returned quickly, hands at her elbows, holding her up.

"Jesus, Deena. You're bleeding. What's happened?"

She looked down at her hands. Blood painted one, a shard embedded in the other.

The door behind Mike rattled and he shot it a worried

look. His gaze swept left, then right, before he pulled Deena away and down a side hall as shouts and laughter closed in from another direction.

"Upstairs," Mike decided, and up and away they went.

Mike locked the bathroom door and led Deena to take a seat on the toilet. After testing the latch, he opened first the medicine cabinet, then the cabinets underneath, in search of a first aid kit. He came away with a telltale white box affixed with the Red Cross logo.

"What happened?" he said. "Who did this to you?"

His gaze drifted down to her hands, halting at the shard streaked in blood. After murmuring something about not knowing how he could miss that, he turned on the running water, rinsed her hands, and yanked the glass free in a single move. Armed with a compress dressing, he applied pressure to her sliver of a wound.

"You're shaking," he said, slight fingers wrapped round her wrist. Like Tak, he had the hands of a man meant to be an artist, slim long fingers suited for music, art, leisure.

"I'm angry," Deena said. "So hurt and angry I can't think."

She was shaking, balling her toes, grinding her teeth, and wishing she could have another go at her mother-in-law. All she could think of was assault.

Her eyes met Mike's. Narrowed and far more set back than her husband's, they had the look of someone frozen in uncertainty. A curious look, Deena thought. For the first time, she felt no pressing need to look away.

She took in his features. The lines and shape of his face stood sharp as a rough sketch, and his eyes—she'd misjudged them—were lighter and softer than expected.

Not a midnight brown, but a soft walnut, ringed in a tinge of sienna. And the downward turn of his mouth. Was it a constant, as sure as this hue of his eyes, or was it because of her and the state he'd found her in?

Mike swallowed, cheeks red as if they'd been rubbed. He dropped his gaze, steadied, then looked up at her once again.

"I think," he said and rummaged in the first aid kit for cotton swaths, "that when people upset us, really upset us, the person we're most angry with is our self. For not seeing, being smarter, or anticipating some flaw or eventuality. We punish ourselves because it gives us a sense of control; it usurps someone else's power. We go from 'you did this to me' to 'I let you do this to me', which is far more reassuring than the idea that things just happen to us and we can do nothing to stop them."

Water on, Mike stuck both her palms in for a rinse. Together, they watched as crimson became pink and pink became clear.

"I see you with your family," Mike said, earning a jerk of the arm from her. He shot her a look, meant to steady and scold, and she went back to stillness for the meantime. "I see you with your family," he repeated. "And I see that you and I are more alike than I ever anticipated."

Deena's underwater hand clenched into a fist. Finger by finger, Mike unraveled it.

"Growing up, I hated when Tak came to visit," he said. "John would throw me off and run straight for him every time. His 'best friend' was what he called him, never mind that I was his brother. They had secret toys and special games and jokes I couldn't understand. Everyone—and I mean everyone—has always treated him like the prodigal son come home. It's Tak that makes me invisible on a good day and intolerable on a bad one." Mike turned off the water and fed her an even stare. "Which one of your family does that to you, Deena?"

"My mother," was what she finally said.

Mike went to work dressing her wounds. If her revelation startled him, he hid it well.

Despite the volume of blood, Deena had only the one cut that required any serious attention. All others took only antiseptic.

"You never told me what happened," Mike said when he rose from the work he'd done.

Deena looked down at her hands. He'd taken his time with them, tending each wound with gentle deliberateness. Oddly enough, she'd been reminded of her own mother and her childhood, reminded of the way Gloria would touch each hurt as if wanting it for herself instead. Deena opened her mouth without realizing it and launched into the discovery of Tak's mother.

When she finished, Mike dropped onto the edge of the tub, heavy with the weight of speechlessness.

"I have this old memory," he said, "old enough to make me wonder if it's true. Snippets come as smoke sometimes, as screaming, shattered glass, and pain. In the dark, a baby cries—he cries enough to suffocate. I want to help him, I want to reach him, but I can't, because my shoulder's shattered."

"It's a dream," Deena whispered. "A recurrent fear of some unknown thing."

Mike yanked aside the collar of his shirt.

There, from shoulder to neck, was a thin white scar of careful design.

"I sustained a broken collarbone at some point in my life," Mike said. "Clearly, I've undergone surgery. Though no one seems willing to tell me about it."

He released his shirt and the simple tee went back to hiding old wounds.

"My aunt doesn't drive," Mike said. "She doesn't even own a car. I asked her once, when I was small, if she wouldn't like the independence that one would bring. She answered that some people lose independence for a reason."

Deena had the sudden, irrepressible urge to clamp hands over her ears, to stave off the certainty of impending horror.

"The Internet is a wonderfully fascinating thing," Mike said. "A search on Tak's mother turned up a record—a very old record—for third degree DUI felony with serious bodily harm."

Her gaze dropped to the ghost wound on his shoulder. Air, she realized, was extremely hard to find.

"She hurt…you?"

It didn't seem right to say aloud, didn't seem even possible, yet somehow those words were the only words she could manage.

The bathroom door rattled off its hinge. Deena swallowed her leap of fear and glanced around wildly for what she'd been meaning to do. Mike, one step ahead, hurriedly shoved first aid supplies back in their box.

"Who's in here?" Tak demanded through the door.

She remembered her smell of alcohol and splashed water

onto her face. Mike, who moved as harried as her, dampened a washcloth and dabbed at her face.

"There," he said, breathlessly. "Like new."

She could feel his heart, hammering away at his chest, and hers, just near it, tearing its way to her stomach.

When the door rattled again, Deena hurled it open.

Her husband sucked in all the air.

They stared at each other, man and wife, smoldering uncertainty between them. Should she try to explain? Should she wait for him? Could she even keep her thoughts together?

"The door," Tak said. "It was locked."

Lies bubbled up to the surface. Easy lies, simple lies that could hurt no one and nothing. So, her mouth moved. Oh, did her mouth move. But not a single sound came out.

"Excuse me," Deena finally said. "I have to…I have to go."

She squeezed past her husband and scurried away, only to pause at the top of the stairwell. She straightened her dress, hesitated, and thought, *I probably shouldn't have done that.* Just a few steps behind her, Mike squeezed past Tak, head down, and hurried to get away.

CHAPTER
fifteen

Boxes of Christmas decorations spilled onto the punctuated marble floor of the entrance hall. Streamers and tri-colored lights, tinsels, and ornaments of varying designs sat pristine and anxious to share the holiday cheer. Motown Christmas classics crooned out of a hijacked radio left by the previous homeowners. Prior to Tak fiddling with it, the kids had been trying out some new dance shuffle to the sound of something obscenely grating.

They lingered near an imported spruce so pompous and stuffed that a tilt of the head and the arms spread wide could take up neither width nor height of the tree. They made plans to adorn it to capacity, seemingly with every ornament, bulb fixture, and figurine sculpted by man's hand. Every opened box brought an argument with it, passionate bickering about color scheme and distribution, interlaced with an endless shuffle of quitting and rejoining the group. As they worked, half a dozen guys moved the piano from ballroom to entrance hall, shouting orders and complaints and threats with every inch. Once situated, they buried the static-ridden stereo in favor of more playing from Tony. He warmed up with scales as the others joined the family in fighting over decorations.

Still, things weren't bad. Not everyone present was Christian. Out there in the world, such a revelation was but a footnote for the day. With her family, it was evidence of some deviation. Before marriage, Deena's greatest fear had been that each holiday season would be a nightmare of contention, grating away at their marriage, grinding it down to bitterness. But the opposite had happened. Her husband, who had once described himself as an ambivalent Buddhist, had neither taken nor demanded, willing instead to leave religion as a choice for each child. Meanwhile, husband and wife celebrated all things together, from the exchanging of gifts on Christmas to the lighting of bonfires at the Obon Festival.

Tony launched into a complicated, full bodied luster of a gentle classic Deena couldn't quite name. Head down and traversing the length of the keyboard, he played as he always did: unobtrusive, serene, angelic. Notes drifted and manipulated once airborne, nuanced, graceful, intimate. Tak, ever the doting father, looked on with unadulterated pride. Tony, as if sensing him, flung a grin his way before tumbling headlong into a bursting cacophony of playful notes.

"Show-off," Tak mouthed and clapped him on the back, to which his son wriggled eyebrows in response.

The music steadied, mellowing out to an upbeat festive number. Tak crossed the room with mischief in his smile, took Aunt Caroline's hand and whispered in her ear. She cocked a skeptic brow and he stepped back, put a hand to his abdomen, and sashayed his hips, eyes closed. Caroline threw back her head and hooted, before allowing Tak to lead her to the center of room. Once there, he took her waist in one hand and drew up their clasped hands in the other, before the two began an exaggerated sway. Small steps to and fro; fractured by cackles of laughter, mashed toes, and accusations of poor dancing.

Deena tried to imagine a man—any man—conjuring affection in old sour-mouthed Caroline. Snake charmer, she thought wryly. Another addition to the résumé of her husband.

"I do wonder where he gets it from," Daichi said, voice low and suddenly at her side. "I've all the charisma of an executioner, while his mother's most content comatose."

He tipped up his glass of orange juice just as Deena stole a glance his way.

"I know," he said. "About what happened in the billiard room, that is."

"I..." she blinked, wondering where all her words had gone.

Tony flashed into a frantic melody, a rush of shoulder-jerking symphony. Tak responded by swinging out Caroline, abandoning her there, and dropping down on the bench next to his son. Tony scooted to accommodate him and the playing of one flew fluid into two. Tak's smooth, raw, deceptively velvet voice slipped in, infected with his inability to stop smiling. Tony followed, voice measured and aware, a musician wielding yet another instrument with care. Son was all shade and delicate harmony to his father's playful torch of emotion.

"You haven't told him," Daichi said, eyes impassive on his son and grandson.

"I—"

Deena halted as the bottom dropped out of Tak's voice as he crooned about the meanness of the Grinch. Tony flooded into the song smooth, seamless, as earnest as if he performed 'Silent Night'.

"Your wife," Deena said, remembering her conversation with Mike. "She doesn't…drive, does she?"

Daichi shot her a look of scalding impatience.

"Ask what you intend to," he said. "I require no preamble."

Fine then, Deena thought, even as ice spread through her belly. She had a relationship with her father-in-law that no one else had managed. They were direct with each other, forthcoming, and she knew more about him than most. If she asked a question of Daichi, she knew that she'd get the answer.

And that was why the fear set in.

"Why doesn't your wife ever drive?" Deena said.

It seemed as good a question to start with as any.

The music slowed. New Orleans blues slow. Jukebox slow. Crawling, gritty, sweat-slipping-down-the-face kind of slow. Tak belted out a roar of ridiculous magnitude, earning a whoop of approval from the Hammonds.

Tony mouthed "Show-off" and proceeded to show off himself.

"The state of Florida revoked her license several decades ago," Daichi said, answering Deena's question.

She let the words hang there awhile.

"Why?" she said eventually.

Daichi threw back his juice.

"Driving under the influence with serious bodily harm. A third degree felony in Florida."

She hadn't been sure whether she'd believed Mike's speculations, even if his tone had been steady and convincing. But this? She had no choice but to believe this.

"Mike has a scar," she hurried on, like one with too much momentum to stop the fall. "Is that where the charge comes from?"

"Partly," Daichi said. "Though Takumi and Jonathan also suffered injuries they were too young to remember."

The baby. The crying baby Mike was desperate to help was his little brother.

"How long has she struggled with this?" Deena said.

Her father-in-law frowned.

"Too long for anyone to be sure," he said. "Off again then on again, then on with no off."

"So, she's always been like this?"

Daichi looked at her in surprise.

"No," he said. "Not always."

Their object of discussion entered the room. Silent, graceful, ethereal, her makeup had been redone in smoky shadows, delicate blush, and dramatic lashes. She'd slipped into a sleek, flattering avant-garde sheath of teal. Deena looked from her mother-in-law to herself in bewilderment. How was it that she sustained not a hint of their earlier altercation, while Deena suffered through a handful of bandages and clothes that required constant readjusting?

"It started with the boredom," Daichi said. "Lonely housewife, unfulfilled. Surely, you've heard of it."

On the piano, Tony had turned his attention to a loping, dramatic melody, all vestiges of holiday cheer gone. Deena recognized it as one of those larger-than-life ballads that graced the Billboard charts a generation ago. When her husband's sonorous quality slipped in, it was with the delicate incision required. Deena was torn between finishing her conversation with Daichi and fleeing, as her husband took a special kind of joy out of mortifying via serenade.

"Boredom?" Deena echoed. "That sounds a little incredible to believe. And dismissive."

"The answer doesn't fit your practical nature, your need for order in the storm." He eyed her with something that bordered on interest. "I met my wife when we were both students at Harvard. Clearly, she had aspirations beyond that of trophy piece. You're a plainly ambitious woman. Would you be satisfied with the domesticated role?"

She thought back to their earlier conversations, back when her relationship with Tak was unknown to him. Back when Daichi functioned as her boss, mentor, and friend even. He'd said that she'd never be sated with the "trappings of mediocrity", with a "subservient role as wife and mother". Did this same fire of dissatisfaction consume Tak's mother? Deena knew that Hatsumi, several years younger than Daichi, had left school to marry him after Tak had been conceived. But so many years had lapsed, years where she threw herself into a bottle instead of resurrecting dreams. It was the mark of cowardice, the mark of weakness to Deena.

When her sister, Lizzie, had been addicted to everything, Deena could work the winding path to her destruction out in her head. Little supervision, suffocating poverty, and exposure to criminal elements were all constant norms. Her choices, while appalling, had explanations backed by twisted reasoning. All Hatsumi had was never-ending boredom.

"You should have left her," Deena said. "When she harmed the children, maybe even earlier. You could have replaced her with a woman of your choosing and given both boys stable homes. Not all of us had the choice of improving the quality of our upbringing."

Daichi looked at her as if she'd just arrived, and unexpectedly at that.

"Tanakas don't divorce. Surely, you've heard that by now."

She looked up then. Looked up as Mike entered the room and Tak hit a false note. Her husband, with angle enough to look from his cousin to his wife, flashed a look of annoyance before burying it in a distracted smile. When their song petered to nothingness, Tak rose, put a hand on Mike's arm, and led him to the hall. Deena and her father-in-law watched them go.

"Tread careful with those two," Daichi said. "Theirs is a game not even they understand."

IN THE HALLWAY, Tak whirled on Mike and buried the urge to punch him somewhere deep. Everything he had in him, absolutely everything, bristled at the resistance to this impulse. But he would be cool. He would not be the jealous, raging husband, as easily subject to paranoia as he was to the latest strand of the flu.

Tak took a deep breath and exhaled.

"Tell me what happened in the bathroom."

Distrust chilled Mike's stare.

"Ask your wife."

"I'm asking you."

Mike rubbed absentmindedly at the spot where Tak had grabbed him to yank him into the hall.

"We talked."

"About?"

Mike dropped his gaze.

"Private stuff."

"Private stuff?" Tak echoed. "You think you can talk private stuff with another man's wife?"

Mike shot him a look of ill-contained exasperation. It reminded Tak of their childhood, back when they were almost OK. Back when Tak would fume for a third go at the Nintendo and his big cousin would give in, because, well, because he really wasn't so bad after all.

"We weren't…doing anything," Mike said. "You must know that. Otherwise, I never would have made it out the bathroom alive."

It was true. All true, and yet he couldn't get past the general unease that always came with Mike. That feeling that since he was the smartest in the room, it was best just to rely on distrust and figure out what the hell he was up to later. He was always up to something.

"Can I go now?" Mike said.

He wore the flat expression of a man expecting undeservedly poor treatment.

Tak forced himself to reconsider. Was he overreacting? He just couldn't say.

CHAPTER
sixteen

D EENA REGRETTED THE DECISION TO do a barbecue
for lunch the second she stepped outdoors to a half
dozen bickering men cloistered around the grill. At the
center was her father-in-law and his brother, unapologetic in
their fervor. Arms waved as faces slipped into varying shades
of magenta. The words "phony", "trailer trash" and "poser"
wafted over to her, before she decided it wasn't the place she
wanted to be. On spotting her cousin, Crystal, by the pool,
she journeyed over to speak to her instead.

They hadn't seen each other since their days of childhood,
when Crystal and her mother, Caroline, lived with Deena,
Deena's siblings, Crystal's siblings, Grandma Emma, and
Grandpa Eddie. For a brief time, Deena, Keisha, and Crystal
even shared a room, crammed into a hell of their very own
design.

Crystal waved her over.

"Sit. Please,'" she said. "Or else I'll think I have BO."

Deena sat and looked around.

"You came with someone," she said after a while.

"Tyson."

The name hung in the air, clinging for recognition. Except, she hadn't said it as a lover would, as if the very taste of each letter was worthwhile. She'd said it cautiously. Maybe their love was new.

Years stretched between Crystal and Deena, years of silence and distance. Their awkwardness felt doused with uncertainty. But they'd been friends once.

"You've done good for yourself," Crystal said. "Tyson can't stop talking about all this."

Deena followed her gaze to the pool, where a dark and rippling man sliced water like an Olympian.

"Oh," Deena said, surprised. "He's…athletic."

"And damned pretty, too. Which happens to be my kryptonite. Judging by the look of your husband, I'd say it's yours, too."

Deena flushed.

"No. I—I'm not vain. I—"

How had this conversation happened?

Crystal giggled.

Deep, toasted even skin, smooth as cream and perpetually flawless. Short, with a compact frame and flaring hips, Deena's cousin was cute in a completely non-threatening way. The sort of girl whose eye shadow matched her handbag, yet would look up in surprise if a man expressed interest.

But she was genuine, with a smile that reminded Deena of winter fires and comfort, of knowing that someone cared.

Yet, they'd grown apart. When Crystal graduated from high school, she'd boarded a Greyhound for Tallahassee, armed with a scholarship to Florida A&M and a determination to never come back.

Deena's gaze shifted to Caroline, who stood at the pool's edge in a yellow one-piece that had her looking like a lemon on legs. A cigarette dangled from her mouth.

"Five years and Tyson's never met my mother." Crystal smiled. "He gets why now."

"Does he?"

A flicker of uncertainty crossed Crystal's face.

"How long did it take you?" she said. "Before...you know."

"Three years," Deena said. Three years and him almost dying before she found some sense, before she let Tak into the world of her family.

Crystal frowned.

"I can't marry," she said. "Marriage brings children and—and the opportunity to..."

Her gaze drifted to the pool.

"To turn into your mother," Deena said.

Crystal said nothing.

Deena gave Tyson a second, closer look as he made strong, smooth scissor movements from one end of the pool to the other. He had stamina and strength.

He'd need it for their family.

Once done swimming, Tyson erupted from the pool with a flood of water, pulling up and over the side before extending to his full height. Crystal was right. He had a sculpted beauty. Tall, dark, and broad shouldered, every inch of him boasted definition, every stretch implied strength. He turned to the women and smiled.

It felt like being laughed at.

"He's sweet. And I adore him. But he knows what he looks like and takes pride in it." Crystal paused. "What happened to your hand?"

Deena looked up.

"Nothing. Really. Just a kitchen accident." She tucked her hand into her lap and smiled too brightly. "Tell me about you. What have you been doing all these years?"

"I'm a social worker," she said and snorted out a laugh. "Ironic, I suppose. Me telling others how their families should be."

It's your need for order, Deena wanted to say. We all have it.

"Tyson's in the Marines," Crystal went on. "He did a tour in Iraq and another in Afghanistan before getting discharged."

Deena looked at him with new eyes.

"Well. Let him know that I thank him for his service."

"I will. Only, he doesn't like to talk about it much."

No. Deena imagined he wouldn't.

CHAPTER
seventeen

Tyson Klein padded into the Aruban mansion on Malmok Beach, trailing pool water along as he went. Two tours of duty in the Middle East would never get him something half as gorgeous—two hundred tours would never do it. Still, he could hardly begrudge strangers who'd given him an all-inclusive Caribbean vacation.

He'd never seen a house so big and he loved beautiful things. Treasured them, as it turned out.

A piano played something forlorn, a complicated symphony that mocked his limited understanding of music. Tyson slipped into the entrance hall and watched as long, slender fingers shared weighty emotion with every note.

"Beethoven's *Moonlight Sonata*," Tak supplied.

Mournfulness whispered what words could not say; each meter weighing in a hopelessness mankind couldn't hope to articulate. "My version's good," Tak said. "But my son's can make the walls weep."

Tyson said nothing, content with the beautiful despair he drowned in. He closed his eyes and felt the span of his emptiness, the insurmountable weight of his own shortcomings. He could never create a sound, a look, any anything as heartfelt as this. Forever, it seemed, he stood shackled to the floor by Beethoven. When notes reverberated long after the last had been played, Tyson knew he wanted to know Tak better.

"It's not that I mind an audience," Tak said, "but my wife would kill you for dripping chlorine everywhere."

"Chlo—"

Tyson looked down at himself and cursed, before Tak came over and clapped him on the back.

"Tyson, right?"

A subtle smirk illuminated the other man's smile. Tyson knew guys like him, had served with them. Easy joy, bottomless humor, charm that rained by the bucket. Lesser knowing people took it as a defense mechanism, a mask for fear made plain on the battlefield. But men like that stood loyal, fought fierce, and found a smile even as they died. He knew. He'd seen it.

"I was about to make a drink," Tak said. "Clean up and join me."

They met in the billiards room fifteen minutes later. Tak stood behind the bar, changed from a blue t-shirt to a white one. He ran a hand through damp ebony hair and shook off the moisture. When their eyes met, Tyson looked away.

"What are you having?" Tak asked.

"Whatever you're having."

Tak fiddled behind the bar before emerging with two glasses of amber liquid.

"Scotch," he said and slid it over.

Good. No pretense behind it.

They went on to small talk the way men do, about alcohol, college days, and sports. Tyson had been awestruck to see Kenji among the guests, but he buried that in a shrug of indifference. He talked instead about a stint on the wrestling team at the University of Southern California.

"Oh hey," Tak said. "You were down the street from me. I was at UCLA."

Which plummeted them to mortal enemies, bickering about every meeting in every sport, right down to men's water polo. Tak shouted about UCLA being the greatest sports juggernaut to ever grace the planet, while Tyson insisted that they hadn't a chance in hell of beating anyone in football. They shouted themselves into laughter and then another round of drinks. When the mania died down, a smile still plastered Tyson's lips.

"What?" Tak said and slid a scotch his way.

"I was thinking," Tyson admitted. "About my time in Afghanistan."

"And that made you smile?"

Tyson looked up at him.

"There was a guy I served with named Ash. Coolest person you'd ever meet. Only thing we ever disagreed on was sports."

Tak smiled. But it was a knowing smile, one anticipating its fall.

"He died," Tyson said. "The wrong way."

The scotch sat staring at him. For a while, there was only it and his hands around the glass.

"He did two tours, like me. Only to get mugged after returning."

Tyson threw back his liquor and winced.

"It's a shit world we live in," he said, feeling the heat spread through his belly. "It's a world where the people you care about—the ones you let get close…"

He shook his head. There was no point in saying more.

"You can't think like that," Tak said, cutting in as Ash Kobayashi would have. "You can't…not let people in. It's not living. It's not life."

Tyson snorted.

"That's what Ash would have said."

Tak studied him with wide brown eyes, indecision painted his face.

"I should go check on the family. But if you ever need to talk—about Ash or your trashy alma mater," he rose and gave Tyson's shoulder a squeeze, "come find me. I'll make sure I'm available."

Tyson promised he would before watching him go. How long he sat there afterward, he couldn't say.

CHAPTER
eighteen

Deena closed herself in the study the second she saw the incoming call screen on her cell. Briefly, she considered rejecting it as she had a few others, but she knew that eventually they'd have to talk.

She answered.

"Collect call from Homestead Correctional Institution. Do you accept the charges?"

Deena took a deep breath.

"Yes."

The call chimed through.

"Deena? It's Keisha."

She found a chair and sat.

"What's happened? Did something happen to my mom?"

A muffled shout distorted whatever her cousin meant to say. In it, Deena felt a stab of fear.

"No. Only, she needs you to get back with her. She says you told her never to call the house, but when she calls your cell, you never answer."

"Keisha—"

Another shout was followed by a rumble of commotion. Deena's cousin spat a rude retort.

"Listen. I'm only calling because your mother asked. She's looked out for me since I've got here. Protected me. Helped me to adjust. I told her I'd get an answer from you."

"Well, you told her wrong, didn't you?" Deena snapped. "Because I haven't made up my mind yet. Now excuse me."

She disconnected the call, stood, and faced her husband.

It was like the steep drop of a rollercoaster.

"Who was that?" he said.

"No one. Just business."

"It sounded personal."

"Fine. Then it was personal."

He watched her as she sauntered for the door.

"Tell me what's going on, Dee."

Going on, she thought. Her mother was going on. Wasn't that always the case?

She opened her mouth.

"Don't," he said. "If it's gonna be a lie."

She hesitated and his eyes went black with anger.

"Fine," he said. "Keep your goddamned secrets," before turning and heading for the door.

"Tak!"

She grabbed his arm without knowing what she'd say. He pulled away just enough to give her a polluted once-over.

"Going after someone only works when you mean it, Dee."

"I do mean it!" She flung her hands in exasperation. Everything was always so clear to her husband, right and wrong, black and white, neat as the lines on paper. Hadn't he ever felt conflicted before? Uncertain? Even his love for her, he swore, he'd known from the start. She'd never been instantly sure about anything, ever.

"Look at me," Deena said. "Look at my face." She felt the desperation creeping in, the nasty voice that said no good things, especially not this man, were truly meant for her. Funny, that the voice should sound like her grandfather.

"I love you. And I will talk to you. I'm just…sorting feelings out for myself."

He stared at her, the hardness of his features seeping into softness.

"I could help you."

She shook her head, then drew up to him, pressing her lips to his. But instead of the familiar warmth she craved, a cold voice crept in instead. Here is where he slips away. Here is where you lose him, because you can't love without controlling.

He kissed her back.

A brush of butterfly wings was what it was. A whiff of fallen snowflakes just there. A whisper of a kiss, swept away by winds of a weak current.

She pressed closer and he swept her into his arms. Solid against her, steady, he was lips and touch and certainty all over.

She had words trapped in her head and oxygen didn't

matter. Her hands raked under his shirt, trailing the hardness of his back.

"Upstairs," Tak groaned and snatched her by the hand.

They scurried up, shut the door and locked it behind them.

Tak pulled her in by the waist and kissed, open-mouthed, fierce, devouring.

She knew his strength, felt it as he lifted her, and experienced crushing weight when they dropped to the bed. Chest to chest, his heart beating against hers.

He dominated her with his kisses, each harder, deeper, and hungrier than the last. They could tangle no more, press one to the other no more; already they were all heat and roaming hands, a single knot of pulsing need.

Clothes came away in hurried snatches, both aiding the other in the need for skin against skin. When Tak pulled away to discard his jeans, it was she who pulled him back, body shaking.

He clamored on top, grabbed her hips and thrust, arching her back violently with the force of his entry. He'd pierced her to the core and kept going, going roughshod till she moaned pitifully.

Words wouldn't come, only air, air that her hands couldn't clench. Deena groped at the bed, wild, bunching sheets in her fist and quivering as her husband rammed tidal waves of pleasure right through her.

Every thrust came with a grunt, every pound a measure of punishment, as he dug fingers into her hips and drilled wrath to her core.

She flooded in spastic pleasure, mouthing his name,

hissing nonsense, far beyond the point of done. He lifted her legs and pinned each back, so that knee touched shoulder on each side.

Impaled, she gave up on not screaming.

He burrowed in punctuated fashion, strokes ragged and hammering to a finish.

She couldn't hold on, couldn't hope to hold on, not when he bucked like a bronco off a cliff. Harder and more emphatic he grew, as if to core her out, till he slammed with a groan of surrender. Liquid heat flooded her, earning a gasp of pleasure from Deena.

Her gaze drifted skyward, ever conscious of the strumming of Tak's heart. In the rawest, most torturous moment of her life, that heart had stopped beating, ceasing hers right along with it. She knew but one thing at the time: that after finding his love, she couldn't bear being without it.

He rolled away from her, sat up, and slipped into his clothes.

"Tak?" Deena said as alarm sliced through her. "Tak, don't just—"

The door shut on her words. Of course, she thought. Of course sex hadn't solved any of their problems.

CHAPTER
nineteen

Finally, the loons had calmed down. A full day of Hammonds and Tanakas meant the full range of manic depression insofar as Tony was concerned. From Aunt June, Mike, John, and Lauren's mom, who squealed and clapped at the slightest joys, to Aunt Caroline, with scowls enough to curdle milk in its breakfast bowl. They had crazy on tap in that household and could conjure up every variety on demand.

Grandma Emma spent her time snoozing in her chair. Even then, she wore the painted smile of a woman with good dreams, or good jokes at the least. It made Tony think of the stories she'd told him, of chickens in the yard and dirt on the face, and soon he was strumming out chords reminiscent of a life he'd never had. Tony imagined that Grandma Emma's heaven, when she reached it, would be something like Eufaula, Alabama, the place of childhood.

Heaven. Funny thing that heaven was. Different to every person and not there at all to some. As a Hammond, he knew that God demonstrated His awesomeness by smiting fornicators, burning down cities, and drowning every living creature when His temper flared. Tony sometimes wondered how many Hammonds He had a mind to smite at the moment.

On the other hand, the Tanakas were cleaved at the center, half Christian, half Buddhist and seemingly uncommitted to it all.

Interesting beliefs Buddhists had. They shied away from questions other religions proved desperate to answer, forgoing the temptation to explain the world's creation or purpose, the afterlife, or whether God even existed. Four Noble Truths, they said, held the key to a life without suffering. They embraced wisdom, patience, love, and tolerance on a quest toward Enlightenment, instead of communion with an omnipotent God.

Both religions had their merits. With Christianity, he couldn't deny the lure of forgiveness no matter how terrible the act. It meant a kid like him, who once rummaged through garbage for a meal, who stole what he couldn't afford to buy, was still worthwhile, was still someone. It meant that Old Tony, sleeping on sidewalks with newspapers, was just as treasured as New Tony, convertible Porsche and all.

For New Tony, nothing had been denied. Not the Porsche, gifted to him for mastering three instruments to his father's specifications, not the weekender yacht parked next to his father's after finishing a series of sailing classes. There were credit cards in his name and a bank account for expenses, though the bulk of his money sat in a trust fund, contingent on his completion of college. When that day came, Tony cleared five million from his parents and another two from his grandparents. On completing an advanced degree, he could get another three, possibly more. These were the things promised and delivered to New Tony, a kid who had the leisure of seeking out wisdom and patience, now that hunger and fear had abated.

"You gonna keep up that racket?" Tony's cousin, Lloyd, snapped from his bed on the other side of the room.

Before he could answer, Tony's cell phone rang. He snatched it up, knowing it would be Wendy.

"You're late," he said.

Wendy snorted.

"I know and I love you, too."

Lloyd's long lean figure rolled over and batted lashes at the sight of his cousin.

"Ready to propose yet?" he said.

Tony gave him the finger.

"OK," Wendy said. "Saints over Cowboys, 17 to 10. Jets over Browns, 3 to 0."

"You sure? Cause—"

"Tony!"

"Alright, alright."

She read off a few more scores for the NFL games he cared about before switching to college football. When done, he cursed.

"Lizard says you have to wash his car," Wendy said. "Topless in the teacher's parking lot."

Tony groaned. Sometimes these games between him and the guys went too far.

"So, what's the deal? You were supposed to call me hours ago. I call you a half dozen times and you don't even answer."

She hesitated.

"Gage came over for a little while. We watched *M*A*S*H*."

Tony felt his jaw set. His lips thinned out in annoyance.

"That all you do?"

"What's that supposed to mean?"

"Don't act like you can't figure it out." He got up, feet pacing without his approval. "Don't act like you don't know what a guy like Gage would want."

"A guy like Gage or a guy like you?"

"Me? What have I got to do with this?"

"Why don't you ask your Jezebel next time you fall into her?"

Tony measured out an exhale.

"You're being silly. I'm just trying to protect you. Gage"

"Isn't half as bad as that girl you chase after."

"Whatever. I know he doesn't like *M*A*S*H*."

"What do you care? Anyway, I thought you'd be glad I found someone else to watch it with. All these years, all you've done is complain about it."

Tony dropped back on the bed, mouth thinned in irritation.

He didn't even know why he boiled. It was as she said: he hated *M*A*S*H*.

"I should go," Tony said. After all, he had to meet Lila.

He jumped in the shower, pulled on a tee and jeans, and slid down the banister. Out front, he handed a fifty to the driver and sat back for the ride.

Fifteen minutes to Oranjestad, to Lila Dahl and her perfect smile.

Except the smile wasn't what he was there for, and he was reminded of that the second she put her arms around him. Oh yeah, he thought as he kissed her. This was what he liked about her.

"Alright," Lila said. "Where to?"

Tony pulled away from her in breathlessness.

"My house," he said and couldn't believe himself, even if he was the one to have said it.

As far as bad ideas went, this was possibly the worst. Not only was there but one place to take Lila without fear of discovery, but that one place happened to be the easiest to get caught. In a house stuffed with people, no place in the house was safe. So, he'd made up his mind on the ride that they'd never actually enter the house.

"Wow," Lila said when the house came into view. She careened her neck for a glimpse through Tony's window, pressing mounds of curls into his face.

He understood her awe and had known it for himself once. After hitchhiking from Bismarck to Miami to find family, he'd stumbled into a world of wealth. Lila wore the face he used to.

"We're going to the gardens," Tony said the second the car stopped.

"Good idea," the driver commented.

Tony scowled. Apparently, although bribing him, a shut mouth hadn't been part of his purchase.

They maneuvered around the side of the house, taking the long way, the safe way, to the gardens. Once there, Tony pulled her into a thicket of Kibra Hacha trees, akin to the African acacias they saw on a safari tour a few months back. He pressed her back to the trunk and kissed her mouth hard, hands everywhere.

It wasn't long before her shirt went up for him, baring full breasts without a bra. Tony pulled her tee away and dropped it. This was it. They would go all the way.

There'd been a close call at a party during the summer they'd met. They'd spent most of it making out, but when his moment came scoring with a drunk girl who might not remember had felt predatory. So, he took her home in a cab instead.

But he wouldn't be calling any cabs that night.

CHAPTER
Twenty

Tony woke to humidity, to sunlight, and to the absence of his pants and Lila's shirt.

"What do you mean, 'they're gone'?" he said.

Lila swept the vicinity with her gaze. Sure enough, his shirt lay where he'd left it, alongside her jeans, but there was no sign other clothes remained.

"Stop playing around, Lila." The sound of laughter too close burned a hole from his chest to his belly. "My family's out there. You need to put on your clothes and leave."

"Don't talk to me like that. Didn't I tell you they're gone?"

In that night, her body seemed glorious, perfected with sensuous mounds. Now it stared back at him, like the banner heralding a hellish nightmare.

Tony rose and searched the vicinity.

"They are gone," he said.

"It's a joke," Lila said. "Someone obviously stumbled onto us at some point. Whether it was when we were…you know, or later. Either way, they made off with some clothes."

He didn't want to tell her how many possible culprits there were. He had loads of cousins in the house, any one of whom might have sought out a good laugh. Even Uncle John or Mike might have pulled something like this, tormenting him for their own brand of enjoyment.

He could spend days interrogating suspects.

He wanted to pray. Pray to God and Buddha and Jesus and Muhammad and the six-limbed Lord Shiva.

The best he could do was hope to pass off his boxers as swim trunks, leave Lila in the bushes like the bare-chested Eve to his Adam, and hope to find her shirt, quick. After that, the hard part began.

Tony took a deep breath and started off toward the house, weaving through the garden as far as it would take him. When he got to the end, his cousins Remy and Lloyd were waiting.

"You should have told us there was a party last night," Lloyd said. "Leaving me in the room like that wasn't nice."

"Yeah," Remy chimed in. "And you know the first rule of bro-dom. It ain't no fun, if the homies can't have none."

"Gimme the clothes. Give me her shirt, at least. You don't want the kids to see her, do you?"

Remy grinned. "No, we want to see her."

"Be serious," Tony snapped. But he looked from one to the other, certainty dimming with each second.

"She's this way, right?" Lloyd said and took toward the garden. "We'll keep her company while you find clothes."

Tony shoved him the chest.

"Stop fucking around!"

But in the time it took for him to shove Lloyd, Remy was already cutting through the trees. He couldn't stop both of them. Lloyd, who was older, taller, and stronger, could floor Tony and step over him. What could he do? What should he do?

Tony saw him in the distance. In fear, hurt, anxiety, he'd come to rely on the name.

"Dad!" he yelled. "Dad, hurry! Come! I need some help!"

Lloyd took off, followed by Remy, who kicked the hidden clothes out from under a bush. So, by the time his father arrived, it was just him, Tony, and a half-naked girl.

Punishment. He didn't need to be told.

CHAPTER
twenty-one

MIKE SET SCOTCH, VODKA, RUM, tequila, gin, and triple sec on the counter. Tak, who had never known that his cousin moonlighted as a bartender in college, sat back to watch him work. Five glasses sat on the countertop, each filled with exacting portions. As Mike worked, he whistled.

"Let's play spades," Kenji said. "I feel like humbling somebody."

Mike came around to dole out drinks as they sorted out the teams: Tak and Tyson versus Kenji and Ken.

Tak drew the high card and shuffled the deck. Almost immediately, Kenji reached over and cut, earning a glare from his brother. Tak dealt, pausing only for a sip of scotch.

"This is bullshit," he said.

Kenji snorted.

In truth, Tak had a stellar hand, but it did little to lift

his mood. Between Tony's antics, Deena's secrets, and not knowing how to feel about Mike, crassness came easy.

Tak stole a glance at Tyson, trying to read the tea leaves in his face. His partner offered a secret smile then looked down at his cards. Good, at least he had a decent hand.

"Kenji," Asami's husband, Ken, said. "How's the shoulder holding up? I saw the game when it blew out, you know. Pretty rough by the look of it."

"The team doctor says the shoulder's garbage," Kenji admitted. "Surgery's set for next week."

He tossed a card and claimed the ones beneath, earning a curse from his brother.

"Team doctor," Ken said. "And Tak with this unbelievable house. You two are more glamour than I can stand. How did you come across this find, anyway?"

"Right place at the right time," Tak said. "The owner was looking to sell."

"And you just happened upon that?" Ken was looking at him now.

"You could say that," Tak tossed out a card and claimed the pile. "The owner's name was Brent Everclear. Maybe you've heard of him."

Ken snorted. "Next you'll ask me if I've heard of the Super Bowl."

Once upon a time, Brent Everclear had been the star quarterback for the New England Patriots. Two rings had been earned under his watch, thanks to a cannon of an arm. Tak looked up to find Mike studying him.

"Isn't that who Aubree Daniels married?"

Kenji snapped to attention.

"Mike, I don't think you should—"

"It's cool," Tak said and glanced at his cousin. "Yes, that's who Aubree married."

"Who's she?" Ken said.

"An old cheerleader, and Tak's ex," Mike said.

"You boys must lead exciting lives," Ken said. "Professional athlete. Unorthodox wife. Cheerleaders. Rivers of wealth."

"Ken," Tak warned. Aunt's husband or not, he'd watch his damned mouth.

"Don't misunderstand me," Ken said. "Envy is what you're hearing." He chased the words with liquor. "I mean, women must fling themselves at you both. Oh, to be one of you." His eyebrows did a little dance before he nudged Tyson enthusiastically.

"I guess," Tyson muttered.

"Listen," Tak said. "We're not about to—"

"Top me off, would you, kiddo?" Ken motioned at Mike with his emptied glass.

Mike rose with his eyes on Tak, who tilted his head in discreet approval. Get the drink, was what that said. Maybe they'd get to meet the real Ken.

"You're modest," Ken announced to no one in particular. "And it's very Japanese, isn't it? Death before shame. Humility and deference." He grinned. "Except maybe for Tak."

"What does that even mean?" Tak said.

Ken grinned. "It means you're good looking and you make sure we know it." He shot a somber look at Tyson. "Lock that Dixie Chick of yours up. They go crazy for this one, you know."

"Nix that second drink," Tak said. "Someone isn't handling their liquor well."

"I'm fine," Ken said and waved Mike over, seizing the drink the second he got close.

"To the boldness of Takumi Tanaka," he said. "And the prowess of his little brother Kenji."

"This would be a better trip," Ken said after a swallow, "if we were back in Miami with you two. Oh, the ladies you must have. Every blonde shade of deliciousness. And nothing turns my head faster than one of those. Cream of the crop, I've always thought. But the way you guys carry on," he spread his palms wide, gesturing to Tak, Kenji, and then Mike, "I think I'm missing something."

"Yeah. It's called marriage to my aunt," Tak said.

For a second, Tak was reminded of the time he punched Mike in face after taking things too far with Deena. He considered doing the same to his aunt's husband, then figured it would make absolutely no difference.

ASAMI SAT OFF the rotunda, legs crossed, and looking out the window. Tissue clenched in her fist and gaze on the rain, the tightness in her jaw looked severe.

This was Tak's aunt and his domain, but Deena sat down anyway.

A few sniffs later, Asami looked her way.

"Well?" she snapped.

Deena blinked. She had never heard the woman raise her voice.

"My husband is a bastard," Asami announced. "He has a child. Six years younger than our daughter."

"Are you...are you certain?"

"Of course. The child comes over some weekends. He has done so for years."

Deena tried to imagine herself in the same position as Tak's aunt, but she got no further than her husband having sex with another woman. Right about there was where she murdered him.

"You think I'm stupid," Asami said.

"No, I—"

"You'd be right. I am profoundly stupid."

This wasn't how the conversation was supposed to go. Deena should have been offering condolences and Asami was supposed to find comfort.

"If you've known this long," Deena said, "why are you upset now?"

Asami's gaze drifted to the entrance of the room, before she turned her attention back to Deena.

"We fight constantly because of this. He says I need to accept things or get a divorce. I don't want to do either."

He give her an ultimatum? She couldn't pretend that any of it made sense.

"They're not as perfect as you think," Tak had told her once. "Some are just better with masks."

"Asami, a child by another woman must feel like a monstrous betrayal. But with counseling, perhaps, you can make peace with it."

Someone snorted.

Deena looked up to see Aunt Caroline.

"That's the dumbest advice I ever heard."

Caroline sauntered through the room, weaving until she found a couch to drop onto. She did it with such force that the furniture slammed the wall, before she let out a throaty exhale.

"What you need," Caroline said, "is to kick his ass one good time."

"Aunt Caroline—"

"No," Asami waved Deena off. "Let her talk."

Caroline leaned in, satisfied.

"With the father of my oldest son, Tariq, I was the other woman and didn't know it. I was sixteen and stupid. Too stupid to know I had no business with a grown man. Turned out the grown man was married. Didn't want nothing to do with me nor my baby, once he got here."

Caroline lit a Newport and took a drag.

"I beat his ass," she said. "Beat him till he shook. And he deserved every lick of the whooping he got."

"But you were sixteen," Asami said. "He must have been larger than you. And stronger."

"Yeah, but that's just a detail, easily corrected with an equalizer and a little motivation. Which gets me to my next point. You sitting here crying. Crying ain't nothing but feeling sorry for yourself. Kicking ass is about justice. When you feel like you need some justice, you'll set about getting some too."

Asami sat up straight. She lifted first one hand, then the other, examining both the front and the back. She stood.

"Asami? Asami! Don't do anything stupid!" Deena cried.

Tak's aunt strode for the door.

Deena tore after her. Into the hall, with a look both ways to figure where Tak's aunt had gone. She heard a noise and chased it to the reception room, just in time to see Asami yank a poker from the fireplace.

"Please, don't—"

She shoved Deena aside and crossed to the billiard room.

Deena burst in just as the poker cracked into Ken's arm, upending him, the table, and a mountain of playing cards. The men scattered.

Her husband fell to the floor in a lump, red faced, cheeks puffed, cursing, and gripping a dead arm. He said words Deena had never known and told his wife to do things she'd never thought possible. Asami lifted the poker again, but Tak sliced in with a cry of "Whoa," and swept her away while in his embrace.

His hands clamped over hers as he whispered. Deena imagined they were words of calm, of encouragement. Slumped on the floor, Ken continued to curse her.

"Get him outta here before I crack his face myself," Tak said, except it wasn't clear who he spoke to.

Mike looked at Ken as if he were a vaguely threatening parasite, while Kenji had only one good arm to begin with. Tyson hoisted Ken up and led him out. Mike went in search of his mother and grandmother, hoping either could calm Asami.

Tyson returned sweaty, but decidedly aloof. When the women arrived for Asami, Kenji used that as a good time to leave with Mike.

"Thanks," Tak said to Tyson. He came over and clapped

him on the shoulder. "The family's not usually this crazy but—"

"Two tours in the Middle East, remember?" Tyson shrugged. "Just glad I could do something for you."

Deena had the feeling of invading some privacy, so she busied herself straightening the room.

"We were going to win," Tak said, turning back to talk of the game. "I can read you. You're cautious. You underbid, so I overbid."

Tyson grinned wide. "That's what Ash used to say."

The two stood there, both on the verge of saying more. Deena excused herself so that it might be said.

CHAPTER
Twenty-Two

Mike sat for a long while in the back of the sedan, ignoring the question that had been posed. Beyond the windows of the muted car, the weather's sudden voraciousness of gloom surprised him and he lived in Seattle.

He wasn't sure if he wanted to do this. And yet, the words fell out just the same.

"Who lived here before?" he said.

The man met his gaze in the rearview mirror.

"An American football player."

"Did you work for him?"

The driver shook his head. "My cousin did some cleaning for them."

Some cleaning for the girl that used to love Tak. Mike slipped him two twenties for the honor of meeting this cousin.

They drove to a blustery fishing village on the south side of the island. There, simple pastel homes cluttered together as if huddled for warmth and comfort. A rickety wooden dock, just within sight, held to it a dozen or so antiquated boats, with a few more pulled right up to the shoreline.

Mike's driver led him up a packed dirt walkway to an unassuming white matchbox of a home. He banged, rattling the hinges, before a stooped and leathery old lady appeared. They exchanged harsh words in a foreign language as raindrops began to fall. Finally, the old lady looked up to the heavens, said something foul, and gestured for them to follow.

They went around the house to a patch of vegetable garden out back. There, a middle-aged woman with threads of gray curling through black hair rose from a row of tomatoes. The driver went to her.

"She wants to know what you want," the driver said.

Mike stepped forward, heart strumming, and handed over a few bills.

"I knew the wife, Aubree. I want to know how they came to sell the house to my cousin."

The woman stood to rake him with skeptical eyes. She fired off rapid Dutch, never bothering to look away.

"She said rich people don't consult cleaning ladies before completing transactions."

Mike dug into his pocket, retrieved the lone twenty he had left and handed it over.

"Please, try harder. I'm trying to help someone. This house was sold to the wife's old boyfriend. Certainly, she's seen him before. He looks like me, except…better."

The woman looked him up and down, then nodded.

"She says she's seen him? She's seen Tak at the house?"

His heart sprouted legs and ran. They disappeared with a look from the driver.

"Done?" he snapped.

"Yes, if she could just tell me how often—"

The driver took off. A brown and burly man, he strode with a limp of gangly steps. Mike scurried after. No door opened for him, and once inside, the driver pulled off.

They rode in silence, back the way they'd came.

WITH THE SEDAN missing from the driveway, Tak set out in a windbreaker and jeans, collar up against the whipping wind. The air cut through fabric and punished him, the sea foamed up against the shore's edge. Still, he needed space. Space away from that house. Time to clear his mind without children careening about.

At the back of his estate perched Malmok Beach, the lone house on their private stretch of beach. Following their graveled path to the boulevard was a hike alone on foot. Once there, he veered south along the shoulder, the Caribbean Sea at his side.

At first, stretches of sand, tangled beach grass, and windswept rocks were all that painted his walk. Seaweed danced in the wind as the skies took on a sinister swirl. Instinct told him to turn back, to avoid the rain that would follow. But it never rained in Aruba. He bid himself to keep walking.

He was more familiar with the island than he let on. He knew not just beaches and tourist traps, but the nestled places of Oranjestad, San Nicolas, Saventa. Long ago, he'd spent tons of time on the island, with Aubree Daniels at the condo her parents owned.

They'd met as juniors at UCLA. Her, the beach blonde cheerleader with indigo eyes; him, the frat boy with a convertible. How could their lives not intersect, when every flick on the planet demanded it? They'd been an on again, off again asset, the inevitable between that came for each of their romances. Never toying with the idea of love, never bothering to mock it, they were all excess and nonsense and sex instead.

He cut things off from her when he moved back to Miami, so annoyed was he with their trite loop of hedonism. What they were required nothing of him, so he never grew and he never changed. That same year, she showed up unannounced at the family's holiday vacation in California. She'd broken up with Brent for the umpteenth time, and for the umpteenth time Tak let her in.

They fought all weekend about Tak dumping her, though technically they had never been together. She accused him of falling in love with someone, which he'd laughed at before asking her to leave. Three separate times she came back, and on each one he rejected her. Under pressure from his family for an explanation on what was happening, Tak took the easy way out, describing their fights as a lover's spat.

The next time Tak saw her was in Aruba at 2 Fools and a Bull. She'd shrieked his name and scurried up ecstatic, only to freeze when Deena emerged, belly bulging with his child.

He'd introduced Aubree as an old college friend, again taking the easy way because it was, well, easy. The unequivocal welcome Deena gave her, complete with a fierce embrace and an insistence that they all eat together, had turned Tak's stomach to ash. But eat together they did.

They talked about one nothing after another, until the house on the beach came up. Both Deena and Tak recognized it as the one they'd been admiring the day before. Later, when Brent went bankrupt and his wife left him, Aubree called Tak to see if he'd be interested in buying it.

It was a tiresome series of events, made possible with the help of one or two lies. Lies that had the ability to morph into something more.

Especially if someone else needed them to.

CHAPTER
Twenty-Three

Deena took tea with Yukiko, Aunt Rhonda, Asami, and June in the room nearest to the north terrace. Mrs. Jimenez, who refused to serve cucumber sandwiches, gave them pepper ones with enough heat to blush the devil. Everyone left theirs to the tray.

"Really, Asami. You must guard your emotions," Tak's grandmother, Yukiko, scolded. "You've made your marriage the entire island's business."

She brushed aside a sheet of silver hair and took an indulgent sip of her Oolong tea.

"Tell us, what is it that you plan to do?" Yukiko asked. "Now that you've satisfied your primordial urge and assaulted your husband?"

"Maybe we should ask what you want to do," June said.

"I mean, you did break his arm. You can't go back to the way things were."

"The way things were," Asami echoed. "And which way would that be? Back to a husband who prefers blondes? One who uses me to satisfy his family? Because I'm eager to get back to that."

Mike came in, the way Mike tended to, as an insect on the wall hoping not to be noticed. He lowered himself onto the chaise by the fireplace and sipped some brown drink.

"You mean to divorce," Yukiko said.

Deena never heard her sound so cold.

"I'm young," Asami said. "And reasonably attractive, not to mention more than capable of earning my keep."

"No one is challenging you," Yukiko said. "Only your beliefs."

Beliefs. Tanakas held onto those like stubborn leeches at times, sucking the life from conviction until conviction was all they had.

"Well, I say it's time for some new rules," Asami announced. "Our 'beliefs', as you put them, would have neither Deena nor Lizzie in this family, let alone their children. I, for one, adore them all."

Deena set down her tea.

"I don't think—"

Yukiko held up a hand. "Asami is being intentionally provocative. It was her favorite pastime as a girl."

Aunt Rhonda sipped her tea. It was the wrong thing to do.

"Tell her," Asami said. "Tell her, Rhonda, that at

times we must follow our own hearts, even if it's down an unconventional path."

"I'd rather not," Rhonda said.

"Fine! Then tell her that men are trash."

Across the room, Mike grinned.

"Asami," June said in that perpetually soothing voice. "You're upset. You don't think that."

"Of course I do. Why wouldn't I?"

"What about the men in your family?"

Asami's gaze fell on her mother.

"My *otosan* stepped out a time or two, didn't he, Ma?"

Yukiko fell a shade past ghost.

Asami looked to Mike next.

"And he's not exactly a saint. He's been pining over his cousin's wife for years."

Deena's face flushed, even as Mike's darkened.

"So the others are then?" he said. "Tak? Kenji?"

Asami laughed.

"Tak a saint? Let his wife answer. She'll know more about it than me."

Deena couldn't shake the feeling that they were teetering at the precipice.

"I...have no problems with Tak," she said.

"No problems you know of," Mike said from the corner.

Deena watched him wide-eyed.

"What?" she managed to whisper.

"Tell me this, Deena. And all you who feel Tak is a saint, feel free to help out. How'd you come by this house? Got a good deal on it, I'd bet."

"Yes."

The word felt very small in her chest, like the punctuation mark for a bigger thought.

"From a gorgeous girl named Aubree Daniels, that Tak just happened to know." He paused, glare triumphant. "Look around you. Look at your family. Correction. Look at his family."

She did. They wouldn't look at her.

"Aubree was—"

"His girlfriend, Deena. His girlfriend for years. On again, off again, right back on again and loving it."

He stopped to soak up her look of dawning horror.

"But, he said—"

"He lied. You'll find he does that sometimes."

"Michael—" June said.

"You've seen her," Mike said. "Seen her over the years, I'd bet. And you just happened on this house at the moment when Aubree's leaving her husband? How do you think Tak knew it was for sale? How do you think Tak still knew her? Don't you think it's a little convenient that—"

No. No more of this.

Deena stumbled from the room. Walls pitched at her as she ran, the floor drew near, and at one point, she stopped to suck in great gasps of air.

But she would not cry.

Instead, she bled from heartbreak.

CHAPTER
Twenty-four

T HE ROOM ERUPTED.

"Why would you do that?"

"What were you thinking?"

"It was cruel! So cruel!"

"All you two do is hurt each other! You and your cousin and your sick games!"

And Aunt Rhonda at the door, shouting after her niece.

Mike pushed past all of them, all of them hurling accusations. He didn't care what they thought. He didn't care what they thought they knew. He had the truth. All things worked to a purpose.

———◈———

TAK BROKE INTO a run mere yards from home just as the rain fell in earnest. Still, the storm at home was worse. Asami attempting murder. Tony screwing girls in the garden. Deena's secrets. Mike locked in the bathroom with his wife. It all had the feeling of standing at the center of a hurricane, while trying desperately not to get sucked in.

When the house came in sight, Tyson flung the door open and held it despite violent rain and wind. When Tak found him in the doorway, it was amidst a cannonade of thunder.

He pushed past him with thanks, peeled off his windbreaker, kicked away his sneakers, and shook the rain out his hair. A look down at his shirt had him sliding that sop off too.

"Everything OK?" Tak said when he saw Tyson was still there.

"Huh? Oh, yeah. I, uh, had something to say. Forgot, I guess."

Tak hesitated, saw nothing further coming, and gave the guy a curt nod.

"Let me know if you remember," he said and clamored upstairs to his bedroom.

Where he found Deena yanking his clothes from the closet.

"Uh, Dee?"

She whirled on him as if scalded. Never—not even in labor—had he seen her so...disheveled. Curls frizzed and half out of her ponytail, blouse askew, button missing. He looked up to see her lips curl back into a snarl.

She slapped him. It was like a branding iron to the face. Whatever confusion he had ignited into fury.

"What the hell—"

"Aubree Daniels is your friend, huh? Just your friend, you whore!"

Of course. Had he really doubted that Mike would tell her?

"Deena, listen to me. I love you. The night I met you was the night I fell in love with you."

"Oh, shut up." She turned to the dresser drawers. Instead of snatching wildly, she rummaged, then stilled.

"If she's your friend, then why do you need this?"

She chucked a box of condoms in his face. The corner sliced the slab of fresh directly beneath his eye, leaving him to wonder if his wife meant to disfigure him.

"Dee—"

"We don't use condoms! We never have."

"Baby, I know. I just—"

He didn't want to say more. Only, he needed to rein this in.

"Tony," he confessed, with the feel of handing her thirty silver coins. "I get them for Tony."

"Tony," she echoed dully.

She looked wash worn, wrung out, and he debated taking the words back.

"He's eighteen," Tak pushed on. "And I know we've encouraged him to wait—but it doesn't change facts. He hasn't waited, so I concentrate on making sure he's safe."

"Tony," she said.

"Yes, Tony!"

"Then why are they here? In your drawer?"

God, he needed this conversation to end. Had he any leverage at all, any, he would have insisted on keeping things between him and his son.

"I give him a few at a time," Tak said. "Just to try and gauge, you know."

Deena stared.

"So you think this is OK?"

"I think what is OK?"

"Our son being sexually active."

Tak eyed her. "I think it is what it is. That's all."

"His father had him when he was sixteen."

"That has nothing to do with Tony."

"That has everything to do with Tony!"

Tak shot her a look an exasperated look before going to retrieve a change of clothes. But the second he snatched up a shirt, his wife grabbed him by the wrist.

"Did you love her?"

Deena's face was unreadable.

He shook his head. She released him and looked him over with the eyes of a skeptic.

"We were something in college, Deena. Never after. Never once. And I was honest with you when things started between us. Honest about how my life used to be."

"But Mike said—"

He shot her a look.

"Never start a sentence that way. You'll wind up looking stupid."

Deena reared back, face bridled with anger, but Tak couldn't help his irritated glare. She, of all people, should know to practice caution with his cousin.

An image of the two locked away together rushed fire through his veins.

"You can't blame this on your cousin," Deena said. "These are your lies coming back for you. Now, tell me. How many times have you seen her since—since we've..."

She choked on the words, body rigid as she worked to swallow the last of them.

What her yelling hadn't done, what the slap hadn't, the almost-tears certainly did. They twisted Tak in the brutal winds of desperation, accosting him with his need to be her everything, all the while screaming he'd failed.

Again.

He'd been emptied out, hollowed to an aching cavern of pain. If she thought this—that he could be with another woman—then she thought nothing of him. Instead of anger, anguish rooted deep, carving a home in the rawness of his fears. She would not—could not—do this to him. The world had already claimed too much; it would not have his heartbeat too.

"Please," Tak said only to realize he'd only thought the word.

"Please," he tried again. The voice that found him wasn't quite his own.

His arms went around her, steady as she resisted, there when she relented. Chin resting on her head, Tak's eyes closed, willing reason, understanding, and clarity to find its way in.

"Don't do this," he said. "I love you too much. It feels like I'm dying."

He brushed the hair from her face and saw that his fingers shook. She wanted to leave; she wanted to set everything he loved ablaze. The realization, powerful as it was, made him cling to her, too terrified of what letting go would bring.

"I want to believe you," she said, voice muffled against his shirt. "It's just that Mike—"

Tak withdrew. Cold.

"Mike?"

Danger coursed through his veins.

"Don't you try to turn this on me. You're the one who—"

"Who what? Had a girlfriend before he met his wife?"

"Except she wasn't a girlfriend, was she?" Deena shoved away from him. "Because you didn't have those. Just a few hundred casual encounters."

He closed his eyes. Told his hands not to pull out all his hair.

"Unbelievable," he said. "After all these years, you wanna ride me about what I did in college? Why don't you get pissed about my prom date, too? Were we together back then without me knowing it?"

"You keep trying to act like I'm crazy. But you're the one who's off if you expect me to believe we got a twenty-three bedroom, fifteen thousand square feet mansion for seven million dollars because you used to be a good lay."

Fuck. He could put a fist through his cousin. He could kill him slow and enjoy it.

"Fine, Deena," Tak said. "You win. You want to believe—"

"I don't want to believe anything."

"No, you do. Because it's what your boyfriend told you. What'd he do, whisper it in your ear while you were locked away in that cupboard?"

"Oh, I was waiting for that! For you to make that nothing into something."

"Nothing?" Tak yelled. "You sneak into the bathroom with my cousin, a guy you know wants to screw you. You lock the door, get caught, and somehow, that's nothing. But I'm on trial for a girl I dated when fanny packs were hot."

"We live in her house!" Deena screamed.

But she could scream at herself.

Enough, Tak thought, and stormed out the door.

CHAPTER
Twenty-five

"YOU SHOULDN'T HAVE DONE IT," John said. "You implied something you knew wasn't true."

Mike studied his fingernails as he leaned against the door of their bedroom, jaw set firm.

"I know no such thing," he said. "And I only told her what I knew. How she took it was up to her."

John stood. Got in his face.

"Except it wasn't really up to her, was it? You made sure she took it exactly how you needed her take it: the worst way possible."

Mike looked his kid brother over. Clumped, bedraggled, black hair. Rumpled white shirt, same as the day before. Even in his own grief, he had time to defend everyone's favorite person.

"Is he even talking to you?" Mike said. He dragged over

to the window and took a seat on the sill. "Last I heard, he'd treated you like a fool for losing your wife. If nothing else, I'd think you'd be glad to show him he's capable of failing."

John didn't answer, so Mike turned to his view of the ocean. Pale blue stretched out to darkness. Rain splattered the surface, falling from a sky near black despite the hour.

"You think I did it because I want her for myself," he said.

"I know you did."

Mike looked at his brother with clinical interest.

"You think it's wrong, how I feel. You think it's a sign of immorality."

John sighed with the effort of a man lacking oxygen. "I think you always want what you can't have."

Mike stood.

"You should have come to me," he said. "When you started having problems with your wife. You should have called on me, not him, when you needed someone to talk. And you should be defending me, not him, always."

"Mike—"

"You always preferred him. Whenever he came to visit, when he called, you forgot me. You forgot plans, promises—"

"Mike," John shook his head. "Is this really the conversation you want to have?"

"Your problems should be mine," Mike said. "I'm your brother. Tak has Kenji. Why should he have you, too? Why does he have everything?"

"He doesn't. No one does."

Mike cut the distance between them.

"The moment I saw you, I knew something was wrong.

I came to you first. I asked you to talk to me. You said there was nothing to talk about. But you talked to him, didn't you?"

"Of course I did."

Mike's hand flailed, crashing a lamp to the floor.

"Why?"

"Because I know Tak. I trust him. Half the time I don't know who you're trying to be."

"I'm your brother. Isn't that enough? Come to me when you have a problem."

"Why? So you'll know that my wife was available? So you can make her think I'm not worth fighting for? That's what you do, isn't it? Before you slide on in to home base."

"I wouldn't—" Mike bit down on his fist. "I had feelings for her first," he said.

"Don't be ridiculous. You never even—"

"She worked in the cafeteria at MIT my senior year. Lunch shift, Monday through Friday. Every day she'd go from there to the Rotch Library, where she studied until eight, sometimes nine."

"Wait. What?"

"I spoke to her—sometimes. As much as I could really. But I never worked up the nerve to do more." Mike lowered his gaze, hands in his pockets, and remembered the Deena from school. "I'm not a lunatic, you know. It's just, she was gorgeous—is gorgeous—and I could never quite find enough courage. Then *oli* brought her around, giving me the second chance I'd never thought I'd have. I didn't know she was with Tak even then. But honest to God, John, I can't help myself. I can't keep myself from wanting her."

"Mike," John said, not without kindness. "Nothing can ever come from it."

"But he's the worst person she could have ended up with," Mike said. "And it hurts, even after all this time."

CHAPTER
twenty-six

DEENA BOUNDED DOWNSTAIRS, FURY sucking and mauling and twisting her into its vortex. She pushed past family, snapping and snarling at anyone who dared gape, before bursting into the library and locking the door behind her. She stood there, chest heaving, eyes twice as large, staring at the lock as if it, instead of her, were responsible for bringing her to that moment.

What was happening? What was happening to them?

She dropped into a seat without knowing how she got there, grateful for the shadows in the room, grateful for the lack of reflections.

There was sense to make of this—sense to make of their anger, their fighting, this thing with Aubree Daniels.

The woman's name was but a blade of agony. Bile bit at

the back of her throat and Deena gagged, pressing the back of her hand and shoving back nauseating desolation.

She hadn't cried in years. Not tears of sorrow, at least. But there, in the dark, with her marriage mangled, tears welled as anguish swept in. Head dropped, Deena clutched fistfuls of hair and let the tears unhinge her.

"DAD!" MIA CALLED as Tak stormed by. "It's raining and the satellite isn't fixed. Everyone in the house is dying."

"I don't care."

"Dad! If you won't call someone, the least you can do is go outside and have a look yourself. Maybe it's something simple. Anyway, it's your responsibility to—"

Tak turned to face his daughter in the hall.

"Mia? Close your friggin' mouth."

She blinked, wide-mouthed from the fleeing of words just there.

"Daddy?" she said.

A door at the far end of the hall opened. Mike stepped out and froze.

"Off to your room, baby."

Tak met Mike's gaze and held it.

"Daddy—"

"Now."

The door slammed behind her.

"Tak—"

That was John, squeezing out of their bedroom, hands already in the air.

"Tak, listen to me. You have every right to be angry."

"That's putting it mildly," Tak said.

"Still, you can't let that temper get the best of you," John said.

"Too late."

Tak went for Mike and snatched him by the collar, using the fabric for leverage to drag his struggling frame back into their room. John hollered for Kenji just as Tak heaved Mike onto the bed.

"You making a run for my wife? What the hell did you tell her?"

"The truth," Mike said. "That you're an old dog with the same tricks."

Tak punched him, hard enough to snap his head back, even if he had been expecting the hit. Mike's gaze flared, darkening his eyes as if the pupils consumed the iris. A thin trickle of blood seeped from his nose and his mouth twisted with malice.

"You're not the only one with secrets about the past," Mike said. "Did she tell you that she already knew me? That she knew me back in college? Or did she let you think that you were introducing us?" He grinned. "Sorry, cousin, I knew your wife well."

"He's lying, Tak. He's just trying to goad you. It's the way it's always been. You know that."

John pulled on his arm though Tak didn't budge.

"What do you mean, you knew her?" he heard himself say.

Mike grinned, emboldened, challenging as triumph glittered gold in his eyes.

"What do you think it means? She was mine before she was yours."

Tak swung only to have John stifle the blow with a bear hug and sweep him toward the door. Legs swinging, he lost balance enough for his cousin to shove him out.

"You're doing what he wants," John shouted from the hall. "Thinking what he wants. Later, he'll say you misunderstood his every word."

"Well, he can say it with my fist in his throat."

Tak went for the door, only to have John drag him toward his bedroom. Clothes still littered the floor.

"Please, cool off," John said. "There are kids everywhere."

As if summoned by the statement, five children burst from an end hall room. Noah led the thunderous charge, only to halt at the top of the stairs.

"Dad?"

A splash of cold water. A dose of sobriety. His child's voice sliced clear to the bone. Here was the truth of being a parent. They watched, always, eager to absorb. All the habits, all the Tak-isms, caricatured in glorious fashion. He wanted to ram Mike's head through a wall, but he couldn't, lest Noah think it fine to do the same to Kenji's sons.

Tak exhaled.

"I'm cool," he said, eyes on a boy who had even mastered his facial expressions. "Just talking to your *oli*."

Noah looked from one to the other, brow bent.

"About...?"

"About you getting lost, knucklehead." John took a swipe at him, earning a peal of laughter, before the boy barreled downstairs.

He turned back to Tak.

"Cool off, OK? Then go find your wife."

CHAPTER
Twenty-seven

NECK STIFF, DEENA STIRRED ON the couch and shifted, slipping legs out from underneath her. The stillness of night hung heavy, cloaking in silence. Across from her sat her husband. She blinked at him, thoughts sluggish.

"What are you doing here?"

"Watching you sleep," Tak said.

She looked down at the blanket draped over her. Her last recollections were of crying. Had she cried herself to sleep?

A single stream of moonlight illuminated half his face. In the dark, he was an isolation of beauty: strong, graceful lines, definition, and a hint of enigmatic perfection. In high school, he would have been the boy she'd blushed at but never spoke to, the one with a smile so brilliant she dropped her books and stared, horrified when he spoke. How had

Deena wound up with that boy? Maybe the incredulity of it all, even then, was what made Aubree Daniels so believable.

"I'm sorry," Tak said. "For not telling you I dated her."

Melancholy laced his voice, and beneath it, strain.

"Tak?" she said uncertainly.

"I can't sleep. Will you come to bed?"

He rose and extended a hand. She took it, body thinking without her.

Upstairs, they lay stiff as two planks of wood, eyes on the ceiling until a fragile sleep found them at last. When Deena woke with a suspicious feeling of tranquility, she looked down to find Tak's arm looped around her waist.

They'd found each other in sleep and knitted so tightly that she could feel every carve of his chest, every thud of his heart, insistent against her back. He shifted, cinching her in tighter, grazing her with his manhood, and her breathing grew shallower by the second. Oblivious lips brushed like butterfly wings at the back of her neck, flooding warmth through her body. Memories of bruising kisses, of him atop and dominating, of her shivering release, had her set to overheat. Deena shifted, as if to slip out from underneath him, only to feel wet lips trail her neck. She whimpered and the hand at her abdomen drifted up, raising her nightgown with it.

He found her breast and caressed before sliding down low, looping a finger through her panties, and pulling.

"Deena," he said and put a hand on her hip, digging fingers in to the bone. Hardness found her and she pressed against it, whimpering when he buried to the hilt.

Neither moved, content instead with managing their

own ragged breathing. Tak pulsed and pressed and strained her walls, burning shivers through her body. She gripped him by the arm. If he slammed into her like before, she could never—

He pulled back, inch by inch, only to slide in.

No. She couldn't take that either.

"Tak—"

She swallowed hard, swallowed so desperately hard, and stuttered on her thoughts. He filled her at an agonizing pace, far beyond capacity, earning a choke of recognition in return.

"Oh, God. Oh, Tak, I need you."

And there was no air, only him hovering in silence, breathing labored. So still he sat for so long that Deena began to wonder what she'd said wrong.

But then he pressed, pressure unrelenting, melting her in a pool of molten need.

Deep, unhurried, insistent strokes followed and she lifted a little more for each one. Sweat-slick fingers imprinted on her hip, as he shoved each time as if resisted. Dimly, Deena registered creaks of the bed, heat, sweat, her own moans. They were close to each other, so close, with his rhythm vibrating right through her. More than the thrill of his body found her as he bathed her in praise. Murmurings about her body, her touch, his love, drifted to her, making her purr like a well-loved kitten.

Long tunneling strokes had them panting, on and on and on, only to burst into bed-jarring bucks. Deena babbled and her whole body constricted to a white hot needlepoint. She called Tak something foul and exploded, a shriek of pleasure consuming her.

Tak froze, body rigid and straining. He jerked once and shoved, moaning as he filled her.

They filled the seconds with gasping breaths and hard beating hearts. Eventually, Tak burst out laughing.

"What was that you called me?" he said, voice teasing. "Son of a what?"

Deena's cheeks engulfed in a fiery inferno that he set about kissing away. His fingertips drifted the length of her thigh, then her stomach, leisurely, exploratory. When he settled, it was with his arm snug at her middle.

"Let's stay like this," Tak said. "All day."

With a frown, she careened enough to face him.

"And the family?"

A small, humorless smile crossed his face, darkening his eyes. She saw a coldness there she didn't know and couldn't recognize. All she knew was that she wanted it gone.

"Let's do it," she said without knowing she would. "Let's lock ourselves in and hide."

He searched her face, uncertain, seeking out the smoke and mirrors. Deena sat up, took his face in both her hands, and pressed her mouth against his. She felt the corners of his mouth turn up against her and soon they were both smiling.

"Call up breakfast," Tak said. "I'll start the shower."

She followed his nakedness with her gaze, drinking up an assortment of hard lines. She straightened her sweaty nightgown, traveled to the door and hollered for a maid to bring breakfast up. She met Mike's gaze in the hall, ignored it, and went to join her husband in the shower.

They showered not as husband and wife did back home when always pressed for time, but as they used to back at his bachelor pad, when gasps and splashes were more important than the soap. Afterward, they took their flambéed crepes Suzette in bed, shamelessly licking at bits of caramelized sugar and feeding each other persimmons.

"How long do you think we have?" Deena said.

Tak bit into a sliver of fruit, running a thin stream of juice down his hand.

"Two minutes, maybe three."

"We could bolt the door." Deena smiled. "Prop some furniture against it."

"Three for sure, in that case."

Footsteps thundered in the hall. Squealing children tornadoed past, close enough to rattle the exit.

"And you wanted six children," Deena said with a snort.

"Wanted? Past tense?" His brows did a little jig.

"Not from my body," Deena said. "Not at this age."

"What? Just a minute ago you had all this need…"

Deena sucked in a mouthful of red-faced horror and swatted him in the chest.

"In case it wasn't clear enough earlier, you don't get to quote what I say in bed."

"How about reenact it? It's not every day that you need someone."

Deena drifted in a fog of almost-comprehension, reaching and not quite grasping what he was really trying to say. She decided to go for the obvious.

"Tak," she said softly. "You can't possibly be ready again already."

He took the fruit from her hand and set it to one side.

"In all these years, there's been no one I've felt more awe

or admiration for. Everything you have, you got with these hands and this head." Tak brushed curls from her cheek and ran a thumb along the curve of her face. "It's been a long time since I felt like you needed me. For anything. So yeah, I could stand hearing that again."

It occurred to Deena that his words were meant to be a compliment. That this was his interpretation of her, that this was his understanding of her life. But how had her own husband got it so wrong?

"I need you," Deena said. "Of course, I need you. How could you even say that?"

"Say what?"

"That!" She hit him. "What you just said."

He withdrew, skepticism knitting his face.

"You love me. It's not the same."

"Try losing someone you love and telling me that. Tell me it's not the same then."

Her father. Her brother. Him. Which one hadn't she needed?

Tak gathered her to him absentmindedly and they fell into a time-worn embrace. Caresses found her before kisses, each one gentle, restrained. Years of urgency, stolen moments, and heat had steamrolled into quickies as their norm.

"I think," Tak said and kissed her, "that you can do without the clothes today, love."

CHAPTER
Twenty-eight

SIMPLE SQUARE MOLDING RAN along the base of the elongated white hall, chain-like and interrupted only by doors. Of all the entryways in sight, the one Mike stared at loomed larger than the others, more prodigious in a way he couldn't understand. It blocked out sound well, and allowed only the occasional flicker of movement through the crevice beneath, an indicator that those inside still roamed. When the door cracked unexpectedly, Mike started, only to see that it was his Deena. She stepped out, shot a wayward glance back, and shut the door behind her.

"Mike."

"Deena," he resisted the urge to smile and failed.

He'd gone all day without seeing her, without breathing, it seemed. Now that he'd heard her voice, he felt sated. Nourished even.

"You and I need to talk," she said in a clipped, business manner. "In private."

She called for a maid to bring her something to drink and she strode off, confident he'd follow.

As if yearning gave him a choice.

Downstairs, a DJ cranked out mindless pop hits. Laughter ferreted upward, interspersed with the occasional splash of pool water. Mike shot a look back at Deena's bedroom. Tak must've been asleep.

He scurried after her, eager.

In the sitting room, a runty, dish-faced girl brought them wine. Mike watched her go, surprised she had an ass worth admiring. But when Deena spoke, he was all hers once again.

"It gets stuffy in here." She fanned herself, scowling, and sent aflutter the delicate ribbon at her neck. A simple shell top tied at the throat, a quick skirt, and she was stunning. "There are some ventilation flaws though. Guess that's why no one uses it."

She looked at him as if unsure how he got there, before pouring herself a glass of wine. Mike followed her lead.

"How would you describe your feelings for me?" Deena said.

Mike froze with the wine at his lips.

"Wow," he said and set his glass down. "Are we really starting there?"

"I think we should."

He swallowed. Steadied his pulse. Swallowed again.

"I love you. I'm in love with you. I have been since college."

"Mike, please. You don't even know me."

"I know you! Aren't you listening? I've known you since college."

Deena stared. Stared until certainty melted from his face. Stared until hesitation found him.

"You may have seen me," she said. "You may have spoken to me. But I don't remember you. You are my husband's cousin. In my mind, you're my cousin."

"Deena, please—"

"I don't know what you hope to accomplish, other than hurting your own blood. But I love Tak. You'd do well to never forget it."

He watched her drink more wine, his eyes on the red liquid as it retreated.

Mike wondered what made her think he sometimes forgot where her love lived. Every smile passed between her and his cousin, every thoughtless kiss, ran like a knife blade through and through.

"He loves you," Deena said. "Even now. Even now that you'd sit here and…covet his wife."

Mike snatched up his wine glass and busied himself drinking, lest he say something he'd regret. Had she really rounded him up just to mock him, just to make plain what he already knew? He couldn't help himself. How else could he? He loved her just as Tak did, and neither needed to apologize.

"I want to love you," Deena said, "as a cousin loves another cousin. But please, put a stop to this. I will never give up Tak for you."

Escargot for roadkill was how she made the trade sound. Mike finished his wine and refilled, hands shaking as he poured to brimming. Cracked ice and mistakes was what his life felt like, broken glass and sharp stabs of confusion. He poured more wine for Deena, splashing her hands even when she told him to stop.

Swallowing made sense. Liquid in his mouth, down his throat, belly warmed, repeat. He wanted words, smart, funny words, Tak-isms on tap. They could knit together fragments of a friendship with them, born in the bathroom but already dead it seemed.

"Mike, please don't—"

Dampness splashed his cheeks, surprising him. He dashed it off and left his seat. The fresh air of a window would clear his mind, reset his thoughts.

Downstairs, the music blared on.

"Tell me what you're working on. What's in that pad you carry around?"

"Oh," she said and hesitated, going on only after he insisted on hearing. She fed him nonsense about skyscrapers, design theories, construction. With his gaze on the pool house, he imagined her there, nude. Mirrored images of him warred with the rage of conflicting feelings. The romantic him stood unapologetic, righteous about his love. Opposed to that was the boy who clung to his responsibility as the eldest grandchild and therefore one day expected to lead, as *ojichan* did, as Daichi does, as Mike one day looked forward to doing.

But who would follow him? Who would follow Mike Tanaka?

Weighted with his own thoughts, he turned to see

Deena. Slumped, a miniscule snore ferreted from her pink parted lips.

Wine stains, he realized. Wine stained her lips. He stirred at the thought.

He looked at her, the door, then her again.

She'd said that the room never got used. That no one ever came; no one ever used it.

Mike threw back the last of his drink to steady the nerves and turned to face her once more.

She sat on the couch, legs crossed on the cushions, with her head on an arm. Her empty wine glass rolled across the floor.

"Deena," Mike said. "Deena, wake up. Do you realize that you're sleeping?"

Nothing.

He took a step toward her, chest heaving, and drank in her every slope. Even this, this unrestricted view of her had been denied for so long. Now he stood, eyes thirsting, devouring her figure.

Alone. Where he could do anything. With no reason not to.

Except that she laid unconscious, unwilling, and married to his cousin.

Do it.

Nerves. Nerves. Damn him, where were his nerves? If he'd had any, he would have asked her out in college instead of—waiting for Casanova to show him how.

"Deena," Mike announced, loud as he dared. "I'm going to touch you. Tell me 'no' if you don't want it."

He edged to the end of the couch. Swallowed. Took her

face into his hands. Delicate, carved, with a pouting little mouth, her beauty framed by tri-colored curls. He could have contented himself to watch her sleep if their love were ever possible. Instead, he had but stolen moments, furtive glances, throbbing need.

It was impossible to want a woman more.

She smiled a secret smile left to a dream he yearned to join. To find her heart, to hold her mind, to be the one that made her smile there—that would be happiness. But happiness wasn't his.

"Tak. Move closer," she murmured. "Don't go to sleep mad again."

At first, he caught the sense of triumph welded to the word "again" and found comfort in the instability of his cousin's flailing marriage. A closer examination of her words, however, had his heart launching into his throat. Did she... did she think he was Tak? Was it the feel of Mike that she truly asked for?

Mike stood and stared at her lips. He bent low, then retreated. Clear across to the far side of the room, where a bead of sweat parted his brow.

God, she was so beautiful.

He returned to her, feet moving double time, only to halt a fraction of an inch from her face.

He exhaled. Inhaled. Exhaled.

Pressed a whisper of a kiss.

And jerked away.

He couldn't stand this. His nerves couldn't stand this violent somersault of emotions, this straining need in his pants. If only he could...walk away.

She'd tasted like wine. Wine and desire and stillness and "Oh God" if he couldn't have more.

He couldn't bear the want, couldn't possibly not nurse this need.

He wouldn't. He wouldn't dare. Not to his cousin's wife. Not to the boy he'd run and jumped and wrestled with. Not to a cousin he loved.

He did love Tak. Only, he'd loved Deena more.

Mike drifted to her. Put a hand to her face. His thumb, content to trace her cheek, her smile, the swell of her lip, drifted lower, to her chin, then the pulse of her neck. Air came in great drenches, vast drags for him. Fire scorched his belly. His gaze caught downward at the opening of her collar.

He teased at the skin of her collarbone. Deena stirred and he froze. Cold seconds of fear ticked. Finally, he clamped his mouth down on hers.

His hand found her leg, bare with the slight rise of her skirt. Mike lingered at her knee, teetered at her thigh, traced fingers round to her ass.

She was drunk enough, he realized. Drunk enough to not wake up if he touched her in the right way, if he did things without too much jerking. He'd seen drunk girls black out in college; he'd seen other guys have their way.

Thrill and disgust shot through him.

He thought back to the holiday vacation where Daichi introduced her as a colleague. One night, Mike happened upon her and Tak making love. He'd seen the fullness of her curves and the power of her want; he'd seen her take desire out on his cousin. To have that, to have the illusion of that—Mike ignited at the thought.

He could fuck her, whether she liked it or not, and no one—no one—would know the truth.

Except he would. He would know that he raped the woman he'd been in love with for years, that he had raped his cousin's wife.

Rape.

That's what it was, wasn't it? While he'd been seducing himself with thoughts of love and lovemaking, he'd been grooming her for rape.

Rape didn't seem like the outcome of love at all.

Over the years, Mike had begged, cried, screamed, and blackmailed for anything and everything Tak ever had. Money, cars, vacations—his parents had nearly lost their home to a second mortgage because he had to summer in Paris—like Tak. And on the rare occasion when no one would give him what Tak had, Mike took it anyway and made it his.

It. Deena had become their it. An object, a thing. One more glittering thingamajig that dulled the moment he seized it.

Except she hadn't dulled yet and he wanted it still. In fact, he could see it through the peek of panties under her skirt. He could put his hand there, his mouth even, and make her moan. But when she did—when she did moan—she'd think of Tak, she'd be with Tak. She was the thing Mike couldn't own. She was the line he couldn't cross.

Mike straightened first her skirt, then her blouse, breaths escaping him in raged fashion.

Rape Tak's wife. Tears of shame pricked his eyes and

choked his throat. *Ojiichan*, their grandfather, looked down on him with shame.

Mike stood and the door opened.

It was the dish-faced girl. She sauntered in, bent to pick up Deena's glass and gave him a view of her ass.

"What?" Mike barked when she faced him, questioning plain in her eyes.

"N—nothing," she said and went for the wine bottle.

It was an expensive vintage and still half full, though she swept it into hurrying hands. Mike grabbed her by the arm.

"What are you doing?" he said.

"Cleaning, sir. Unless you—"

"That wine cost more than you make in a week," he said, tasting cruelness and liking it.

"Can I pour you another glass then?"

She held out the cup from the floor. It shook.

Her tremble coursed power through him, more power than he'd ever felt, perhaps.

"You drink it," Mike said.

She looked around. "But…there are no more glasses."

Mike took the bottle from her and pressed it to her lips. She stared at him, eyes watery.

"Drink."

She opened her mouth, sucking like a babe. He was reminded of a time in junior high. Clustered in a locker room with boys much hairier, it seemed that he alone had yet to develop. With his slight pale frame and hint of ribs, Mike was the brunt of taunting each day. "Whoa, what an ugly girl!" "Hey ugly girl, choke on this milk. It'll help you grow." He had choked on milk that day, as they poured and let it dribble down his chin, chastising when any spilled.

He heard those taunts as he force-fed her wine, as it dribbled on her heaving chest, as Deena snored. When Mike set the bottle aside, he saw it. Fire. Ambivalence. Intimidation.

"My room," he said and opened the door, taking the last of the wine with him.

He watched her walk into the hall. Square shoulders, sausage legs, a dwarfish sort of frame. Had he thought her ass okay before? Deena, he knew, had supple round curves, each one weighted and feminine.

In his bedroom, Mike locked the door, took the wine and drank. When he wiped his mouth, she reached for the alcohol. He handed it over and watched her drink.

Once she'd had her fill, he set the bottle down, leaving a swallow at the bottom of the glass. Mike shed his pants, backed her to the bed, shoved up her skirt and mounted.

He recognized the look on her face, knew it for what it was. She would have preferred the other Tanaka, it said. No matter, he could say the same.

He'd had a hard-on since rubbing Deena's lips, and already it threatened soreness. Pressed together, crotch to crotch and padded by clothes, Mike humped the maid, eyes closed.

The first girl he'd ever fucked had been no Deena Tanaka. She was a pudgy little gimp with frizzed red hair and a spit-pooling lisp. Freckles smeared like dirt on her face and narcolepsy plagued her. Chana McGhoul from Somerset. They'd been in the Science Fiction Club at MIT together.

On first meeting her, Mike hadn't given her much thought, except to tell her to try harder at not being a walking joke. At every meeting she made a point of detaining him. Eventually, she asked him out for pizza. When they went, she ate most of it.

She wanted him to walk her back to her dorm, which felt laughable since she was bigger than him. Once there, Chana invited him in for coffee and served it from a pot stained with grease. Not that it mattered that grease floated in his drink. The moment he sat down, she asked to make out.

Mike had never made out before, had never even kissed. But with a greedy, awkward, grease-drinking Chana, he felt emboldened, like he couldn't go wrong. So, he moved in, mouth open and winced at the taste of onions he'd picked off his lone slice of pizza. Pulling back, withering in disgust, he was caught by the button of his jeans. Chana yanked it, springing him free. Never had a hand other than his own been there, and he couldn't have anticipated the flood of sensation she'd give him. She gripped him through the boxers and jerked twice and he choked out a cry of pleasure in response.

She'd shoved him in her mouth next. No preamble, no overtures. Just him in her for a minute. When he came free, he shoved her on her back. Mike, treated to another whiff of onion, closed his eyes and concentrated on the softness, but faltered at the sound of her coarse breathing. She'd shed her clothes. A pump had him in, then a pause. Another pump, then a pause, bare skin stuck to bare skin.

Apparently looks had little to do with how good a woman felt.

Her breaths had been all dragon snarls and groans though, making him cringe even as he dug in. Six hard shoves were all he could manage, before spilling out and hurrying for clothes. A week later had him back with Chana, with eight pumps over last time's six.

This girl wasn't much better. She didn't smell, but she had a body like old laundry.

The sounds coming from her mouth grated him, so he clamped a hand over her lips when it came time to thrust.

She was dry and he told her. She was ugly and he told her. He hated this and he told her that, too.

He hated this girl.

Eyes clamped tight, he said it was Deena, and that she didn't want him, that he'd shoved into Deena anyway.

She-had-no-choice.

Mike gave a single savage thrust. Her back arched, neck corded, she whimpered behind his hand. Glistening, wide eyes stared back at him. Accusing. And *ojiichan* called from the end of a tunnel, from a place too far to reach him. Mike's lungs couldn't find enough air.

Fire shot through his veins, unrelenting. He bathed in the ragged up and down of her chest, thrilled at the unchecked fright in her eyes.

"I'm hurting you," he said and slammed in.

She screamed into his palm, back like a bow, raising up as if to meet his assault.

He took away his hand and kissed her hard on the mouth. He yanked down her shirt and kneaded one triangle of a breast clear down to the ribs. He repeated with the other, twisting both until they reddened. Tears painted her cheeks.

Mike asked her if he should stop.

"No," she said firmly.

Nothing about her said that she enjoyed being used. Not the tears in her eyes, not the trembling lip. Still, she told him not to stop.

He hated this girl.

Mike gripped her waist and rammed, then held with insistent pressure. A gasp escaped her and she shoved at his abdomen; he dug until fresh tears sprang.

Deena, he thought, unable to stop him from having her. A thrill shot up his spine. One brutal stroke followed another, before a savage rhythm found him. She sobbed, filling the hand that covered her mouth with saliva.

Deena beneath him, legs open, he told himself, and ignited on a hammer of vicious pumps.

He didn't care what she wanted. He didn't care who she loved. She had no choice but to make him come.

Mike erupted on a tide of brutal strokes.

CHAPTER
Twenty-nine

Punishment. That's what his father called this. Chained to a room all day and all night with a narcissist who found his own voice captivating. No satellite meant no television, though Tony did still have his phone. Trading insults via text with Lizard did nothing to lift his mood. He wanted to call Wendy—she could always cheer him—except calling her meant explaining what he'd done.

He couldn't do that.

Tony stared out his bedroom window. For a while, he'd tried to content himself with the sounds of his family having fun. But when that fun came at his expense...

Lloyd cleared his throat. Standing in the vanity mirror, he straightened the collar of his button shirt and grinned at his reflection.

"Aren't you going to ask me where I'm going, roomie?"

Tony shot him a look.

"No. Because it's obvious you want me to."

Lloyd turned to face him. With one hand on the vanity stand, he leaned into it, and took in his younger cousin.

They weren't so many years apart, Tony, Lloyd and the other two brothers that flanked him most days, Remy and Damien. The oldest of them, Damien, was twenty-two to Lloyd's twenty-one and Remy's twenty. But they aged like Benjamin Button. Why he hadn't thought of them when the clothes went missing Tony couldn't know.

"I've got a date tonight," Lloyd said. "And I'm prettying myself up for a pretty little girl."

"Who could you be seeing? You don't even know anyone."

Lloyd's eyes danced as if delighted he'd finally asked. "I know one girl. A bare-breasted-in-the-gardens kind of gal."

"Lloyd—"

A grin played across the older boy's lips.

Lloyd turned back to the mirror. "You're not her boyfriend, are you?"

He smiled at Tony's sheepish expression. "Exactly."

He went back to adjusting the shirt. On squinting, Tony realized it was his.

He stood.

"I swear to God, I'm gonna pound you. If you don't quit playing, I'll—"

Lloyd sauntered for the door, arms swinging, pep in his every step.

"How are you gonna do all that from there, little cuz? Lord knows you wouldn't try Daddy."

Tony's nostrils flared. But as Lloyd said, he rooted into his spot. Not daring to cross the threshold.

"Night, night, little one." He shut the door behind him.

Tony kicked it, then cursed.

Lila. His Lila.

No, she wasn't his girlfriend, but he had a claim on her nonetheless.

Didn't he?

Tony turned in a circle. He needed out of that room. He needed to see where Lloyd was going, what he was doing, and for how long. He needed to know if Lila had turned to his cousin and away from him.

He wasn't fool enough to think that she was his alone, especially when his visits were sporadic. Still, he held on to the notion that Tony in Aruba meant only Tony with Lila.

He ventured to the window. A jump straight down could chuck him onto a terrace table, shattering it and ending his chance for answers. He'd have to slither down the wall for results. Which, of course, was stupid.

There was only the door.

CHAPTER
Thirty

Tony's door swung open with deceptive simplicity. He stood there, Adam's apple mobile, and contemplated retreating. His father's punishments were notorious, brutal in their creativity all the while delivering an unequivocal message. On the day that he got his Porsche, he'd stayed out two hours past curfew. The next night, he did the same. On coming home that time, he found a note attached to the door. In his father's large, lazy script were instructions he never forgot: 'Step One: Open the box on the porch. Step Two: Remove blankets and pillow. Step Three: Sleep in the hammock out back. Next time, there'll be no box.'

Still, Tony stepped out, a single step, and cocked his head for a concentrated listen. He frowned at the silence.

Door closed behind him, he started for the stairs. The hall stretched on in a magician's trick that never ended. Door after door, mile after mile, until his heartbeat assaulted his ears. A moan of ecstasy drifted toward him. Tony's mouth curled down with repulsion as a single word rattled plain in his head: gross.

He put a hand on the rail and a foot on the stair. Too many to go down, too certain to creak. A glance down showed a scurrying maid. He hissed at her. She stopped. Looked up.

"Help me," Tony said. "I need to get out. Is anyone down there?"

She made the sign of the cross and ran.

Coward.

He started down the stairs. Music from the backyard drew near. Bass-laden old funk gave a cover that could only help, masking the sound of his descent.

He made it to the entrance hall and cast a glance left then right for his sister. She was the only one he'd trust to help him, the only one he felt sure of.

Tony slammed into Mia on turning a corner.

"Watch where you're going," she spat, skateboard tucked under one arm.

Then her brows knitted for the long look.

"What are you doing down here? Dad'll murder you, you know. Turn you into kielbasa sausage or something."

Tony's cheeks warmed. While he'd wanted his sister's help, now that she stood there, he couldn't form the right words.

"Lloyd. He—he says he's going out on a date with Lila."

Mia's face wrapped into a scowl, before she dropped her skateboard and mounted it. She shoved wild, jet black coils from her face, only to have them spring back in. A resonated sigh later, she shook her head.

"I've told you about that girl. Over the summer, I told you—"

"That was the summer, Mi. Now could you keep it down? I've got to know what's happening."

"What's happening is that you're obsessed with some skank because her knockers are huge. You, like every other guy, use her appearance to bolster your ego." Mia shrugged. "I don't get it. But maybe in a year or two I'll look like Mom, guys'll go in heat at the sight of me, and then I'll understand."

Truth was, boys were already half gone over her. Truth was, his kid sister, straddling the fence of puberty, had begun a not-so-subtle shift that hadn't escaped notice. Boys left notes in her locker; one once wrote her a poem. Tony trashed them and ran the guys off with threats of mutilation. It wasn't that he liked or particularly wanted the stereotype of fierce older brother. It was only that in thinking of Lila, in the way he thought of Lila, he had no stomach for his baby sister in a similar role.

"Tony," Mia said, voice softened. "Did you see if the sedan was out front? If the driver's here, then Lloyd's here and probably in the billiard room playing Pac Man."

She was right.

All three brothers huddled at the Pac Man machine, with Lloyd at the center, jerking it and kicking. To the left of them was the button up he'd worn for Tony's benefit, draped across a chair unwrinkled.

Remy saw Tony first, then nudged the others.

The laughter started. Deep, rolling guffaws that landed

one boy on top of the other. Smacks of the thigh and belly clenching, they were bent over and howling with it.

He thought of the old Bugs Bunny cartoons, where the brunt of a joke would have his head transformed into a massive red sucker. If that weren't bad enough, the massive lollipop would have "SUCKER" printed across it.

"Look at his face," Damien gasped. "We need a camera. We need a picture. Lloyd said you'd be a—"

"Sucker," Tony supplied.

"And it was true," Lloyd said. "Only, you got here too early. I had plans for lipstick on my shirt, a bit of perfume. Anything to watch you go ape up the walls, little cousin. You're just so good at it."

Tony thought back to the boy who'd been desperate for a family. The old him who'd hitchhiked from Bismarck. He wanted to tell them that this wasn't exactly what he meant.

"I should pound you," was what he said instead.

But Lloyd only turned back to his game.

"You've got a temper, little cousin. Counseling might help."

"You actually thought he'd sleep with your girl," Remy said, smile now fading. "Your own cousin, messing with your girl? You must think so much of us."

And the tide rushed back, shifting fault from them to him. He was the one who disappointed. He was the reason the joke worked.

Tony groped for tendrils of victimhood, sought ways to plead his own case. They were Hammonds, he wanted to say, and in their family worse things had happened. Except none of those things involved them, so who knew how it all really went? Everything involved dead people with versions never told. They had nothing of the anger and envy that ripped their parents' generation. The most they felt was a scratch of annoyance when the grown-ups harped on old things.

He decided to leave. But not before cursing each one: to an accidental step on a rusty nail, to a growth of man boobs in their prime.

Then he started for his bedroom.

"Wait," Lloyd said. "At least let us help you get back up."

Tony blinked once, in surprise, before following his cousin's lead.

CHAPTER
Thirty-one

Tak ROLLED IN BED AND COLLIDED with a patch of ice. A hand across white sheets confirmed that his wife had abandoned their hibernation. But she couldn't have gone far. Gelatinous legs were no good for walking, and he'd given her a pair on that day.

He climbed out of bed. Mike in the house meant Mike into mischief and the need for a closer eye on his wife. Naked, Tak pulled on a gray tee that said 'Big Easy' and slipped into wrinkled jeans from the floor.

A sweep of the house gave Tak a glimpse of John lying on a couch in the entrance hall staring at the wall. It took him to Tak's father flipping through *The Discourse That Sets Turning the Wheel of Truth* in the library, smiling as if it were the Sunday comics, and it took him to Aunt Caroline and

Aunt Asami, drinking beer in the reception room. Neither had seen Deena.

More searching brought him to his grandmother seated with Grandma Emma, both women caught in a smile. Tak resisted the urge to join them and hurried onward in his hunt. His wife had to be somewhere. That somewhere had better not be with Mike.

A head in the pantry revealed the backside of a tall, dark, thrusting figure, jeans pooled at the ankles. Pale legs wrapped his waist, arms wrapped his neck, and the face at his shoulder was familiar. As for the guy, Tak couldn't think of which cousin he might be, but the girl was definitely Lauren. A tall white shelf stacked to overflow with cans, supported both their weights. It jerked and jerked and a can sprung free. Bush's Baked Beans with extra brown sugar rolled to Tak's feet.

He backed out the way he'd come.

And collided with Tony.

"Jesus, kid!" he cried and snatched shut the pantry door. Heart heaving, he looked back at it with an expectation of betrayal.

"Dad," Tony said. "You've gotta come."

It was then that Tak remembered who was who and that Tony, not him, should fear detection.

"You're out of your room. I told you that if you come out again—"

"Mike's on the roof, Dad. He's gonna jump."

"Wait." Tak's mouth snapped shut on a reprimand. "What?"

"Hurry," Tony said and ran.

CHAPTER
Thirty-Two

THEY TORE THROUGH THE HOUSE, toppling a wild-haired bust before sliding through the entrance hall and spilling into the driveway. Tony pointed upward.

"There," he said. "Stand back to see him better."

Tak kept his face skyward, but walked back, just as his son had instructed. On the roof of his house, Mike stood, a silhouette against the moon, hair flapping.

"Go get his dad," Tak said.

"No! Get my parents and I'll be dead before they get here. I don't want them to see me."

Tak dropped his gaze to Tony, who stood in taut expectation. Eighteen years of life shrank to insignificance; he needed his father to tell him what to do.

Tak turned to the roof.

"Listen to me," he said. "Let's talk. We're still family. It's not too late."

Mike came all the way to the roof's edge. Only his head jutted out for Tak's view.

"You don't even know what you're talking about," he said.

Mike drew back, leaving Tak to stare at a gaping darkness, a void where his cousin had been.

"Mike." Tak heard the fissures in his voice. "Mike, I'm going to come up now."

He searched for how his cousin had done it, but saw nothing to aid understanding. A quick study of the house showed him grooves good enough for scaling. He stepped back, got a running start and leaped to latch on to the first floor balustrade. Their house, hoisted on a foundation, meant that even the lowest floor stood a little tall.

Tak pulled himself up with a yawn of muscle, before swinging a leg onto the ledge. He looked up, grabbed the grooved end of the French arch separating first floor from second, and used it to hoist up yet again. He repeated for the second floor, before feeling for a column that ran to the roof. Tak used it to scramble up to a smaller window, feet pedaling in the throes of a near-slip. Finally, he grabbed hold of the roof, pawed around for the parapet, and used it to heave himself up.

Chest heaving, Tak flopped onto his back and blinked at the multitude of stars.

"You climbed the house," Mike said, voice strained, as if Tak were a lab rat who'd grown a massive penis. Disgust tinged with fascination.

Tak looked around.

"How'd you get here?"

Mike pointed to the side of the house, where the top prongs of a ladder rested.

Great.

He turned back to face Tak and studied him as if he hoped to learn.

"You came to stop me," Mike said. "After all I've done. But if you knew the half of it, you'd shove me off this thing instead."

Tak's stomach instinctively clenched. What he shoved back was a myriad of possibilities. Mike had done something or a series of somethings so vile that he wanted to die. Couple that with his general inability to conjure up contrition and Tak's hands wanted to cover his ears.

"Tell me," he said instead. "Tell me why you're up here."

Mike shoved both hands in the pockets of his jeans and turned to face an oversized moon. It was the kind that a kid on a bicycle pedaled by, with an alien in a basket heading home.

"I think about old stuff," he said. "Swimming in Blue Lake Reservoir. John hurling on Mister Twister. Us running away to try and sign up as rodeo clowns." He shot Tak a grin. "That meat we tried to feed the lions at Denver Zoo. You were there for all of it, I realized. Me and John's best memories."

Mike turned on him abruptly.

"I want you off this roof."

"No."

Tak clamored to his feet.

"What am I supposed to tell my best friend when you

jump? My aunt and uncle? My grandmother? That I left you up here so you could kill yourself properly?"

"So, you're here for them."

"Yes, I'm here for them!" Tak cried. "I'm here for you, too, you moron."

Mike's nostrils flared.

"You're not here for me. You don't even like me."

Well, he had a point there. Tak sighed.

"Not liking you is not the same as wanting you dead."

He had the same memories as Mike. Splashing in lake waters at summer time, gnawing on candy coated apples by the bushel. Once, they'd camped in the backyard and told ghost stories, after which Tak felt too paranoid to sleep. On telling Mike, he sat up, flashlight in hand and guarded the tent with darting eyes until Tak found rest at last.

"I misled you," Mike said. "When I said I knew Deena. I did, but she didn't know me. I admired her, left gifts for her sometime, but never did I find courage enough to speak."

Tak felt none of the usual burn that accompanied Mike's confessions of unrequited love. Instead, a slow sorrow spread through him.

"You don't have to tell me this," Tak said. "You don't have to—"

"I think about her," Mike said. "I have, every day since college. She magnified in my mind, until no other woman could compare. Deena couldn't compare to the woman I made her out to be."

"Mike—"

"You feel sorry for me," Mike said. "I hear it in your voice. But if you knew how much I fantasized about—"

"Shut up," Tak said. "Stop trying to make me push you."

Mike fell silent, chest rising and falling heavily.

"You said you wanted to know." He paused, as if giving Tak the opportunity to refute this.

"After she left your bedroom," Mike went on, "she asked me if we could talk. We went into the sitting room, for privacy, and shared a bottle of vintage wine. She only loves you was what she wanted to tell me, as if I hadn't gathered that for myself. She fell asleep as we talked after drinking too much."

Tak's breathing suspended mid-inhale, giving him a floating, buoyed sensation. He saw Mike before him, but didn't see him, staring through and numbed by his words.

"I would have done it," Mike said, gaze level on Tak. "I didn't do it, but God knows I wanted to. I touched her—a little—and kissed her—and then…"

Nothing moved for Tak. Not the air in his lungs. Not the blood in his veins. Everything, cemented still.

"I stopped myself," Mike said. "I saw myself and I stopped. But then this girl came along, this maid, and I took it all out on her. I hurt her, Tak, and I liked it. I liked not caring what she felt. I hurt her and hurt her and hurt her and, God help me, I couldn't even stop."

"Where is she?" Tak said. "Who is she? Tell me something so I can get her some help."

Mike didn't bother to wipe the tears, snorting instead with derision.

"She liked it, too," he said. "If you can believe that. She liked me treating her like shit. Turns out, I can't even get being a monster right. I belong right here on this roof."

She liked it. That gave Tak one reason to exhale, even as he backpedaled to another thought.

"My wife, Mike…"

Every inch of Tak's body felt vice tight. His fingers curled into hammers. He had flung himself onto the roof; he could easily fling Mike off.

"I caressed her face as she slept. I kissed her. I ran a hand up and down her body. I—"

Tak shoved him. A rocket of a move not even he anticipated had Mike pitching back. A plummet on his ass. A fistful of tile. A wide-eyed realization of truth. He'd almost fallen off the roof and he hadn't wanted to.

Tak stormed for the ladder.

Mike screamed after him. First his name, then the begging, and finally, the pleas for forgiveness. Not just for Deena, but for candy, marbles, old lies.

CHAPTER
Thirty-Three

DEENA SAT AT AN OCEANSIDE CAFÉ, twisting a napkin until her hands turned red. Furtive glances at the window revealed nothing. Her waitress returned with a fourth refill of coffee.

Women like the one she waited for were used to an anticipating audience. They made fashionable entrances and were forgiven, though Deena didn't feel so forgiving.

White. Of course she showed up in all white. Tall, tanned, and with a body so narrow, so slender, that the wisps of white she wore did nothing but flatter, emphasizing flawlessness. At the swell of pert breasts, at the flat of a perfect stomach, at the width of hips that were barely there. Aubree Daniels was perfect. Damn her for knowing it.

Aubree sat down across from her and smiled. A piteous thing, really, heaped on Deena in a flash of common courtesy.

A wave of a hand brought a once disinterested waitress, who took her order with alacrity.

She wore the ring.

The Tanaka ring.

And smiled when Deena noticed it.

Deena looked down at her own hand and noted she wore it as well.

Her cappuccino arrived, but she ignored it.

"Deena," she said in a voice that mocked sympathy. "You must find a way to cope. After years of letting him…drift, you mourn now that your husband's lost at sea."

"I did not let him drift," she hissed, only to have Aubree smile small. "Our problems are no worse than any other couple's. I don't see why you're here."

Aubree began to fiddle with the Tanaka ring, spinning it round and round her finger as she admired it.

"Deena. Let's be reasonable here, shall we? You were so inexperienced. Your virginity must have been an enticement, I suppose. But after that? You can't think a man as skillful as Tak would be…pleasured by your fumbling?"

Deena's cheeks caught fire.

"If you know what's good for you—"

"Oh, but I do know what's good for me. See?"

Aubree held up the hand with the ring.

"You're inattentive, angst-ridden, self-involved and…" a critical gaze swept over Deena, "only moderately attractive. You couldn't have expected to keep your husband forever."

Deena stared at her blankly, certain that her every pimple, blemish and scar had magnified one hundredfold.

Her oversized breasts sagged, her stomach softened to pudding.

"You're talking about my career," Deena said. "You're alluding to some backwoods misogyny that criticizes female work ethic and aspirations."

Aubree blew a raspberry with plump, Marilyn Monroe lips. "I'm talking about you sucking at being a wife. I'm talking about you sucking at everything but your husband's—"

"Shut up," Deena said. "Shut up before I slap you. Who are you, anyway? Some tramp my husband's forgotten?"

Aubree smiled as if delighted at finally being asked.

"Who am I? Why, I'm your better, Deena Hammond. You should always note your betters."

Deena woke to a twist of sheets. Mummified, her limbs flailed until she found a suitable escape. She was in her own bed, in yesterday's clothes, though the last thing she remembered was wine with Mike.

Tak sat in a chair drawn up to her nightstand. Fatigue made shadows of his face. In his lap was a tattered copy of *Architecture Digest*, face up, unopened.

"What did you dream?" he said.

She sat up.

"Nothing."

He looked at her, expression revealing nothing except fatigue.

"Your phone rang," he said and tossed it to her. "First thing in the morning, non-stop."

Deena caught it in mid-air and turned it upright before swiping through to the missed call screen.

A Miami number. Unrecognizable.

"Well?" Tak said.

"Nothing. It's no one."

She tossed the phone aside.

"They left messages."

"OK."

"Check them."

"Later," Deena said.

"Check them now," Tak said.

She stared at him.

"No," she said quietly.

Tak tossed aside the magazine and walked out the room.

CHAPTER
Thirty-four

JOHN WOKE TO THE SIGHT OF A GUTTED room. Mike's side had been stripped of all luggage. His bedding lay folded in a corner. It was Christmas Eve and thunder boomed like the prelude to a B-List horror flick. With the window cracked, a single sheet of paper took flight, gliding from the writing desk to the floor.

John clamored to his feet, picked it up, and went over to Mike's open closet.

Emptied out. The nightstand clock next to the stripped bed said 9 a.m., though outside it looked closer to midnight.

With the note in hand, John took a seat on the edge of Mike's bed.

John,
By the time you read this, I'll be on the first flight out. My plans are

to travel until something feels like me. For so long, I've chased what others wanted and what it seemed like I should have. I have no idea who I am. I have no idea what I like. It's like Shakespeare once said, "God has given you one face, and you make yourself another."

I don't know when you'll hear from me again. I don't know what I'll say when you do. Convince the family that I love them and that it is best for me to be away. I am sorry. There's more on the dresser. Read it. Burn it. Forgive me.

Mike

John went over and pulled a wad of papers from the nightstand. On it were a laundry list of deeds, listed in Mike's tight and orderly script. Toys purposely broken. Mean words said. Lies told. And at the bottom were the things he'd done to Deena in her sleep and what he'd done to the maid.

John sat with the papers as lightning illuminated the room. John sat with the papers as thunder quaked and windows rattled. He read them once more. Afterward, he ventured down to the kitchen and lit the sheets one by one on the stove.

CHAPTER
Thirty-five

Tony rose in the morning to the sight of his bedroom door wide open. In the adjacent bathroom, running water and Lloyd's nasal falsetto meant that his temporary roommate was up and ready to start his day. Maybe the open door was a sign that he had made amends with his father. After all, he had saved Mike's life. Or alerted others to do it. Same thing, he figured.

Lloyd emerged from the bathroom, freshly spritzed in a fragrance Tony knew. His cousin extended tree branch arms and grinned.

"Eh? Eh? Look good, don't I?" he said.

"You'd look better in your own possessions," Tony said.

Lloyd went for the closet.

"Hardly. Especially when yours are so much more

expensive. I mean, look at all these Jordans. Half of these I've never even seen before."

"They're custom made."

"Custom—?" Lloyd looked from him to the closet. "Wow. Just wow. Kids in my neighborhood knock off heads for a used pair of sweaty feet. Meanwhile, you've got Air Jordan himself knitting some for you."

Lloyd went back to admiring the two neat rows of gym shoes. Tony wouldn't tell him that those were his Aruba collection, only a fraction of what he kept at home.

"I tell ya," Lloyd said. "One shift in the gene pool and it would have been me with the Jordans and you trying to figure out next semester's tuition bill."

"Your tuition isn't paid?" Tony said as Lloyd disappeared into the closet. "What happened to basketball?"

His cousin attended Florida International University on a basketball scholarship. He'd been a flamboyant point guard who missed as many shots as he made, though seemed not to notice.

"Coach cut me," he said from what sounded like a cavern. "I've been off the team since last spring."

"But you can borrow money, can't you? Enough to—"

Lloyd emerged with Jordans in fire limestone green. He held them up to his face for inspection.

"These are nice. Brings out the green in this shirt. Flashy, but I like it." He looked over at Tony as if remembering he was there. "You can only borrow money when you make progress. And I haven't."

Lloyd dropped down on the edge of his bed and jammed

a foot into Tony's sneaker. They were identical in height at 6'1" and apparently identical in shoe size at 12.

"See that? We could be twins. With me being the much handsomer one, of course."

"You should ask my mom for help," Tony said. "Tuition can't be much. She could write—"

"You going to open up those letters you hide in the drawer or you want us to bury you with them when you die an old man?"

Tony followed Lloyd's gaze to the desk drawer where four envelopes sat. One from Harvard, one from Julliard, one from Yale, one from Berklee.

"You act like nobody raised you," Tony said. "Like you haven't got respect for property."

Lloyd looked at him expectantly. Tony released a weighted sigh.

"I can't bring myself to open them, okay? They're the best schools in the world. I was dumb to apply."

"You're dumb for not reading them."

Lloyd marched for the desk and snatched it open. Tony leap-frogged to grab his arm.

"I'm serious! Don't—"

They fell into wild grappling, with Lloyd reaching and Tony slapping. Slapping at arms, slapping at hands, until the two tumbled to the floor. It was Lloyd, the athlete, who found his footing first, snatched up the envelope and waved it triumphantly.

"Lloyd, please—"

"Open them or I tell everyone in the house."

"No."

"Remy! Damien! Come see what Tony's hiding!"

Tony rushed for the door to lock it.

But it was the wrong move.

Now Lloyd had all the letters.

"Lloyd, please."

How could he explain Old Tony and New? Or the difficulty of not knowing whether he belonged? All decadence and jet-setting for the boy who'd once found meals in the trash. Here was the dilemma of his life. In those letters were stark truths: that he was a charlatan and pretender, an upstart waiting to fall down.

He wasn't ready to fall just yet.

Lloyd cleared his throat, letter open.

"Dear Mr. Tanaka—"

"Don't!"

"Dear Mr. Tanaka—"

"I won't listen."

Tony headed for the door, with vomit building like stacked Legos. Higher and higher it all went towering, until—

"You got in."

He hadn't heard that. He hadn't heard this cruel attempt at—

"You got in, dipshit. Are you listening? Big surprise, you got in."

It wasn't true. Another of Lloyd's tricks at his expense. Another game he didn't want to play.

"Listen," Lloyd said and Tony heard the crinkling of paper. "In the real world, nobody gives a shit if you spend your nights in dumpsters. Well, your girl might, but that's about it."

"That's not something I joke about."

"Whatever."

Lloyd sat down at the desk, where he opened more envelopes.

"Like I was saying before you forgot your manners, talent is a pretty good equalizer. Somewhere in this world is a kid with thirteen years of music lessons to your seven. That kid just got rejected to Harvard, Yale, Julliard, and Berklee."

"Why would you say that?"

Lloyd held up the letters, grinning shamelessly.

"Because you got into all of them," he said.

CHAPTER
thirty-six

RIOTING SET OFF THE MORNING OF Christmas Eve. Shouts and the thundering of a thousand feet rocked Deena's bedroom. She had the skull howling pain of a wine hangover, Tak had an attitude, and now this. Ingrates traipsing like a buffalo herd. No question as to who it was.

Deena jammed her feet into slippers and marched out the door.

Tariq's children were making a racket again. Three of them rushed up and down the hall, hooting in bare-faced glee while banging every door they encountered. They dog-piled one on top of the other with Tony at the bottom, toppled into the wall and repeated.

Deena stalked to the end of the hall, where they jammed like five o'clock traffic.

"This is ridiculous," she said. "And I've had enough. Enough of—"

"They're letting dummies into Harvard!" Remy hooted. "Loons into Yale!"

"Hooray one time for Tony!" Lloyd cried. "Hooray two times for a fool!"

Deena blinked. "What?"

Tony stood with considerable effort, shoving older, bigger cousins off his body.

"They mean me," he said. "I got in. Early decision at that."

"You got in where? Harvard?"

"And Yale," Remy said.

"Julliard and Berklee, too," Lloyd supplied.

Deena stood up straighter. Frowning.

"But how do you know?"

"Pardon me, Mrs. Tanaka, but is it possible—"

Deena whirled to see a tall, slim woman with liver lips and a thin smile. She wore the black and whites of a housekeeper.

"Whatever it is will have to wait," Deena said.

"But Mrs. Tanaka—"

Deena turned back to her son.

"How do you know your admission status? I mean, you're here."

"That idiot's been carrying the letters around for days," Lloyd said, just as the maid departed with a surly look in their direction. "He's been too afraid to open them."

Deena shrieked and her head paid the price. Still, she shrieked some more. For Tak, for Mia, she even shrieked for Noah. Then she swept Tony up. He was his father's height and well over Deena, but she choked him to her bosom just the same.

"Mom, don't—don't cry," he said and twisted in her arms. Even that word, 'Mom', made the tears fall freer.

Meanwhile, he'd turned the color of rich rhubarb and stayed like that till Tak extricated him.

"Harvard," she said. "Yale, Berklee, Julliard."

Tak let out a low, impressed whistle.

"Top shelf," he said and messed Tony's hair.

They exchanged a quiet, intimate sort of smile, before Tak snatched him in, too.

Deena felt it then: the thing always between the two; the thing that had her as a perpetual third wheel, sitting in on a conversation among friends in a language she didn't know. Words passed between them in their embrace, words that no one else heard, and once apart, Deena saw both their eyes glistening.

She headed back for their bedroom alone.

She loved that they loved each other so. She loved that they were indivisibly close. Whenever contrariness about it came to her, she reminded herself of these facts and repeated as often as necessary.

Deena dropped down at the stool of her vanity and gave herself a good hard look. Her son—and that's who he was now—was eighteen years old and on his way to college. His transgressions over the years didn't even hint at the possibilities for wrong. Breaking curfew, too much time on his cell—those were the infractions her son had committed. And the possibilities for bad? Endless. All the wrong choices lay before him on an ever-intersecting path of realities. But her son had made his own way: the right way. She could only find joy at the thought.

Tak came in, closed the door and leaned against it. Like always, he looked at her with eyes that knew too much.

"You okay?" he said.

She wanted to snap, "Yes, yes, of course."

Except her mouth wouldn't comply.

The bed creaked under the weight of her husband.

"He looks like him. More and more every day, I think," Tak said.

There was no need to say who or even why they were talking about that.

Still, Deena didn't trust herself to answer.

"Sometimes I ask myself if I could ever let Kenji go," Tak said. "If I could ever be okay without my doppelganger."

"And what did you realize?"

He looked at her. "That I hope to never know."

He rose and pulled her over to the bed, where they sat together.

"He needs you, too," Tak said. "He needs a mother. I can't be that."

Deena dropped her gaze, scarlet illuminated her cheeks. "I know."

She thought he would kiss her there. It was such a Tak thing to do.

Instead, he rose and went for the door.

"Breakfast," he said. "Because the sooner we start the day, the sooner we can finish it."

CHAPTER
Thirty-seven

A FTER LEAVING MIKE ON THE ROOF he'd gone and put his wife to bed, locked the door, and headed to the billiards room for a drink. Eventually, Tyson had joined him. They had drinks, talked movies, and insulted each other's sports teams. It was almost as good as being with John—John before the divorce, that is. Tyson, who mentioned Ash a few times, seemed to be feeling wistful himself. They'd parted on a good note.

Tak had slept that night with his wife in a vice grip, her head on his chest and both his arms around her. More than once, he woke with his pulse skittering, only to have it calm at the sight of her sleeping still. His dreams had been filled with Mikes. Mikes raping and confessing and pillaging and plunging to his death. And when at last Tak gave up on sleep, he took a chair to watch his wife dream of Aubree Daniels.

Her name was like a broken whisper in the dark, a swept cobweb, a bit of shattered glass. Tak knew no more and no less, only "Aubree Daniels" said once.

Then there was her, and a phone that held secrets.

It gave him childish wants, that phone. It gave him impulses. He wanted to rummage through it, smash it, and stomp it in abandon. He wanted to spit misogynistic things at her, to remind her of what her bible said about her husband's role in her life. But none of that was him.

He hadn't been honest with her. Not when he retrieved her sleeping body from the upstairs sitting room. Not when she woke from her dozing in the middle of the night. Everything was fine. All was alright. That was what he'd said.

He'd made up his mind not to tell her. Whether it was best for her, he couldn't say. Only, that it wasn't possible for him to say the words—words that meant Mike had touched her without permission, violating her. His throat constricted at the thought, as if to squeeze his Adam's apple up and out.

She would be okay, he told himself. She was obviously okay.

Downstairs, breakfast had already begun. There were great heapings of meat and breads, complemented by cheeses, eggs, and Belgian waffles with two dozen options for toppings piled high on table after table, a spread worthy of Buckingham Palace. Tak sat with his wife, alone. When Noah came over, Tak ushered him downstream with a tilt of his head, where he fell in with a few Hammond kids.

John came next but sat down gingerly, as if the seat itself fueled his discomfort. He had food before him but he didn't eat, and promptly told them that Mike had gone.

Tak and John exchanged a careful look, only to find Deena studying them.

"I'll leave you two to your breakfast," John said. "Anyway, I hear there's a knucklehead I need to congratulate."

Deena spoke the second he'd gone.

"You two look as if something happened," Deena said. "Although, I suppose my telling Mike off is something happening."

Tak buried himself in his juice, one gulp, then another, until Tony entered the room. It exploded into whoops and jeers and a dozen or so clamored around him. When at last he emerged again, his cornrows had frizzed and his shirt was twisted, and lopsided.

Tak took in Deena's bewildered look.

"What?" he said.

She looked at him as if trying to focus.

"It's just…it was nothing like this when I went off to college. No one cared. No one."

He wanted to tell her that these were different people; that her grandfather was dead and Caroline was but one in the crowd now. No family was the same at any two points in time, anyway. Families shift, grow and shrink, while priorities and how they perceive life changes with them.

"Mr. Tanaka?" a maid said.

"Not now," Tak said.

"But Mr. Tanaka—"

"Is it possible for me to have one meal with my wife without being interrupted a hundred friggin' times? Unless you're coming to tell me which one of you has been lifting all the liquor, I don't want to hear it. And who stands over people when they eat, anyway?"

"Tak—"

"Sir, it's only that—"

"Take the day off," Tak said and turned back to Deena. "Take more if you like."

The maid snorted, mouthed off something he couldn't make out, and stalked away. Tak stared through the plate before him.

"Baby?"

Boy, was that an annoying look. The one people gave when they wondered if you'd finally succumbed to the voices in your head. Tak looked pointedly at Deena.

"What?"

She saw it. That his question wasn't even a question. It was a statement, a command. Leave me alone, was what it should have said. But like everything, it softened for her. I need a second, was what he'd told her.

He felt a mountain atop them, a mountain of misunderstandings, lies and secrets. But this was no mere peak of stone, therefore scalable. This was comprised of something so delicate, one cinder could ignite it all.

"Tak?"

He returned to his food, smashed the eggs around a bit, and shoveled some in his mouth.

Cold.

He added it to his list of disappointments.

TONY'S FATHER HAD granted him a last minute reprieve after news of his college acceptance. The second he'd done so, one word whispered in his mind: Lila. A phone call, a shower, hurried breakfast, and three thousand claps on the back had brought him to that moment. Tony climbed from the sedan like a man jumping bail.

She stood at the spot they always met at: the cluster of squat adobe fixtures, in turquoise, pistachio, and white.

Lila ran to meet him. A tall, raven haired figure pressed into a fitted black tank and tights. She threw arms around him and showered him with pecks, body sinking into his so tightly that he felt every curve, every hint of flesh. She murmured something in Dutch and pulled back long enough to grin. Then the kisses started in for a second time, one long and luxurious after another. Tony's arm found her waist and cinched it, mouth against hers and working.

"Somebody's been lonely," she said and unraveled from him with a teasing grin.

"You mean me," he said and felt the smile slip from his face.

"Yes, you," she said and tousled his hair.

Tony took her by the wrists and placed her arms aside. Only one of them had been lonely? He pushed the thought from his mind.

"How'd you get free?" Lila said. "That man seemed so angry. Who was he, anyway? Kinda cute for an older guy."

"My dad," Tony snapped.

Her face went slack, as if presented with an

insurmountable problem. Then it brightened. "Oh! So, you're...adopted?"

He didn't like the way she said it, as if it were something subject to xenophobia, some puzzling otherness she hoped never to have the misfortune of catching. There was some vague pity there, too, alongside the implication that he must be deprived of the truth concerning his identity.

It occurred to him that they didn't talk much. That she knew nothing of his home life, of how he grew up, of what he wanted. She'd never even heard of Lizard or Wendy, though they knew something of her.

Lila batted over long lashes at him and wrapped her arms around his waist.

"I've ruined the mood," she said. "But I know how to make things fun. Let's go shopping. Then you can spoil me."

His mouth curled down on an exhale.

"How about we talk?" Tony said. "Or take a walk on the beach?"

She cringed.

"Really? You sound like an online dating profile."

"Fine. You think of something. But I didn't earn early release just to take you shopping."

She coiled up to him again, slipped an arm around him, and let red painted lips brush his ear.

"We could go behind that building over there." She tilted her head in the direction of an evening café. "Have a little fun."

Despite his better judgment, Tony's breath caught as the thrill of arousal snaked up and down his body.

"Outside?" he breathed, and like that, his flush of abandon evaporated.

Outside. An image of Lila topless, of him on her, of his father stepping from the shadows turned him cold, all titillation forgotten.

"Yes, outside," Lila said, to which he extricated himself a second time. Unlike the first, she held on, resisting his urge to be free. With his hands on her wrist, he was able to forcibly remove himself and give her a hard, bewildered look.

"What's with you?" he said.

"What's with you? You're all into me one second and throwing me off the next. If I didn't know better, I'd think you didn't love me."

She crossed her arms and huffed, bottom lip springing out before stealing a cautious glance his way. They'd never talked of love—love wasn't possible—hell, he didn't even know where she lived.

"You don't love me," she said, in what she only thought was a voice tinged in hurt. Instead, she sounded like his kid sister, back when she lugged eyeless baby dolls around. She'd lose them and demand his help, which grew tiresome quick. When he stopped, she'd accuse him of not loving her.

Except, he did love Mia, so that always worked, whereas with Lila, he felt only…urges.

"So, you love me?" Tony said and held eye contact. "You're honestly trying to say that you love me?"

They didn't keep in touch when he left Aruba, they didn't write, they didn't call, they didn't email.

She swelled at his question, chest rising, chin rising, eyes lit.

"I can't believe you have to ask," she said, but as she said it she dropped her gaze.

His mouth thinned in irritation. It tended to do that whenever people avoided his questions.

"So," he said. "Just to recap, we've established that the answer is 'no'. I don't love you and you don't love me. We're just two kids having a good time."

"That girl you call when you think no one's looking," she said. "The one back in Miami. She's the one you love."

Tony started down a side street toward a row of shops; Lila fell in step behind him.

"Where are you going?"

"Away from you. You're annoying me."

"You're annoyed because you're hearing the truth?"

He stopped. They stood in the shadows of a two-story building. A YMCA, he realized belatedly.

"You don't even know what you're talking about. You've never even met Wendy. You didn't even know her name until I just said it."

"I know she must be pretty important."

She looked proud of herself, as if she'd made some great point.

"Yeah? So?"

A Honda hatchback rolled by. Tony recognized it as belonging to Tito, one of Lila's best friends. As inseparable as him and Wendy, last summer there'd been only a few occasions where they'd been without him.

Tony watched him drive off.

"Are we meeting him?"

She pursed her lips at the question, snapping off an "Of course not," that seemed unduly irritated.

"You've picked the worst time to start an argument," she said, making him wonder who had done what. "If you knew what I needed to talk to you about, you'd feel horrible for how you've been treating me."

Tony's eyes narrowed.

"I think you should let me be the judge of that."

She took a deep breath and extended a hand to him. He let it hover, staring.

They stood like that, with traffic milling by and the sky rolling toward darkness.

She'd let it hang forever, it turned out. So with a sigh, Tony accepted her hand.

She looked up at him with eyes that were more honey than brown and wider than he recalled. Mixed with a thousand things, he thought. All the islanders seemed to be.

Against his better judgment, he pulled her in by the hand and took her into his arms. His body responded to her even if his mind didn't, and soon their mouths met. She responded to him as expected, their heat never ceasing.

"I'm pregnant," she said between kisses.

He ran a hand under her shirt, then froze before pulling away.

"What?"

"I'm pregnant, Tony. I'm carrying your baby."

His cloud of lust abated, making room for understanding.

"How can you be?"

Her mouth curved into a smile. "Tony, be serious."

"I am being serious!" He turned, as if to leave, only to double back. Dumb shock had blazed to fury. "I am being serious!" he yelled again, because he could think of nothing else to say.

But then he took in her features: her bloodless face, her searching gaze. His reaction shocked her, but why it did, he didn't know.

"Tony, don't be mad. I mean, I know it sounds like bad news, but—"

"It sounds like bullshit."

"What?"

"I said, this is bullshit. That you're on some bullshit." He roped in a thousand thoughts organized on a deep breath, and moved forward. "You may be pregnant," he said, "but you're not pregnant by me."

"Are you really doing this?"

"It's not possible, Lila. What'd you do? Conceive on Monday and call me on Wednesday? Good scam, I can see you thought it through."

"I'm not talking about what we did this week!" She shook, furious under his glare. "You and I both know what happened between us last summer."

"Nothing happened between us last summer."

"Tony, come on. Tito's party?"

"You got drunk," he said. "We made out. After that, I put you in a cab. I wouldn't take advantage of a girl like that. I couldn't."

Lila snorted out a laugh. "Be serious."

"I am serious. Unconscious girls aren't my thing. So, I don't know who got you pregnant. But I do know who it wasn't."

Tony stalked off, in search of a cab ride home.

CHAPTER
thirty-eight

Deena's umbrella drooped with the weight of insistent rain as it battered and clawed at her only defense. Howling winds cut, first one way and then the other, so that ice water sliced in sideways, buckets of permafrost hurled at her back as rivers rushed through the street.

She burst into the café and found a double pair of wide eyes staring back at her. The woman behind the counter stood tall and pale, red hair like a flickering flame. She offered neither smile nor greeting. Deena turned to greet the other person present.

"I didn't think you'd come," Allison Tanaka said. "You sounded like you wouldn't on the phone."

Deena tossed her freshly bent umbrella to the floor and dropped into the seat across from her.

"I'm here," she said. "But why?"

John's soon-to-be ex-wife sat back. Unlike Deena, she seemed unfazed by the rain. Dry, neat, clothes clean. With her flaxen locks pulled high into an absentminded ponytail, the lines of her face looked severe, windswept by time and worry.

Allison drummed fingers on the narrow café table, the faint line of her ring finger betraying her secret.

"You said it wouldn't affect our friendship if I left him. You said you'd be okay with it," Allison said.

"And it hasn't."

"Yet, you talk to me like this," Allison said. She waved over the ghost-lady behind the counter.

"Two cappuccinos," she said before turning back to Deena.

In need of something to fiddle with, Deena plucked a napkin from the silver display and turned it round and round in her hand.

"I'm not angry about you leaving him. Like I told you before, you're the one who has to live with him, sleep with him. I have no opinion on that." She looked up. "But for the love of God, Allison, did you have to do it right before the holidays? And after all these years, couldn't you have told him to his face?"

"Like he told me about his secretary to my face?"

Allison 1, Deena 0.

Deena tossed her napkin.

"Like I said, it's no business of mine. If you can't stand your husband, you can't stand your husband."

"I never said I couldn't stand my husband. Only that I couldn't stand the idea of him with another woman."

Both of Allison's hands sat on the table, pale, open, veined and shaking. Like her face, they'd aged since the last time Deena had seen her friend.

"I'm not judging you," Deena said. "I wouldn't be able to stand the idea of Tak with another woman."

She thought of Aubree Daniels and quickly shared what happened, up to and including her discovery of condoms and throwing Tak out.

But Allison only rolled her eyes.

"I warned you about Mike years ago."

"Yes, I know, but—"

"And what did I tell you?"

"Allison, what you said is completely irrelevant to—"

"You think a man being in love with you is irrelevant to what he tells you about your husband? Really, Deena, you're supposed to be brilliant. Or something like it."

Deena sighed. "I know he misled me. But—"

"But nothing. Your marriage to Tak is fine as long as the two of you keep the world out of it. He is so in love with you. Still. Do you know how rare that is?"

Rare?

"Allison, the question has never been one of whether John loves you—"

"You think infidelity isn't a question of love?" She accepted her cappuccino with a snort. "I should have asked you that when you thought Tak and Aubree were bed buddies."

Lightning scissored through the parking lot. On its heels was the boom of thunder. A car alarm protested in the distance.

"I can't speak to your husband's motivations," Deena said. "He betrayed you. You have every right to be heartbroken and furious."

"But?" Allison said. She looked, not at Deena, but to both of their untouched drinks.

"But John doesn't talk. He barely eats, or grooms, or sleeps from the looks of him. He has bags under his eyes and hopelessness in them. He's ruined. Whether it's what he deserves or not is a matter for you to decide. But, for the record, he is heartbroken."

Allison's gooseberry eyes narrowed to slits.

"I didn't call you here to be his advocate."

"No," Deena said. "You came to Aruba to spy, to feel nearer to your husband. You called me here for the same reason."

Allison blew a gust of air from her mouth, sending wisps of ash blonde hair adrift.

"Deena, I hate his guts."

"I don't blame you."

"But I love him. And I feel so weak for that."

Weak. Allison Tanaka, the powerhouse divorce attorney that made her living by terrorizing wealthy philanderers. In some sick quirk of fate, her husband had turned into one of them.

"Maybe it's what I deserve," she said as if reading Deena's mind. "This misery. After salivating at the mention of divorce all these years, maybe I deserve the most heartbreaking, gruesome variation possible. I've done nothing but delight in the irreparable damage of matrimony."

Deena exhaled.

"You said you love him still."

"Yeah?"

"So take him back."

Allison sat back, face drained of color.

"Deena, no."

"No?"

"I can't. I won't. My parents. My family? I couldn't bare the humiliation."

"But you can bear to see him marry another woman? To see him move on?"

Allison gasped. It was as if she'd never considered it.

"My sister would gloat," Allison said. "You've met Claire. You've met her husband Broderick. They're perfect."

Perfect, Deena thought. No doubt Asami and Ken were perfect.

"Are these really your concerns? Embarrassment? Because that's temporary. Divorce is forever."

Allison scowled.

"You're like everyone else, chock full of answers when none of it concerns you." She rummaged in a purse seated on an adjacent chair and slapped a few dollars on the table.

"Allison—"

"My husband slept with another woman, Deena. I can't take him back. I can't even look at him, okay? I just pray that you never know what this feels like."

Allison rose, grabbed her purse and umbrella, and strode out. Deena stayed to finish her coffee.

CHAPTER
Thirty-nine

DEENA MADE IT BACK IN TIME for lunch. She dropped down in a chair across from her husband, just as the soup was served. His gaze was on a point just past her. His mother.

"Tak?" Deena said, an edge of worry in her voice. "Is everything alright?"

He looked at her. "Where'd you go?"

She opened her mouth. Let it hang. Then her cell phone throbbed.

"Are you going to get that?" he said.

She swallowed. "No," she said and brushed bangs from her face. "I'll check it later."

Of course she would.

The phone continued to throb. Tak clenched his teeth and shoved back a mocking voice of doubt. So, now he could add disappearances to a list that included secret phone calls and secrets, period.

No matter. Tanakas didn't get divorced, he reminded himself. So, whoever stayed on his wife's phone would be shit out of luck. He'd deal with it, whatever it was. That's what he told himself, at least.

His wife.

His.

Tak stood so fast he toppled his chair. He went over to the oversized stereo in the corner and turned it on. A medley of pop emerged from the speakers. Tak returned to extend a hand to his wife.

"Dance with me," he said and whisked her to open floor.

One song ran into the next and Tak slipped in, only to be rewarded with a livelier, demanding beat made for dancing. A wry smirk crossed his lips before he tucked into a straight line. Already, the music melted the edges of his sharp irritation.

She came to him, palm to palm, and their fingers laced. They stood close enough to kiss and smiled. Close, Tak thought, but they'd get closer still.

A child cart-wheeled by.

He wrapped one of Deena's arms behind his waist, before tucking his in behind hers, so that their bodies cinched together, tight. His wife grinned. They moved together, snug, in a sharp, seamless flow that poured from his body to hers. It was borne of lessons together and practice, of making love to the same person for years.

Tak whipped her, dipped her, and drew her up slow, warming to the thrill of closeness and smiling when they pressed nose to nose. They kissed before he released her again, parting just to whip her in quick, surprising her. She laughed, reminding him of old days, freer days, when they'd never last a song at home before he had to have her—against a wall, somewhere, anywhere.

His feet moved without thought, gaze steady on pretty pink lips. Soft lips, full lips that knew every part of him.

Every part.

He brought a thumb to them and traced, other arm still snug at her waist, still conscious of the music, somehow.

He'd been in love with her hair first. Rivers of cascading chocolate, honey, and chestnut, weaving a waterfall as lustrous as spun glass. Admiring her from afar might have been enough, had she never looked at him, spoken to him, saved his life on that first night. He'd been so hopelessly, irrevocably gone from the start that, by the time he made love to her, he'd known what she'd be to him—even then.

"I wonder," Deena said, "if we could slip away unnoticed."

"Oh, they'd notice," Tak said, thumb still at her lip. "Not sure I'd care though."

Deena's gaze skated toward the exit.

"Me either," she whispered.

His mouth made a silent 'o'.

Hand in hand they side-sidled from the ballroom to the entrance hall, where stairs would take them up. At the moment she reached for the rail, Tak snatched her back, claiming her mouth for his, pinning her to the balusters.

Maybe he wouldn't wait for upstairs. Maybe he wouldn't chance running into someone with some problem, some insistent thing that needed to be said.

He pulled her into the coat room and shut the door.

She met his kisses, hungry kisses, desperate kisses that probably meant more than he could make out. Still, she pressed into him with each one, arms around his neck, mouth ravenous. His hands found her backside and squeezed, before shoving up her dress, looping fingers through her thong and tearing.

Deena shuddered, strained against him, core to the crotch of his jeans. Fingers—his fingers—fumbled at his waist, shed his pants, and felt his breath almost come before he thrust into her with the hardest of strokes.

She gave way like butter.

He ran a hand down the side of her body, pausing so both could adjust. But she was so sensitive, so sensitive everywhere, that already he could sense her tremors. So close to release. Had the thought of him really brought her so close? The idea was enough to unhinge.

Tak kissed peek-a-boo nipples through the sheerness of her shirt, before coming down harder to suck. Deena yelped, back arched, fingers winding in his hair.

Tak groaned.

"Hold on," he whispered. "I'm gonna…"

Gonna what? Try to hold on himself? Or try not to find a tempo where the whole house would know he was doing his wife in the closet?

Tak shook off the thought and thrust. She rewarded him with an outcry of pleasure. Another cry gave him a moan of the same. Tak pulsed, no longer moving, and even that minute movement earned a whimper from his wife.

"Baby," he whispered and sunk fingers in her flesh.

There'd been a warning on his lips, but it slipped away the second she moved against him, grinding and burying to the hilt.

Too much.

Tak yanked her up by the legs so her back hit the wall and sunk. She grabbed him with both hands and pulled his mouth down on hers, both kissing as if it were much-needed CPR. He remembered how to breathe again, though air dragged in and out of his lungs, forcing him to steady with a hand above her head, heart hammering.

"I love you," she whispered. He grinned as if it were the best thing he'd ever heard.

In fact, he knew it was.

They were up against the wall, moving and pulling at each other and way too desperate. Coats rained down and a fedora from another generation tumbled from the top shelf to the floor. They worked up a frenzy. God, he realized, he could have run her through the wall; they couldn't go hard enough, fast enough, deep enough to tame him.

He took her to the floor, mounted her, knees bent, head cowering from the brush of jackets and sweaters overhead. Her legs went up again, not wrapping his waist, but further, until her feet scraped the bottoms of fabric and she yanked him down for what should have been a kiss.

Instead, she moaned his name into his mouth. He plunged.

He went in like a riot and she buried her mouth in his neck, stifling her cries to muffles. Fingers in his hair, running, then clutching, as his strokes grew rough and frenzied. He was close, desperate, hurtling towards the finish line.

Deena cursed and shook until she curled against him, a hot, pulsing sheath.

He couldn't explain the sound he made.

This woman, he thought. Forever.

She held on to him, damp with the sweat of them both, body trembling. Tak's forehead pressed hers and he tunneled deep, driving against her earthquake, stoking it more, until he exploded in a place he knew well.

"Yes," she whispered. "Exactly yes."

They lay there, crammed into the closet, hearts slowing, breathing labored. Tak shifted, only to have her touch his shoulder.

"Not yet," she said and drew him into her embrace, eyes closed.

They had so much they needed to say, so much they needed to talk about. But not then. He could drift away, he realized. There in her arms, as content on a closet floor as he was in grandeur. So long as she lay next to him.

He'd needed this. This—her—in that way. In that gasping, drowning, never-able-to-recover kind of way. It made the worst seem surmountable. It made the world conquerable.

"Dee—" he said, then stopped. As he had no idea what should come next.

So, he kissed her forehead, then her lips, because it was impossible to see them and not want to. But his mouth continued on a plan all its own, tracing a path to the pulse of her neck. A sharp rap at the door stopped him.

Deena clamped a hand on her mouth, eyes wide and alight with laughter.

Tak cleared his throat and did his best not to look at her.

"Er, yes?" he said in his most formal of voices.

She giggled, leaning on him. He tried to shove himself free, only to give up when her laughter claimed him, too.

"Would you stop?" Tak managed, and sat up straighter, as if it might help him keep the straight edge in his voice.

"May I help you?" he said too loud and heard the absurdity of it all.

Her laughter was unbidden this time.

"There's a girl here," John said through the door, "that needs to talk to you about Tony."

CHAPTER
forty

Tony stared at Lila, unable to believe that she had the audacity to come in the house after what she'd just told him. After what she'd just tried. Yet, there she was, head high, eyes bold.

"Who is this, Anthony?" his mother said, looking from him to her.

'Anthony.' Great.

Tony cleared his throat and studied the tiles.

"Her name's Lila."

"Look at your mother," Tak said. "And try again."

Tony took an exaggerated breath before meeting her hard gaze.

"Lila," he said.

"And Lila is…?" Deena said.

"His girlfriend," Lila supplied.

Tony shot her a look of venom. Oh, he'd be her everything now. Now that she was in a bad way.

"Your girlfriend says she's pregnant," Tak said. "Did you know that?"

His voice stayed even, gauging, studying.

"Baby's not mine," Tony mumbled and felt flames lick his cheeks.

"What?" Deena said.

He looked up.

"I said, it's not mine. I don't know whose baby she's carrying. But it isn't mine."

Tony glared at Lila until she dropped her gaze.

Deena swallowed and folded her arms.

"You had sex with her," she said. Not a question. An accusation.

Tony nodded.

"Then you'll take responsibility," she said.

"I'm not taking care of some other dude's kid!"

"Anthony." His mother took a step toward him, face pinched as if dealing with some hidden ache. "How can you, of all people, say that?"

"Deena—" Tak said.

She shook her head and tried again.

"Anthony, really. You should be ashamed. Your own father treated you no better."

Shame. Furious shame. Shameless fury. It slithered on heavy as a coat, snug as his skin. Tony stared at his mother as if just seeing her, really seeing her, before the smallest of doors shut between them.

"Tony," Tak said, and his name was a whisper, a regret, a want.

He shook it off and tore upstairs to his room.

Gone.

Gone from that.

Gone from her.

TAK STORMED FOR the front door.

"We'll be in touch," he said and yanked it open for Lila.

The girl rose and treated Tak, then Deena, to a thin-lipped smile.

"I should tell you that I need—"

"And I should tell you that I've already said that we'll be in touch."

The girl flounced out on a sniff of exasperation, hair bouncing, hips twisting too much.

The door slammed behind her. It opened just as abruptly as Lizzie went out.

"What the hell was that about?" Tak said to his wife.

"You're mad at me? When our son is out there being reckless?"

"Oh, come on. Why don't you bother to get the facts before you open your mouth sometimes?"

"Oh, I've got the facts. Or did you miss the one about the girl carrying our grandchild?"

Tak grunted.

"Some strange girl comes in here talking crazy about our son and I'm supposed to believe it?"

"Who'd lie about that?"

Tak stared at her. Really stared. Once, he'd found her naïveté to be the sweetest part of her, given the reality of where she'd grown up. Now, it just seemed absurd.

"Open your eyes," he said. "Look around you and see for yourself why she'd lie."

His wife's mouth fell open.

"So, what? She's poor and automatically out for his money? Is that how it works? You must have thought the world of me!"

Tak's hands clenched into a fist and then opened, over and again, as he groped for calm.

"Don't do that. Don't even try it, Deena. You and I both know there are all kinds of people out there. Let's wait to see what sort she is before we turn on our own son."

"Yeah. Meanwhile, Tony's child goes without prenatal care and Lord knows what else. Another Hammond without the start in life he needs."

"It's not even his!" Tak yelled.

"You don't know that! You don't know anything about this!"

Tak walked off, turned around and came right back.

"I know I've had a dozen conversations with him about sex and protection and responsibility. How about you? Ever do any better than shouting?"

Deena stopped.

"This is your fault. You should be discouraging him from having sex."

"He's eighteen!" Tak thundered. He threw up his arms in disgust. "Just because you were frigid—"

Shit. Did he really just say that?

The look on her face said he did.

"Deena—"

He reached for her. She took a step back.

"Deena, I didn't—"

"Just because you carried on like a—like a whore—"

Tony stormed by, buffeted by a whirlwind of ferocity, swinging limbs on a straight shot, barreling for the door.

Tak snatched him by the arm.

"Don't go out like this," he said. "Go back upstairs and cool off."

Tony's teeth clenched. "I need air."

"There's air upstairs on the terrace."

Tony snatched free and strode for the door.

Lizzie saw the girl when she'd sauntered up the driveway, windswept hair, long legs, determination. She'd listened to her as she explained herself, first to John, then to Deena and Tak. Now that she strode back out on foot—Lizzie rushed out to catch her.

Lila whirled the second she heard her.

"What do you want?"

All pretenses of the doting, scared girlfriend were gone. Here was the real woman, all cold, all steel. This was what Lizzie had expected.

Lizzie grabbed her by the arm and resumed the walk. Belly jutting before her, they took a pace twice as fast as before.

"I want to know how much," she said. "How much you'd planned to clear."

The shift in her was subtle, uncertainty quickly blanketed by impatience.

"I don't know what you're talking about."

Lizzie stopped. Rummaged in her purse until she found her checkbook.

"I'm talking about you spotting a mark and cozying up. I'm talking about you expecting a payday. You're not pregnant. So, I'll give you two choices. Name your number and stay the hell away from my nephew or we march inside and you do a pregnancy test. I'll sit with you until a maid comes back with one."

A blush crept into the girl's face.

"It wasn't my idea," she gushed. "My parents kicked me out, and Tito, my boyfriend, took me in. Sometimes he has me do things for cash…but I do like Tony. It's nothing personal. I figured he'd just give me money here and there, no harm done."

Lizzie waited, pen poised. "How much?"

"A grand?" she said uncertainly.

Lizzie scratched out the check and handed it over.

"Can I get two grand?" Lila tried.

Lizzie looked her over. "Take it," she said, "before I tear it up and tell my sister what you just told me."

Lila snatched the check and started off, on foot, toward the boulevard. Lizzie sent the driver after her with the assumption that the girl hadn't enough for the return cab fare.

TAK CURSED AND took off after Tony, bumping into Lizzie on her return. Father and son spilled out into the driveway before Tony whirled on him.

"I've never even met him, you know."

"Tony—" Tak took a deep breath. "Listen. We've talked about this. I know how you feel. But now isn't the time to—"

"I've never met my dad," Tony said. "And I never want to. He was nothing. A bum and a thug."

"Tony, don't talk about this when you're already angry."

"I hate him," Tony went on. "And I'm glad he's dead. Did you know that? I'm glad he's dead."

Tony froze—froze as he stared at a point just past Tak's shoulder, at a place he really didn't want to look.

Deena.

The world had officially collapsed.

Tak's hands found his hair and he willed himself not to yank by the very roots. He took a deep breath, then another, and wondered if he should take a third.

"Dee, go back in the house. Let me handle this. For once."

"I don't care if she heard me," Tony said. "And Dad, you know it's true. How long should we pretend my biological father's so stand-up that he's some guy we're all supposed to mourn? He sold drugs and he hurt people. He tried to hurt you, Dad."

"No, Tony," Deena said in a voice Tak didn't know, so strained and anguished was it. "You didn't know him. You never knew him. If you did—"

"Then I'd be dead or in prison or something. Certainly not Ivy League-bound."

Tak knew that he needed to say something. What that something was, he couldn't say. People were drowning, he thought, and here he was forgetting how to swim.

"Tony," Deena said. "I don't understand. You're so angry and I—"

"I'm tired, Mom! Tired of you not facing facts. Tired of you seeing what you want."

"I don't—"

"Yes, you do! You've got your mind made up about every Hammond and every Tanaka, and what you come up with has nothing to do with what's actually happening."

He took a step closer.

"When Lauren needed money for school, you practically shoved it down her throat. Tuition, room, board, book money—the whole thing in one check. Then Uncle Yoshi made that bad investment, and you, you had plenty for him, too."

Tak shot Deena a quizzical look.

"You've got all the money in the world for a Tanaka. But your own blood—"

"Don't. You don't know—"

"I know plenty! I know Remy and Damien have had to beg and borrow their way through college. I know Lloyd's gonna have to drop out."

"No one told me—"

"That they were in school? No surprise. It's not like you're the easiest person in the world to approach. You've got all these ghosts and demons in your head. All these dead people. We're all just our parents to you, anyway. We're all their mistakes."

"Tony!" Tak said. "That's enough."

"You think I'm stupid," Tony said, taking a step closer. "Stupid as my dad. So, you hover over me, so sure I'll do what he did. And when this girl shows up, you're oh-so-ready to believe it. Why? Because I look like him. I thank God I don't look like your mother. You would've murdered me on the doorstep."

A sob cracked the air. His mother didn't bother to hide it.

"You wanna know why I'm closer to Dad?" Tony said.

"That's enough," Tak said. "You've made your point. Can't you see that she's crying?"

He reached for his son and Tony snatched away.

"I'm closer to him," Tony said, "because he doesn't look at me like I'm some ghost or a second chance. I'm me, not your trash little brother."

She slapped him: a ringing, slam of a slap that swiveled his head like an exorcism.

Then she ran indoors.

CHAPTER
forty—one

T AK SLIPPED INTO THE BILLIARDS ROOM with a game of pool on his mind. Any distraction would help. Anything to clear his mind.

He was glad to find Tyson behind the bar, already preparing two drinks.

"Hey," he said when Tak entered. "Hope you don't mind my jumping back here. I kind of figured you could do with a pick-me-up after all that's been going on."

Tak waved a hand dismissively, before retrieving the pool balls for racking. He picked out a cue stick and plucked his drink from the counter. Scotch straight up. Just the way he took it.

"You must have heard us," Tak said and took a sip of his drink.

Tyson grabbed his own and joined him at the pool table.

"I did, but don't feel bad. I'm military, remember? I know everything."

Military, huh? Military hadn't known Tak's wife was getting molested.

"What's wrong?" Tyson said. He watched Tak pull a coin from his pocket.

"Heads or tails?" Tak asked instead of answering.

Tyson hesitated. "Tails."

Tak flipped his quarter and flashed the results. Tails had it. He left Tyson to break the rack.

Tyson leaned forward, cue in hand, and connected with the balls in a swift sleight of hand. With a clean run of it, balls scrambled in every direction, hitting the walls of the table before coming to a stop.

Tak weighed the cue stick in his hand.

"You never told me what was wrong," Tyson said.

Tak went for his shot. A smooth one, he pocketed two balls, both from his suit.

"I never said anything was wrong."

Tyson took his time with his, weighing and studying, but sunk nothing all the same. When he stood upright, it was with his cue stick as a crutch, gaze sweeping over Tak.

"I can tell something's bothering you. You're like Ash that way, it paints your face."

Tak went for the table again, sinking another ball from his suit. He stood and realized that he wore a scowl.

"You must think I'm an asshole," Tak said. "Here you are trying to check on me and I…" He shook his head. "Tell you what. Come visit me in Miami sometime. That's a standing invitation. I promise you it won't be half as crazy as it is here.

We could go to a game. Do some deep sea fishing, whatever. Maybe then, you'll get it all out of me."

Tyson's gaze softened.

"I'd like that," he said. "Although, it is possible to get away here, too. No need to wait for Miami."

He had a point: were the rain to take a permanent vacation, Tak could charter a boat and sail, clear his mind for a spell. He said as much to Tyson. Silence followed, and in it, Tak had the feeling of being watched.

"What?"

"Nothing. Only," Tyson cleared his throat, "it still bothers me sometime. Losing Ash."

Tak exhaled and, in his mind, the word 'asshole' appeared like a puff of smoke. Here was a man in mourning after losing his best friend. Nothing he was going through compared to that, none of it even came close.

And to his horror, he looked up to find Tyson teary-eyed.

Tak set the pool cue down.

"Hey, listen man. I—I know what it's like to lose someone," he said, groping for the right words. "It feels like the pain will never get better, but I swear, one day it does."

Tyson wiped at his face with the back of his hands, embarrassment plain in his smile.

"I'm sorry. I just—"

Tak clapped him on the back. He thought better of it and went in for an embrace. After all, this was a fellow human being. The least he could was act like one, too.

Only, something went wrong. Something went horribly

wrong, as Tyson turned into him and Tak jerked from his mouth.

"Hey! What the—"

He fell back, edge of the pool table on his spine, as he escaped what might have been a kiss, what looked like a kiss. Meanwhile, Tyson looked as if he'd just been spat on.

"Tak, please," he said. "I know it feels strange. I was the same way with Ash. But after seeing what you're going through, I know I can make you happier. If you'll just…give it a try—"

"Give what a try?"

Tyson reached for him. Tak jerked wild, scrambling up onto the table.

"Please," Tyson said, desperation edging his voice. "I can make you so happy. I understand you so much better than her. If you just—"

He dropped a hand on Tak's knee. Tak flung it and scrambled from the room.

CHAPTER
forty-Two

Tyson stormed into the bedroom and closed out the world with a shove of the door. Heart wild in his chest, he grasped for the calm just beyond deep breaths and found it slow in coming. He cursed, closed his eyes and concentrated on breathing. He saw Tak's bare chest, rippling and dripping with pool water. And that lazy smile, as if he knew he needn't bother to try for more. Damn him and that body. Damn him and those lips.

Tyson opened his eyes to see Crystal staring back at him. "You alright?" she said.

He brushed past her for the bathroom, not because he needed it, but because it gave him a semblance of privacy. Once inside, he locked the door and ran cold water, splashing his face with the hopes of getting his brain in gear.

All the signs. All the words. The inadvertent touches.

Had he really read it all wrong? Was it possible? They'd connected, right from the start, from the very first second, and Tyson had felt that here, in this house, was where he'd find what he needed. It had been so long since Ash, so long since he'd felt anything. And for Tak to come along and—

"Tyson? Tyson, are you okay?"

She tried the door. He struck out in blind panic.

"Get the hell away! Leave me alone, why don't you?"

Crystal said nothing. Silent Crystal, with those eyes always watching.

"Is this about Ash?"

She knew Ash, of course, knew him as Tyson's best friend and the guy who'd had his back in service. When he'd moved from Austin to Daytona Beach, just to be closer—just to die—

"It wasn't your fault, Tyson. What happened to Ash—"

Except it was his fault. His fault that Ash moved to Florida and his fault that he was where he was, picking up a six pack for Tyson, when a punk decided that he could kill him for spare change. And the worst part was that there'd been beer in the fridge, just not the kind Tyson liked.

Crystal talked, trying her hand at comforting with empty words. Sweet, sweet Crystal; she was the girl he'd marry. Not because there was some profound romantic love—but because they were perfect for each other, in the most pragmatic way possible. Tyson cared for her, loved her even, in the best way he could, but even he knew that that love was familial more than anything.

He'd come there believing he'd made peace with the loss of Ash. He'd come there ready to propose to Crystal in the presence of her family. But what he hadn't counted on was Tak: Tak turning his head and waking his heart so completely. Ash was the only man he'd ever been with and there'd been a few women before Crystal. Over time, he became convinced that his relationship with Ash had been a chance quirk of fate, love sprouting between two without regard to who or what they were. He wasn't gay and with Ash their roles had always reflected that. It meant that Tyson gave and Ash received, always without variation. But then Ash died and time moved on, committing their time together to memories. He came to Aruba next, where he met Tak, and Tyson found his heart turning yet again. He found his old rules melting away. He wanted Tak's touch, Tak's love, and he didn't care how it came. Tyson realized it: he wanted Tak completely.

He'd thought Tak wanted that too. They talked and drank and spent time and Tyson thought, Tyson knew, that this man, this man that he wanted so desperately, wanted him too.

Except Tak didn't and the thought of it repulsed him, sending him careening across the table like a spider, breaking things in his panic to get free.

"Tyson? Is there something I can get you?" Crystal said.

He flung open the door in response.

"Space," Tyson spat. "You can give me space."

She stared at him, her eyes transformed to two shimmering, full moons.

"Is this about—"

Tyson rushed for the exit, eager to slam the door on her question.

CHAPTER
forty-three

Dᴇᴇɴᴀ ꜱᴀᴛ ᴡɪᴛʜ ʜᴇʀ ꜰᴀᴛʜᴇʀ-ɪɴ-ʟᴀᴡ as the rain ran torrential. What a horrible Christmas Eve, she thought, and got a streak of lightning in response.

"I'm retiring," Daichi said. "And leaving the company to you. I'll begin the transition as soon as we return."

He said it as if it were nothing, as if he hadn't spent his whole life dreaming about, then creating, the firm. She stared at him before breaking into a knowing smile.

"You're absurd. Leaving the firm? To go where? To do what exactly?"

Daichi picked up his mimosa and sipped before crossing rain-splashed legs pricked in dark hair.

"To do pleasurable things, Deena. Surely, you remember those."

Fire lit her cheeks. The first retort on her lips was an

admission that she knew pleasure well, thanks to his son. But she buried it for the crass thought it was.

"You're serious," Deena said, with dawning realization.

The idea of him leaving that monster of a firm to her was stomach-clenching. Even if she had prayed for it *ad nauseam*.

"You're a god to most people," she said. "And I'm the daughter you dragged to the top."

Both knew that wasn't the half of it. Both knew that Daichi paved the hardest paths for those he cared the most about.

Plaques covered the wall in Deena's office. A nearly top-level suite with a panoramic view of Biscayne Bay on three sides. Young Architect of the Year. Innovator of the Year. The Conscientious Designer Award—twice. But they were puffs of smoke to the Picasso of their day. He left no path for her in making her his successor; she could only disappoint others.

"If you are so determined to fail, sell the firm, break it up. I don't care," Daichi said in that slicing, no nonsense clip of his. "Buy an island, if you want. It's none of my concern."

Deena stared. For twenty years he talked of leaving his life's work in the hands of another Tanaka. He'd tried to push Tak into architecture and failed. He'd pushed Kenji into architecture only to find that art without love led to disaster. Through Deena, his dream had been realized: Tanaka to Tanaka for the next generation.

Never had they talked of selling.

Then she realized it. He'd tipped his hand. Obviously, this was a joke. She said as much.

"*Musuko*, listen to me," Daichi said. "My wife is ill. She's in the throes of addiction. We are not young. Therefore, it is time I tend to private concerns. You understand that, don't you?"

In the throes of addiction. She knew it from Lizzie, who'd once used cocaine and heroin. To pry an addict from her fix was to pry fingernails from fingers. After eight years of attempting to force sobriety on her kid sister, Deena had thought it impossible. Then along came a certain Tanaka whose love was the shove she needed. Maybe, Daichi could be the same for his wife. Maybe.

"You can't cure her," Deena said. "No matter how you wish it."

Daichi studied her. As usual, he saw what simmered beneath.

"She's not Elizabeth."

"And you're not Kenji," Deena snapped.

Daichi pressed his fingers together and brought them as a steeple to his lips.

"Is that what you believe? That the power of love is what cured your sister?" Mockery dripped like venom.

"No," Deena said.

"Then your Jesus?"

She shook her head.

"Not Him, either."

Daichi splayed his hands.

"Then I'm fresh out of options, I'm afraid."

Deena lifted his drink and drank it, earning a smile from him. Only when it was empty did she return it to the table.

"I wait for the day," she admitted, "when Kenji calls me. When Kenji calls and says he found her shooting up, he found her snorting coke. It hangs over me like a promise, like a prison sentence, certain to come down."

"And yet it's been so long."

"Not long enough," Deena said. "Forever couldn't be long enough."

Her father-in-law turned his gaze to the ocean, absorbing crashing waves till their blue reflected in the dark pools of his eyes.

"You and your husband are having problems. You disagree so much now. On childrearing, on issues of trust, on what modicum of truth can be offered."

Deena looked at him. Really looked at him.

"What does it mean?"

Unlike most kids, her parents were parted through murder, not divorce. Without friends growing up, there'd been no buddies caught in a custody battle to comfort, no personal experiences with divorce.

Was this what it looked like? All nasty arguments with sweet moments between, until the nasty and the sweet bled together, infecting good times with bad?

"You're unhappy. Both of you," he said.

And it was true. Misery found them more often, pulled up a chair and stayed longer each time. Perhaps one day, it would never leave.

"This is how marriages end," Deena said.

It was never just the other woman or the slap across the face that did it, but the thousand little cuts—every unwitting discouragement, every scathing remark. So many had passed between them already.

"Yes," Daichi said. "But he would never leave you. Even if he no longer loved you. You realize that, don't you?"

Some part of Deena, the fatherless and impoverished part still buried deep, had found Tak's belief in the infallibility of marriage anchoring. She held on to that belief for the stability she needed early on, back when her marriage was so new she didn't know if she was doing it right. Even now, that voice hung in the back of her head. No matter what she said, no matter what she did, he'd never leave her.

But he could stop loving her. He could fold into himself and into his work, leaving her outside the warmth of his existence. They could become Ken and Asami, with him taking on a mistress and another life, this second preferred to the one that kept him tethered. Or maybe he would break tradition and leave her. She was living proof he didn't prescribe to everything his father insisted upon.

"He could leave," Deena said. "If Aubree Daniels…"

She dared not say more. She dared not say that the name of Aubree Daniels sat in her stomach like the burning embers of jealousy, never quite content to peter out.

Daichi looked at her.

"Your question is not one of Aubree Daniels or not. It's of Deena Tanaka or not, isn't it?"

She didn't know how he expected her to answer. With some confession of hidden inadequacies? With a sobbing declaration that meant she couldn't survive without her husband?

She wouldn't.

Because neither was true.

Deena, like any other person, had shortcomings. But

a hard life had shown them in sharp relief: a need for acceptance, love, to belong. Deena had once yearned for acceptance in that painful way another required food after a hunger strike. It made her do stupid things, banal things, things born of cowardice, in the hopes of finding her place among the Hammonds.

But then she gave up on that. And she'd been just fine.

That had been her greatest secret among all things. Not just that she'd moved on from needing a place in a family that thrived on dysfunction, but that she had moved on and been just fine. In a world that had claimed her mother, father, brother, and in many ways, her sister, Deena had survived nonetheless. Maybe this, the world's eventual claiming of her happiness, was the one thing she'd actually anticipated.

Deena looked up to find a short sprite of a housekeeper in her cleaning whites powering toward them with a scowl of deliberateness, Mrs. Jimenez on her heels. When she reached their table, she took in a deep breath.

"Mrs. Tanaka, we must start preparing for the storm."

"Storm?" Deena said.

"Yes, ma'am. The city's preparing for a hurricane that's changed course and is barreling in our direction. They'd said it would land due north of here, all the way near the Bahamas, but it's changed and picked up speed at that. We're going to get the brunt of it."

"When?" Daichi said.

The girl looked as if she wanted to keep the words in her mouth. It escaped anyway.

"Tonight."

CHAPTER
forty-four

THE FIRST FLIGHT OUT OF ARUBA WAS a nonstop to Buenos Aires. Mike settled immigration's entry fee with a phone call and credit card authorization, presented his passport, and purchased a ticket for onward travel at the airport.

He expected a large plane, not the rickety forty-seater he'd been required to venture outdoors to board. Nor had he anticipated the single narrow aisle with two seats on the left and the right, stopping short after a meager ten rows. Mike dropped down in his window chair with a swift intake of air, held it, and exhaled as he stared out at the island.

No one waited for him in Argentina. He knew neither good neighborhoods nor good people. His college Spanish meant he could conjugate an arsenal of verbs, but forget what they meant and how to use them. Yet, calm settled over him just the same. He'd spent the night packing, allowing the tears to come under a blanket of solitude. Maybe time and distance could wash away his urge to swallow a pharmacy's worth of pills.

A bronzed and petite woman with a plump, heart-shaped face and rivers of black hair dropped into the seat next him. She had the look of a woman eager to read his fortune.

"*Buenos Dias*," she said and inclined her head.

Mike tilted a nod in her direction.

"Good morning." It was best to get the mistaken assumption that he spoke Spanish out of the way. That way, they could get to ignoring each other in peace.

"No Spanish?" she said, with a trace of humor in her voice. "And you go to Argentina?"

Mike lifted a shoulder and wished her elsewhere. "I'll learn."

She smiled.

"What else do you come to learn, Michael Tanaka?"

He froze. "How do you know my name?"

"Here." She pressed a finger in his lap, where his boarding pass sat face up. "Is where I read it."

Mike snorted something close to disgust and turned back to the window, but most of his reaction was for show, he supposed. She was attractive, with a pixie face and ample bosom. But women were the last thing he needed. Detox. That was the prescription.

"Did you vacation in Aruba, Michael Tanaka?"

Orange-vested figures fiddled with a cart full of luggage

on the ground. The woman next to Mike touched him at the wrist with a single finger, then dragged it up his arm.

He looked back at her, eyes wide in disbelief.

"I asked you a question, Michael Tanaka."

He plucked her hand from his body and dumped it in her lap.

"Mike. Not Michael."

"Then Mike."

He rubbed his head tiredly in response. Were he back in Seattle, wanking off to the tune of his own loneliness, no woman would have spat in his direction let alone drag her fingers up his body. But as it was that he'd sworn them off completely, he supposed they would fling themselves at him nonstop.

He had half a mind to move.

"Yes," he said, remembering her question. "I vacationed in Aruba."

She raised one brow.

"My name's Carmen," she said. "It is impolite to speak so long without asking my name."

Mike rolled his eyes and turned to the window. He would feign sleep all the way to Argentina.

"You're better off," she said, after some time, "without the thing you left behind."

He turned, faced her, studied.

"You don't know what you're talking about." But even he heard the strain in his voice.

The stewardess who stood close enough to touch greeted them in the PA system. First in English, then Spanish. Mike wondered why she bothered. Given the attendance on this flight, she could have gone up and down the aisles and shaken each person's hand for a while.

"Did you hear what I said?" Carmen said. "You're better off."

Mike's gaze narrowed. "Do I already know you or something? Because the dark-haired mysterious woman thing is kind of a tired trope. Give me whatever premonition you've got and move on. I'm missing my nap."

Carmen smiled.

"No premonition," she said. "Only, you coming to Argentina, alone, without so much as bothering to learn a few phrases, speaks of a man on impulse. Also, your eyes are so burdened, your shoulders slumped. Maybe it would help to talk about what troubles you. I've no…skin in the tournament."

"It's 'game' not 'tournament,'" Mike said. "And no, I don't want to talk."

"No, I don't want to talk," Carmen echoed. "Not, no, I'm not running."

Mike closed his eyes and rested his head against the window.

"I think this is the last flight out of Aruba," Carmen said. "Before the airport is shut down."

That opened his eyes.

"Why would they shut—"

"The storm, silly. Mandatory evacuation for all tourists. They are expecting brutal conditions, you know. Good thing you made it out, Michael Tanaka."

"But my family," he said. He shook his head and began

again. She had to be mistaken. "They don't know about any storm. They're beachfront. What can I do?"

Her dark eyes glimmered with mischief.

"Pray," she said and slipped her hand in his.

"*Oh, Señor, hazme un instrumento de Tu Paz.*

Donde hay odio, que lleve yo el Amor.

Donde haya ofensa, que lleve yo el Perdón.

Donde haya discordia, que lleve yo la Unión..."

Mike's mind drifted in the lull of her recitation. When she finished, she released his hand and exhaled, smiling as if rising from a nap.

"Better?" she said.

Oddly enough, he was.

"I have no idea what you said. But I did make out 'Amen.'"

He smiled at her and she returned it, broad as the ocean on horizon.

"It is the Prayer of Saint Francis of Assisi. I have prayed with you, so that the Lord may make you an instrument of peace. So that you may bring love instead of hatred, harmony instead of discord, truth and faith instead of error and doubt, light and joy instead of shadows and sadness."

Mike swallowed. The engines of the plane revved just behind him, but it was a distant sound, unimportant.

"How did you know?" Mike whispered.

Carmen pulled a small flannel blanket from a bag just under the seat in front of her. She draped it over her lap, making him wish he'd brought one for himself. As if reading his thoughts, she unfolded it until it covered both their laps.

"Your regrets are plain, for anyone paying attention," Carmen said. "And I, it seems, am paying attention."

The flight attendant went through safety regulations while being ignored. The man on the left of Carmen, across the aisle, flipped through an in-flight magazine. The child next to him had headphones in her ears.

"This will be a new life for you?" Carmen said. "In Argentina?"

His nostrils flared. This woman was all questions. All he knew of her was that her name was Carmen. But Carmen what? Diaz? Sandiego? Electra?

"Is Argentina where you live?" he asked. "Where your family lives?"

The aircraft began to move. An easy stroll that belied their eventual summit, they taxied away, picking up speed with the drone of an engine.

"My family immigrated to Argentina." Her gaze skated the cabin. "From Bolivia."

Mike looked around, as if to uncover the thing she looked for. "Is that…a problem?" he said.

She smiled weakly. "You are a foreigner, no doubt here for a short time. You will find that Bolivians are not…crowd pleasers in Argentina."

"That sounds disgusting," Mike said.

"It is like that in your country, right? With Mexicans?"

She stared at him with wide open eyes. She didn't appear to be teasing.

"People have issues with illegal immigrants," he said. "But it's a divisive issue. There is no unanimous sense of xenophobia. Especially for people like me."

"Like you?" she said.

"People who can remember when their race was the least favored."

Mike faced the window again and sucked in a gust of air as they took flight. The running taxi glided up in glorious flight, veering as sparkling waters shimmered endlessly. There was liberation in flying, in defying limitations. It said to him that it mattered not how or where he'd been born. It said to him that innovation, ingenuity, perseverance would prove more reliable than circumstances of birth. It said that the premature child of a barely legal adult and community college dropout could be anyone, live anywhere, and do anything.

Including saving his family from Argentina.

For hours, Mike listened to Carmen, unsure if she paused at the moments he snored. In sleep, he contorted into a seven-headed demon, desperate for a woman to ease his bestial satisfaction. A monstrous phallus was what he wielded, complete with spikes on the tip. Any woman, no matter her appearance, was in danger the moment she grew close. When one did, he impaled her on sight and dropped her, dead, the second he'd been sated.

A monster. Him.

Mike woke gasping. Carmen still talked.

"So where are you staying?" she said, eyes on him expectantly.

"St—staying?"

"Yes. Certainly, you've made arrangements."

He had the sneaking suspicion that she'd laugh at him if he said otherwise, and for someone used to being laughed at, it bothered him immensely.

"Yes. A hotel. I have money for a hotel."

For a little while.

"And your family? By the time we land, it will be too late for you to send them warning. The storm will be upon them."

He'd thought of that before falling asleep, but so far had come up with nothing better.

"They could die," Carmen said, as if he needed reminding.

He snapped at her, something insulting, and an image of the seven-headed demon came to mind. Mike apologized.

"You are frightened," Carmen said. "It's understandable."

But when he looked down at her hands—weathered, beaten, roughhewn, he saw that they shook, too.

"What is it? Why are you shaking?"

She shook her head. "It's nothing. The work in the textile factory is harsh. I developed this while there."

The textile mill. He searched his inventory of stories for one that matched. Ah yes. Her brother Mateo came over to Argentina first. Found work for himself and his siblings, including Carmen, then sent for them. The three of them worked in a textile mill that promised room, board, and good pay. What they got was one hundred dollars a month and a work day from 6 a.m. to midnight, six days a week.

He'd been nodding when he heard it and had hardly responded at the time. Now that he gave it the attention it deserved, he felt his fists clench in response.

"Is there nowhere else you can go? Nothing you can do?" It was a stupid and obvious question, one she no doubt asked herself time and again after five years of servitude.

Carmen smiled warmly, as indulgent as an old woman

would for a child with questions that had no answer. What is time? Where is God? If I speak to Him, will he answer?

Once, Mike had asked his *ojiichan* those same questions. The old man sat on his stoop in Denver and pulled him into his lap. Of all the children, he had loved Mike best. He always felt it. But Mike suspected that all the others felt loved best, too.

"Michael," he'd said. "You think so much and you worry even more. Worry is a stone in your belly that you can't stop rubbing." He messed his hair in that way that was all *ojiichan*'s, broad-handed enough that his finger fell in Mike's little boy eyes, even as he wrecked every strand of hair. "Be free," he told him. "Try to be free."

Mike's gaze had fallen on Tak then, wrestling in the dirt with Mike's baby German Shepherd, O'Toole. Even O'Toole liked his cousin better.

Ojiichan had followed his gaze.

"Not free like Takumi. Free like Michael Tanaka was meant to be."

Carmen slipped the whisper of fabric from her shoulder to reveal an angry red gash. Eyes wide, Mike's fingers drifted to it, hovered, then dropped in embarrassment. The factory, he realized belatedly.

This was his weakness. Women. Beautiful women. Bonus points if they had scars of the physical or emotional variety. What man's primal instinct didn't swell at the notion of being needed, of being a rescuer?

He stared out the window at open seas, toying with an idea, then buying it. Deciding it was his moment to be free.

"They pay you $100 a month to work at your factory," he said.

"When they pay."

"I'll give you $400 if you help me figure out how to save my family. Agreed?"

He stuck out his hand to shake. Carmen looked at it doubtfully. For all her talk, all her prayer, she knew charlatans more than Jesus, it seemed. Eventually, she slipped her hand into his.

"I will help in any way I can. I will not accept payment in return."

THEY LANDED AT Ministro Pistarini International Airport early that afternoon. The trip through immigration took two hours. He stood in line behind Carmen, and watched her present a Mexican passport with Elena Salvadore as her name. He tensed, sensing the wrongness of it. The official who examined her passport excused himself momentarily. Carmen kept her gaze down. Mike followed suit. Minutes eked by as if kept by a broken clock. When the official returned, he waved her through with a nod. Mike exhaled, presented his passport without looking, and watched Carmen hurry away.

He was ushered past almost immediately, and rushed to catch up.

"You're illegal," he said in a rush of air.

She shot him a murderous look but said nothing. It was confirmation enough.

He allowed her to lead him to the luggage carousel, his opinions vacillating wildly from righteous indignation to sorrow and uncertainty. She had no right sneaking into a country illegally, no right to utilize the resources hardworking citizens made possible. He should turn her in himself. But just as he thought it, a contrary vision came flying on its heels. One of a young Carmen, fleeing the poorest part of the poorest country in South America. Of course she fled. Why should she stay there? To waste her life in squalor, in hopelessness?

Mike claimed his luggage as Carmen went for a single ratty, stained suitcase. He took it from her and stared at her expectantly. He had questions. Questions about what she was doing in Aruba, who she'd been seeing. But his family came first.

"What do we do?" he said.

Carmen shook her head. "About your family? I'm not sure. I don't have many resources, Michael, but let me think."

For a woman supposedly so deprived, she had access to international travel, a good command of English, and, perhaps, a few other surprises in store. The constant curiosity that bolstered him tingled in desire to know. Who was this woman that drifted between border patrols without making a scene? Which of his assumptions about her were wrong?

"You can't keep them out the storm," Carmen said. "The best you can do is send help as quickly as possible."

"Help?" Mike echoed dumbly. The bags in his hands grew heavy. He set them on the floor.

"I am talking of a rescue effort. You must call someone and alert them to their presence."

"Of course," he said. But who?

He chewed on his bottom lip. His mother and father were there. His grandmother, brother, and sister. Deena was there, he thought, and shut the door on what followed that.

Some sort of boat or plane, he supposed. One willing to take them a long distance. Or a short one, if the hospital were needed. One willing to transport forty or fifty people in harsh conditions on short notice. What would it cost him? How would he pay it?

"Why were you in Aruba?" Mike said.

He thought she'd recoiled at the question. But as fast as he'd seen the wrinkle in her brow, it was gone, causing him to question its existence.

Carmen dropped her gaze.

"We are talking about you, Michael. You and the help your family needs."

Michael. He didn't know if it was by means of attrition, or what, but he didn't mind her calling him Michael anymore. Before, the usage reminded him of his *oli* Daichi or his grandmother. But Carmen had made it all her own, saying it as if he were the godfather himself. Maybe it was the accent. It had an exoticism beyond belief.

He stared at her. For seven hours she'd talked his mind to numbness about her mother and father and three brothers, one of which worked for an airline and lived well in the United States. She'd told him of everything from childhood scrapes to the slave-like conditions in the factory, never even flinching when showing lashes she'd received at work. A slip of fabric off a bronzed shoulder, another in the front near her cleavage. None of that had been too much. But Aruba—there was where she drew the line.

"I see," Mike said.

"What time's the storm to hit?" he said.

"I couldn't say. End of the day?"

End of the day.

He wandered over to a row of seats and pulled out his cell. Like every other airport he'd been to in the world, Wi-Fi was available. Mike logged on and went to search for helicopters he could charter. He made the first phone call, eager, and explained the situation to the operator.

But she was all facts and figures, estimating space and fuel necessary, without hearing the urgency in his voice. When she quoted him a cheerful $41,000, plus tax, Mike hung up. He didn't have that kind of money. He'd never seen that kind of money.

He rooted around in his phone for Daichi's office number, dialed and got voicemail. After hanging up on that, he called the firm's answering service and asked to get put through to Daichi's personal secretary—who turned out to be absolutely unavailable because it was Christmas Eve.

With a sigh, Mike dropped his face in his hands. Who did he think he was, anyway? Tak? He hadn't the ability to save himself, else he'd be back there with them, facing death where he belonged, instead of sitting in Argentina with nowhere to go.

"Maybe a boat?" Carmen said.

A boat! It was bound to be cheaper than a plane, he thought, and immediately went searching for companies online.

Private, temporary yacht rentals were available for specific activities. They transported up to twenty-five people in most cases and would take them snorkeling, deep sea fishing, or to watch the setting sun.

Mike sighed.

"The Embassy," Carmen suggested with a clap. "They are American citizens, like you, no? The Embassy will help them, for sure."

"Of course!" He could have kissed her. He would have kissed her, if he weren't on a forced sabbatical from women. More searching on the net turned up the American consulate in Curaçao. He put in a call and explained the situation, emphasizing that not only were they American citizens, but prominent American citizens. "My uncle, Daichi Tanaka, is quite famous," he said for the umpteenth time. "He's been on *Time, People, Newsweek*. He's won the Pritzker Prize. The man's like the Nelson Mandela of architecture."

Okay, yeah, it was a road too far, but he was saving lives here and that's what mattered.

"Whatever the cost is," Mike said, "the family can pay tenfold. Just ensure you have someone to get them out. There is a pregnant woman and several small children. Their deaths would be a scandal of epic proportions. It would raise diplomatic concerns, I'm sure."

He wasn't sure, of course. He wasn't even sure if it would conjure more than a memorial cover on *Architectural Digest* and a scrolling headline along the bottom of CNN, but hell, he was in this for the gold.

They assured him that they would alert local authorities and follow up to ensure that something had been done.

Mike took the name of the woman on the phone and hung up, feeling a sense of accomplishment for once.

He turned to face Carmen who smiled a little too brightly.

"See there? American problems solved with American ease. Now, I must go."

Mike stood, darting straight up stupidly, and looked down at her with concern.

"Go where?"

"To the factory. It's where I live and work. I've explained this already."

Maybe it was the cold steel of worry lodged in his throat, a thousand worries about the safety of his family. Maybe it was the sight of a young and beautiful woman with lashes on her body and hands akin to his grandmother's. Maybe it was him, aching to prove he could be human, whole, and kind with reciprocity. Whatever it was, his mouth moved before he could stop it.

"Come with me," he said. "Don't go back there."

Carmen blinked, stared, then chucked him a brittle laugh. "You don't even know where you are going."

"To a hotel. Somewhere close."

She shook her head. "And do what? Be your whore till you tire of me? No, thank you."

Mike smiled weakly. As if a guy like him could tire of a woman so beautiful.

"Actually," he said. "I've sworn off women. So, if that's your only objection…"

Carmen's brow creased. "What does this mean? 'Sworn off?'"

"It means I don't want to be with them."

Her eyes widened. "You mean that…you prefer men? Because in Argentina—"

Mike's cheeks colored. "I am very much attracted to women. I am very much attracted to you. But poor decisions teach me that I should be alone for a while. I am…searching for the truth in me, I guess."

Carmen studied him as if trying to determine whether she had translated properly. Finally, her face smoothed.

"You ask for everything and offer nothing, a few days of comfort in exchange for my livelihood."

Mike lowered his gaze. It was true. He could offer her nothing. Not without gaining employment. He thought of his job at IBM, the one where he hadn't bothered to put in for more than vacation time. They had a location there in Buenos Aires, though, and he had enough seniority to press for relocation.

"What if I hire you?" he asked. "To show me around? To be a tour guide, translator, to help me find a job?"

Carmen's eyes sparkled. "And when all that is done?"

Mike grinned. "To teach me Spanish, of course."

Carmen's mouth spread into a wondrous smile.

"*Estoy loco*," she groaned and slipped her hand into his.

He didn't know if she meant that she was crazy, or he was, but whatever the translation, he suspected both were right.

CHAPTER
forty-five

DEENA RUSHED INTO THE HOUSE WITH her father-in-law on her heels. They were late. So late that whatever meager supplies existed on an island scarcely thirty miles large—an island that somehow managed to never get storms—would no doubt be beyond their grasp. Still, she sent two housekeepers into the city with orders to get whatever non-perishables they could. Three others were tasked with gathering whatever flashlights, candles, matches, portable radios, and first aid kits they could find. Two more hunted down bottles of water, filled jugs, and as many discarded soda bottles as they could manage.

"The house," Daichi reminded her. "The house itself…"

A silent conversation passed between them, one where he reprimanded and she accepted it. On buying the house, Deena knew that it lacked the proper fixtures for adequate storm protection. Combine with that the reality that it sat wedged in the Caribbean Sea and she really had been careless. Except, it never rained in Aruba. Or so she'd thought.

"Wood," Deena said. "We need as much as possible."

"*Musuko*, you must know that—"

"Tell everyone to find an armful of wood." She spoke directly to Mrs. Jimenez then. "I don't care if they have to tear up the furniture to do it. Board every window. Protect every space. Have all the supplies delivered to the drawing room. When the storm starts, I want everyone in there until it ends."

Daichi looked at her.

"And if…conditions deteriorate?" he said.

"There's an upstairs linen room. It doesn't have windows."

Daichi eyed her.

"I see."

And she knew he did. He was, perhaps, the only one who did.

To Tak, it made no sense to wreck the furniture when they had a forest of trees in the backyard. Had his wife been the one to discover Tony and his half-naked minx, she might have remembered that. But, since she wasn't, it was Tak who strode for the gardens with little more than a chainsaw.

"That's a really bad idea," Tyson called, falling in alongside him at once.

Tak doubled his speed. If Tyson took the hint, it wasn't apparent.

"I'll bet that you've never cut down a tree," he said. "Which means you're guaranteed to get hurt. Let me grab some supplies from the garage and help you. I don't…want anything to happen to you."

Tak wished he wouldn't say things like that. He really wished he wouldn't say things like that.

He watched him go, repressing the urge to fling himself into the task of assaulting trees ignorantly. Anything to avoid the awkwardness with Tyson.

Tyson returned with two sets of goggles, helmets, gloves, a few wedges and something Tak couldn't even identify.

"Come on," Tyson said. "Your furniture's pretty expensive. Let's chop a few trees and save you guys some money, huh?"

Tak nodded, but still he stood, gaze sweeping the landscape for someone—anyone—to accompany them.

At least he'd said "you guys", an acknowledgement of Tak's wife—an acknowledgment of his marriage. That had to be a sign of improvement in their conditions. After all, Tak wasn't a homophobe. Once Tyson accepted the platonic nature of their relationship, there was no reason to think they couldn't find friendliness again.

That's what he told himself.

They made it as far as the tangle of trees and their looming darkness before Tyson selected one good for cutting.

"It's already leaning," he explained. "So, we'll go with the lean, not against it. It's small enough to come down easy."

They set to work in silence, with Tak following his lead, moving away brush and scattered limbs from their landing site, then deciding on the direction they would move when the tree gave way. After that, Tyson sawed in a small undercut on the bark about two feet up from the root, an incision he explained would aid the tree in falling safely. He followed it with a careful cut, uniform all the way around the tree.

"I owe you an apology," Tyson said as he worked.

Tak studied leaves on the ground.

"Uh huh."

"I'm attracted to you. I thought you were attracted to me, too."

Tak felt his face go hot.

"So, you're saying I gave you some kinda gay vibe."

Tyson shot him a look.

"I'm not gay."

"Uh…yeah you are."

Tyson set down his saw.

"Listen to me. What I had with Ash—that was different."

"Yeah, okay. I gathered that much myself."

Tyson looked him over with eyes that weren't quite the way Tak remembered them. What he'd taken to be astuteness now looked like naked interest.

"I'm not gay," Tyson repeated. "I only thought that we connected in some meaningful way. I only thought—"

"Look. Let's just cut the wood, okay?"

"I'm not asking you to choose between Deena and me. She doesn't have to know."

"I'm leaving," Tak announced and tossed his helmet to the ground.

Only Tyson grabbed him by the arm the second he moved. Tak snatched free.

"Look, I don't care that you have some kind of identity crisis. Or even that you think I'm your soulmate. Chop the damned wood, already," Tak said, "or I'll forget my manners and plant that chainsaw in your skull."

Tyson stared, stared until there was nothing but the violent rise and fall of Tak's chest and the wild way he looked at him. He opened his mouth to say more, then closed it and returned to the tree.

"Tell Crystal," Tak said. "Tell her today. And stop making a fool out of my wife's cousin."

CHAPTER
forty-six

THE SKY SMOLDERED A COBALT BLUE and streaked in fitful bouts of lightening, as they stood on the terrace boarding back windows. The wind was fierce. An old fierceness, as ancient as God.

John was a menace at carpentry. He'd hold a plank and affix it with a single ill-placed nail, then balk when it swung and crashed to the floor.

"The one side has to hold so I can get to the other. What kind of wood is this?"

Of course, Deena thought. The type of wood. The chemical consistency. That was the problem.

Thankfully, others worked faster, which meant that Tak found the means to help John. Which meant that two bumbled for the price of one.

"Oh really," Deena snapped in a moment of impatience.

She took the hammer and nails, stuffed both in the pocket of her skirt, and snatched the bit of wood out of John's reluctant hands. A well-placed nail and a few snaps of the wrist had her protection up on one side. Quickly, she moved to the other and repeated the same. Rain sprinkled her.

"Show-off," John muttered.

Deena turned to demand more wood and her phone rang.

She saw it then. The tense crease of her husband's mouth. The set of his shoulders. They'd been reduced to this, she realized. Not trusting. Suspicious of even a phone call. Deena thought of her conversation with Daichi.

A slight peek into her pocket revealed that Allison called. Deena snatched it out, as thunder rocked the room.

"You're still here?" she said.

She turned her back to John, who stood waiting with his next piece of wood. Tak, stoic as he watched, had both hands loose at his side.

"Deena," Allison said breathlessly. "They've cancelled all remaining flights, including the one I was meant to be on. We're marooned and I'm terrified."

Deena shot a look at John, who wore his crumpled white shirt for yet another day.

"Come here," she said.

"I can't. After all that's happened—"

"Come here now, Allison." John snapped to attention. "This is your safest possible option. Of course, John would want you here."

Now neither John nor Tak moved. Deena, whose

heart beat with the insistence that she'd been too bold, too presumptuous, pushed the thought from her mind.

"You need to get here any way you can. Bribe someone. I don't care. It's getting scary out there."

"There's no one to bring me."

"No one to bring you? There must—"

"Where is she?" John demanded.

Deena paused. "I don't know if—"

"Where is she?"

Hurriedly, she told him the hotel. John tossed the last of his wood and bolted for the door.

"John's on the way," Deena said and hung up the phone.

"The driver hasn't left yet," Tak explained. "He's waiting as long as he possibly can, in case we need something. John will probably have to drop him off and sort it out with the chauffeur company later. He's a lawyer, though. He'll think of something."

Deena retrieved John's discarded plank.

"They better hurry," she said. "We'll have to bolt the doors soon."

In simulated recreations, hurricanes were always disciplined circles of torment traveling in a neat, predictable path. Tony knew, because he'd studied every storm that had formed in the Atlantic Ocean since his moving to Miami. "Studied" seemed too mild a word though. He agonized over those storms, writhed over them. He imagined every one as 'the one'—the one that would shred every manmade structure in its path, hack at every human limb. This storm, he told himself at every single one, would raise the floods of Noah and bring locusts to their mangled bodies.

His phone sirened every time a smidgeon of a signal fought its way through. Lizard and Wendy checking in on him again. Tony texted them when he could, but found that every word, every act in reaction to the mania outside only fueled the pump-pump of his heart and the nonstop swallowing he kept up.

The wind shrieked its hysteria. Glass doors, doubled down with planks of wood and reinforced with duct tape, might as well have been wisps of white, lined paper. Every bit of glass in the house rattled like the barred cells of the innocent, rabid creatures on the other side, wild in the need to unhinge.

Dinner on Christmas Eve was to have been an elaborate event, a twelve-course meal dwarfed only by the twenty-one-course one scheduled the next day. Now, family sat huddled together in the ballroom, scarfing down cold soup and lukewarm duck, all the hired help from the island now gone. Everyone that remained cast dark, expectant glances at the boarded up windows. Where endless banter and wild whoops had been the norm, plate-scraping silence now dominated.

Tony looked at his cell, unable to help himself as he force fed. There, he found a message from Wendy.

'Wish I were with you.'

With him. Not in safety, but with him. Selfishness struck Tony and he wrote:

'I wish you were too.'

Not Lila, he realized, but her. He wanted Wendy there with him, desperately.

Tony knew what it meant. Not only that, he knew what

his anger about Gage Sawyers meant and hers about Lila. He could go so far to say that he had always known what it all meant.

He was in love with his first and truest friend. And she was in love with him.

Simple as that, the last puzzle piece of his life fell into place.

So far, they'd had only howls and threats. With nightfall descending and the true storm hovering in the distance, Deena and her husband eked out their last moments alone together in bed. It was their final stab at privacy, while privacy was still an option.

Deena lay on her side, studying the silent figure beside her. He was stiff in a way that felt foreign to her, in a way that followed no fight they'd ever had. Something occupied his mind.

"Are you worried about the storm?" she said. "I know the preparations were rushed but—"

"No," he said gruffly.

"Then what?"

Tak's lips parted before a puff of air escaped.

"Tyson," he finally said.

Deena blinked. They'd fought over so much that week. What happened between her and Mike in the bathroom. The extent of his relationship with Aubree Daniels. Tony. She didn't even know that her husband knew her cousin's boyfriend.

"What about him?" Deena said.

Tak stared at the ceiling, stared through it, if that were possible.

"I don't want to say."

"Please do."

"Why?"

He looked at her.

She had no right to say what she was about to say, no right to assert anything given the fierceness with which she'd guarded her secrets. Still, she felt the need to try.

"Because we're married," she whispered.

"Married." He snorted at her words as if they were mere conjecture.

An afternoon of silence passed between them.

"He tried to kiss me," Tak said.

"What? Like a Frenchman?"

"No, Deena. Not like a Frenchman. You know what? Forget it."

"I'm trying to understand."

"The man's gay, that's what I'm telling you. He was hoping I'd be gay with him."

"Well, he can't be gay, he's with Crystal!"

Tak sighed. "Tell him, not me."

Deena stared at her husband. He had all the rigidness of someone expecting a cobra strike. She ran a hand along his arm and trailed fingers to his, laced them, and heard him exhale.

"I'm not—a homophobe," he said as if the point had been pressing him. "It was just...I'm sitting there doing bro time. I don't expect one of the bros to try and tongue me."

Deena smothered the urge to laugh, then thought about her cousin and felt it dissipate altogether.

"What should I do? Talk to Crystal?"

The idea nauseated her. Five years they'd been together and Deena could shatter that with a few words.

"I told him to tell her or I would," Tak said. "But by me, I really meant you."

Deena looked at him.

"Maybe it was a mistake," she said hopefully. "You know how you guys are with your zealous masculinity. Tyson violated some unspoken code and now you think it means something it doesn't."

Tak looked at her, his mouth a single thin crease in his face. All the blood had rushed away, leaving him blanched in its wake.

"The man thinks I look like his dead lover, Deena. He wants me to replace him and not tell you. You don't need it clearer than that?"

Her mouth rounded out to a lower case 'o'. Her husband snapped up like a rubber band, snatched on a tee and crumpled jeans. Deena followed him with her gaze.

"What are you doing?" she said.

"Checking on Tony. You know how he gets about these things."

He gestured vaguely to the atmosphere before stepping out the door. It slammed soundly behind him.

Outside the wind howled like a legion of the damned. Deena closed her eyes and focused on the pummeling rains, a tempestuous brew of turbulent, roaring showers. An insane urge came over her to run out, throw her head back and let the rage have her, full on as it came through.

Deena pulled on clothes and rushed out the door. She intersected with Tak as she passed Tony's room and ignored his calls for her.

Downstairs, only two doors remained unsecured. They were strategically identified escapes should the storm make departure necessary. She headed for the one that served as the servants' entrance and threw it open. It battered back shut in her face. When she shoved it a second time, it took both hands to keep it wide.

Blustering winds beat her to blindness with the first step, whipping and tearing at her hair, plastering it with rain to her eyes. Midnight descended like a cloak. The sound of rain filled her ears to capacity, water pouring on concrete, ceaseless, resolute.

Minutes of stillness had her drenched and shivering, with storm water running arctic currents down her face, flooding her mouth, and painting clothes to every curve and crevice of her body.

"What are you doing?" Tak yelled from the threshold.

Deena shot him a grin and let the storm engulf her.

With all life's planning things happened, the heavens opened and destruction found a way in. All that lived came to die. All that was one day ceased to be. Every moment of her life had bathed in meticulousness, the careful work of a girl craving order. But that meticulousness, that careful planning had carved none of who she came to be. Wife. Mother. The things important to her. Even planning had its limitations.

And so, she stepped out into the storm, threw her head back and her arms heavenward.

Never had Deena done something so reckless.

Never had she felt so free.

CHAPTER
forty-seven

AT MIDNIGHT A WINDOW EXPLODED, leaving the sound of cannon fire blasting into the mansion. Those who had been upstairs rushed down to see the damage, before Tak and Daichi ushered everyone into the drawing room.

"It ripped the boards straight off, I swear," Lloyd was saying as Tak gave him a shove in the back, parting him from a horror-stricken Tony. "It was like peeling steel off a skyscraper. Those winds must be, like, 400 miles per hour."

Tony stared, wide-eyed and rooted to his place.

"We'll be fine," Deena said and squeezed her oldest son's shoulder. "Better than fine, in fact."

They were the first words between them since the blowout and both seemed to be testing the waters since then. Deena with her words of comfort and careful touch, Tony with his look of latent remorse.

Noah careened past them as they spoke and cheered as another clash of thunder rocked the room. Mia came in sullen, not far behind, skateboard under her arm, no doubt sour at the closed in space. Any place that wasn't big enough to skate was bound to put Mia Tanaka in a foul mood.

Tanakas, Hammonds, and the hired help that had traveled with them, pressed into the room: a room with a single, wide-paned, boarded-up window. Grandma Emma, parked by Aunt Rhonda in the corner, had already begun muttering scripture.

"Behold. God is my salvation. I will trust and not be afraid."

Tony found a seat at her feet.

"For yah, the Lord is my strength and song. He has also become my salvation."

Mia sat down next to Tony, skateboard in hand, and said something for his ears only.

He smiled.

"Therefore," Grandma Emma continued, "with you joy, you will draw water from the wells of salvation."

Her gaze stopped on Allison as she entered.

"Glad you could make it," Grandma Emma said.

Allison's cheeks flushed an enthusiastic purple.

John entered next. Allison looked up, as if not knowing he was so close behind, and glued her gaze to her husband.

There was no one else in the room. No one else on the planet. Even their hurricane melted away in the look those two gave each other, a silent want mingled with naked pain.

John said nothing. Allison said less. Deena waited, spurring her on in her mind. Go to him, do something, fix this, she thought, even as her own problems mounted in a rearview mirror. The singular nature of adultery seemed so simple compared to the problems that she and Tak faced. Forgive or not forgive the one act: that was what needed to be decided. But for Tak and Deena, half a dozen, two dozen grievances, stacks upon stacks it seemed, stared back at them—more than either could hope to address.

Someone coughed. Allison crossed to Deena, saying not a word to her husband.

"Thank you for letting me come," she said. "After all the flights were cancelled and the hotel was evacuated, I wasn't sure what to do. Even the taxi cabs had stopped running. I swear, it was like this storm…came from nowhere."

She was babbling: babbling because she had the attention of everyone, babbling because she wanted to look at her husband and didn't want to look at her husband, lest he realize how much she wanted to look at him. But the lights flickered out and all that was forgotten.

A whirring sound sliced through the groans. A promise of lights followed that—there and then gone and then there once again. Electricity returned.

"Thank God," Deena said. "Let's get the matches and stuff together. In case the backup generator goes out."

CHAPTER
forty-eight

Tak slid an arm around his wife's shoulders, pulling her in until she pressed hip to hip. With his free arm, he tugged on Mia until she nudged closer, even as she busied herself drawing on her skateboard with a sharpie. Only Tony, sitting on the other end of Mia, needed no prompting, moving in closer to his sister, then telling her he would protect her as best he could. But his kid sister didn't even bother to look up, so engrossed was she in getting the shading proper for the front fakie flip she re-imagined on her board. Not bad, Tak thought, as he watched her technique and felt a stab of pride at the skill she exhibited in shading. Noah, never one to be left out, bounded rough into his father's lap, earning a grunt, before curling up for a nap. He paid no heed when Mia barked that he was too big and in the way.

Gold whorls ran through the stark white carpet of the

room they occupied. John, being careful not to look up and therefore directly into Allison's eyes, busied himself tracing the pattern on the floor. On seeing this, Yoshi crossed the room, stopping only to yank on his pants so that his belly flopped up, and then dropped down on the floor next to his son.

"You're being a fool," he said.

John looked up. In his face was the weight of hurt, the toll of divorce. Shadows cast his eyes in dark relief and cheek bones jutted anew.

John went back to tracing patterns.

"I don't understand," Yoshi said. "Why won't you fight?"

His father's voice always carried. He was the sort who'd shout your business in what he thought was a whisper, only to look up and see even the postman grinning. John stole a glance at Allison and saw her head snap downward, eyes averted.

"She wants to leave, *otosan*. It's not like the old days. You can't make a woman stay."

His father scoffed as if hearing the overtures of a snake oil salesman. Or worse, a fool.

"You can make a woman stay by making her want to stay." Yoshi slid in even closer. "You are a man," he said. "Can't you remember passion? Desperation for the woman you love?"

Tak forgot to pay attention discreetly, and found himself leaning in for the response, breath absent.

"Maybe it's too late," John said, fingers still married to the whorls on the floor. He hazarded a glance at his wife, studying her as she concentrated on looking away.

"And maybe you saved all your passion for the wrong woman," Allison spat.

"Okay," Deena said. "I'm going to take the kids out. They can gather some toys or something."

"I don't mind staying," Mia announced, looking up for the first time.

Deena rose and ushered out a half dozen children. When she turned and demanded that Tony help her, she was met with a cry of outrage.

"Dad?" he said.

"Hurry," Tak answered. "Before you annoy me by questioning your mom."

He needed the kids gone so he could see how this ended. Certainly, if these two could find some way to begin anew, then optimism for his own marriage felt possible.

"I didn't—" John cringed with the force of a man trying to crawl inward. "I didn't give my passion to the wrong woman." His gaze darted from face to face, with him questioning each on how they'd earned a front row seat to his humiliation.

"So, you don't regret what you did?" Allison said.

"I didn't say that either."

"You did."

"I know what I said! And if you'd listen for once, you'd discover that you don't know half of what you think you do."

Oh boy. Self-righteous indignation wasn't the best course of action. Not when trying to get a woman back.

Allison dashed back a lock of messy blonde hair from her face. Never had Tak seen her so frayed, with hair sticking here and there and clothes that needed straightening.

John turned on his father.

"You see? I told you. It's over."

Yoshi stared, incredulity etched in his every pore. A minute passed, maybe more, of him searching his son's face for something.

"Fine. Your marriage is over. You win. Do you like your prize?"

Yoshi jumped up, strode across the room and flopped down near his wife.

"Daddy, marriage is just an artificial attempt at validating—"

"Shut up," Yoshi and June both snapped. He rubbed the entirety of his face with a hand. "Please, shut up," Yoshi added.

Eventually, Deena stuck her head in, found all silent, and returned with the children.

CHAPTER
forty—nine

Aubree Daniels stood before reading what should have been hidden in Deena's purse.

"I take it that you have received my other letters and now know that I'll be out on parole soon."

Her eyes did a little jig.

"As you know, budget cutbacks mean that the usual halfway houses are practically nonexistent." She hesitated for effect. "Meaning, I'll be out on the street once released."

Aubree tut-tutted and made a show of considering this dilemma.

"You've asked so much of him. First, to hide from your family for years because he's Japanese—which is really racist, by the way. Then you reject his overtures for marriage time and again for the exact same reason."

"I never—"

"Oh come, Deena. You always held him in the palm of your hand, controlling him with your melodrama."

Aubree waved the letter from Deena's mother as a smile found her red-painted lips.

"This is too far, you know. It's why you haven't told him. Why you can't tell him. Your murdering mother under the same roof as his children? His children are where he draws the line. And you'd put them in danger just to settle an old debt."

"I wouldn't—"

"But it's what you've promised, isn't it? A home for your mother because she saved your life."

Aubree let the paper cascade to the floor. In its drift it accentuated her slight flare of hips and long, pale legs stacked in stilettos.

"She's not dangerous," Deena said. "And I haven't promised her anything."

"But you will."

These words for her were but luscious fruit, dripping with delectable juices. She could have said them a hundred times, squeezing sweet taste every time.

"She's in prison, Deena. Of course she's dangerous. How else do you think she's survived? She's made alliances. Hurt people. Nothing she's not used to doing. She'll be out by the time you return," Aubree continued. "And here you are, having not said a word to Tak yet."

"I will. When the time is right."

Aubree's smile broadened, wide enough to make the Cheshire cat blush in parental pride.

"He'll leave you. He doesn't trust you and he knows he

can do better. You know he can do better. He certainly has before."

"Tak loves me," Deena said.

"No, he fucks you. You're not stupid enough to think it's the same."

Aubree strutted across the room, effortless in monstrous, needle heels sounding off on wood. Except the room wasn't a room anymore, as the roof melted back. Deena looked up to open skies, a blue expanse of perfection. Wind twisted her hair and she smoothed it with a cautious hand. Aubree's gold locks stayed in place. Her body looked thinner and even more curvaceous than before.

"Your husband," Aubree whispered as the wind found rage, "loves me. Still."

Deena opened her mouth to contradict, only to find it flapped aimlessly—also on her side. A croak escaped her.

And the world exploded.

CHAPTER
fifty

Tak yanked Deena to her feet, ripping her from her dreams. With feet like cinder blocks, she took one step, then another, before realizing her pants were wet.

Rain.

The light flickered ominously.

"Dee, come on. The window's gone. We've got to move."

Only then did she see her family bottlenecked at their only exit.

"I was asleep!" Tak shouted over a roar like a wind tunnel. "Everyone was. Then the sound woke me—I can't believe it didn't wake you. Then I saw this hole in the wall where the window used to be."

Deena examined it. The yawning gap into night was where a respectable window once stood, low enough that water rushed in on a steady stream.

Tak ushered the children out, then latched on to Deena, half running, half pulling, the last out the room. Upstairs and into the linen room they crowded, a vast open area with shelves stacked high on all four walls. No windows, thankfully.

"Did anyone bring the candles?" Deena said.

Tak cursed.

"I'll get them," John offered. Allison reached out, then withdrew her arm, cheeks hot.

Her husband opened his mouth, choked on something painful, and disappeared downstairs.

Long minutes passed. The rumbling and wild banshee of the wind felt ominous.

Too much time stretched on.

"I'll go for him," Tyson said. "I should have gone anyway."

Tak stood. "I'll go. He's my cousin."

Tyson stopped, brows drawn and knitted in pain.

"Just…stay with your family," he said. "Please."

Tyson disappeared and the minutes droned on. When he finally did return, it was with a saturated John and a fistful of slick candles.

"Something's wrong," John explained. "There's too much water down there. Too much to be coming from the one window. And it rushes like a river."

Deena and Daichi looked at each other just as Grandma Emma began to pray.

Allison inched over to a dripping John and asked if he was okay. He nodded, said something covert, and both burst into laughter.

It opened a door and a hushed conversation flowed

between them. The absence of tension in either of their faces said it was a nonsensical one, light and avoidant of problems. And then it changed.

"I missed you," John said.

Allison looked away, eyes glassy.

"Hey." John took her by the chin and steered her so that she looked directly at him. "I missed you," he said again.

Allison slapped him.

"Damn!" Lloyd cried from a corner.

Even Deena winced.

"You think you can just say that after—"

"Allison," Tak said. "There are kids around."

"Oh shut up," she snapped. "You're always protecting him."

"Shutting up," Tak said.

"Actually," John rubbed the line of his jaw, "he's been pretty crappy to me. You know, since you left me. He blames me, I think."

"He should!"

"I didn't really say—" Tak started and Allison shot him a warning look.

"Keep quiet," Deena told Tak. "Before I lose my temper too."

Friend or not, she had one more time to yell at Deena's husband.

"Listen to me," John said. "Listen good. I never cheated on you. Ever."

"Don't." Allison held up a hand.

"I didn't! I don't know how to explain it. I just wanted you to think it. I wanted to get you riled—to—to just get you to stop. To slow down. To realize that I'm worth something, too. That I have options."

"Options, huh?"

"You're obsessed with divorcing people," John pushed on. "You get this rapturous delight in—in the failing of other people's marriages."

"Don't be silly."

"You do. And then you come home and can't decide if you're interested in me or not."

"Interested in you? Like I'd be interested in the six o'clock news? I love you, John. What the hell are you talking about?"

He frowned.

"Really? Because I thought—"

"I accused you of cheating with your secretary, you idiot. You never even denied it."

John shrunk. "Well, I didn't expect you to go straight for the divorce."

"This is the part where they either slap each other or kiss," Tak murmured.

"Both is my guess," Deena said.

She looked up to see Tyson looking at her husband. Her gaze narrowed to accusatory spikes. He studied the carpet instead.

John and Allison kissed.

"You need out of those wet clothes," she said. "Show me where your room is. I'll...er help."

"Of course you will," Deena said.

Allison kicked her on the way out.

CHAPTER
fifty—one

Grandma Emma started in on another bible verse. "Quit that, will you?" Tariq said. "It's creepy."

"I agree." Aunt Rhonda clasped a hand with her wife's.

Deena cocked her ear, straining to hear beyond the fury of the storm.

"Maybe you could play something, Tak. Give us something to listen to besides this storm."

He went for their bedroom down the hall and returned with his guitar. Tak began strumming and fell into something mournful. Moods crept in that way. He shifted again, to a mimicry of Tony's symphony.

"It's a good sound," Tony said.

"A great sound," Tak affirmed.

"I should have added a little something at—"

"You wrote that?" Lloyd said.

Tony nodded.

Aunt Caroline shot an accusing look at her grandson.

"See there? He's got talent. Some sense. Not sitting around shooting rainbows out his ass, trying to get noticed."

"What does that even mean?" Tony said.

"She's talking about me losing my scholarship," Lloyd explained. "It's her favorite topic."

"Fool out there trying to audition for And One. You're in college," Caroline said. "Play like you got some sense, dummy."

"Really, Aunt Caroline," Deena said, "at least he's trying to do something. More than I can say for a lot of people in this family."

Tony groaned. A few of the younger ones shifted uncomfortably.

"Who you talking about, Deena? Make your voice known," Caroline said too loud.

Deena felt the feverish flash of embarrassment and shoved it back. Never mind. Some things needed to be said.

"I had no idea he was in college," she began. "But there's something to be said for it. At least he's trying, instead of pursuing the poor choices we have all around. Drugs. Teen pregnancy. Prison."

"There you go again," Caroline spat. "After school special on the microphone." She lit a cigarette despite constant admonishments that she wasn't to smoke indoors or anywhere around the children. "The way you carried on all these years, you'd think we beat you. That we forgot to feed you. Judging by the size of this house, we did alright by you."

"Oh no," Deena said and near-choked on the flare of fury that followed. "I did alright in spite of you. Not because."

Caroline took a leisurely drag.

"I guess you raised yourself," she said and flicked ashes to the floor. "Worship her, for she is worthy."

"Shut up, you old tub of lard. And put that damned cigarette out."

Deena felt Tak's hand on her shoulder and cooled at the place he touched her. Sensibility set in like a fog, unclear and settling little by little.

"You really should shut up, Caroline," Rhonda said.

"Oh, here we go. I've been waiting on you. Good thing you spoke up, too. I was starting to think you had a little too much fun last night and your tongue went numb."

Rhonda melted into the wall, leaving her wife to gasp.

"Aunt Caroline, please. There are children," Deena said.

"Who don't know what the hell I'm talking about."

From her wheelchair, Grandma Emma mumbled about popcorn and diapers.

"Anyway," Lloyd said, and shot Caroline an impatient look, "I'm not going back to college."

It was as if his grandmother hadn't even heard.

"You and this one here," she said, gesturing to her daughter, Crystal, "want to run, want to hide from us. From your family. Dysfunction, you say."

"Definitely dysfunction," Deena said.

"Except look where you ran to. These Tanakas got as many problems as us. And you, you fool," Caroline looked her daughter over as if she were just that. "You ain't no better. You can't even see that your man's just gay."

Deena shut her eyes, fury spiking and plummeting all in the same breath. Had Aunt Caroline just done that? Whatever shot of anger she'd felt at calling Tak's family out on their problems, she, of all people, sank to the basement of humiliation the moment she outed Tyson.

Maybe she'd heard wrong.

Deena opened her eyes.

Nope, she hadn't.

Eyes and mouths gaped at Tyson. Only Tak looked at the floor. Crystal had neither wide-eyed shock, nor angry disbelief on her face. She had nothing. She was a blank canvas, waiting to be filled.

She'd already known.

"I'm not gay," Tyson announced, brows furrowed into a scowl of a V.

"Sure you aren't. Only, you been spending every minute of every day looking like you want to eat Tak's ass with a spoon."

"Aunt Caroline," Tak moaned, sinking as if to go through the floor. "Come on."

"Baby, I'm sorry. You know I say what I mean." There was amusement in her apology.

"Well, I wish you wouldn't," he said.

"This is awkward," Lauren said. "But it underscores what I've been talking about. Heterosexuality is a prison of fictitious design—"

"Hush!" June snapped with a wave of her hand. She leaned forward enthralled.

"You and Ash," Crystal said to Tyson, voice low. "Not just my imagination, right?"

Tyson answered by lowering his gaze, before excusing himself from the room.

Caroline shifted, long gaze affixed on Deena.

"You know, I know what you been up to. Keeping money on Keisha's books. Paying lawyers. Asking your momma to look out for her. Can't see why though, the way you carry on about us."

Neither could she.

"I'm grateful you do it," Caroline said. "Whatever the reason."

"Well," Deena said, frowning as if she'd swallowed something sick. "We are family."

Caroline snorted. "That what we are?"

Deena's aunt looked her over.

"I don't kid myself about what goes on around here," she said. "About all the mistakes I've made, that others made. In fact," she paused, "I'm not even sure you'd call 'em mistakes."

Caroline drifted toward an abyss, poised on a cloud of distant thoughts.

"I hated you," she said. "First time I saw you, if you can believe that. I hated a child." Deena's aunt laughed. "But you looked like that damned Gloria, who took my brother away."

She brought a shaking, wrinkled hand to the bridge of her nose and paused as if forgetting why it hung there. When the hand dropped away again, Deena found tightness in her jaw and her lips muscled into a knot of silence. Still, she could see the tremble there in that button of a mouth. Caroline swallowed once emphatically. Only then did Deena see the dampness of her eyes.

"When I heard that he'd died…" Caroline shook her

head. "I would tell you that you don't know what that's like, except you ain't so fortunate. You know exactly what that's like."

She took her time piecing together the next thought. Steady, somehow oblivious that even the storm hung in wait for her words.

"In my mind, you weren't kin to me," Caroline said. "Nothing with her blood could be kin to me. The kids…the kids just picked up on that. Picked up on my hate and made it theirs."

Her hands rubbed together, hands that creased in ways Deena hadn't noticed, hands that shook just so and lined from the passage of time.

"I wish I had a lot of stuff back to do over. Wish I had the last thirty years to do over. I wouldn't let hate eat me alive, if I did. And I'd kill that goddamned Snow in his cradle."

If she realized that this would have meant being without a grandchild that sat before her, she didn't notice. He stared back at her blank, Snow's son. Not speaking. He never did, really.

"All that was my fault," Caroline said. "What he did to Lizzie, Keisha, Anthony, the kids. You say what you want, but Anthony was killed for loving his sister, for trying to protect her from what he knew was out there." She looked directly at Tony as she spoke. "Who wouldn't do that? You?"

Tony dropped his gaze, eyes filled with a thousand contrary emotions. He stared at his hands as if uncertain of their purpose, before inhaling what he looked unwilling to exhale.

Caroline turned from him and cast a questioning stare

at each of them, daring one to contradict her. Only Deena and Kenji noticed the tears that filled Lizzie's eyes. Kenji put an arm around her and she curved into him, earning a ghost of a smile from Deena.

"He was a child trying to protect a child," Caroline said. "It should have been one of us, out there, putting a bullet in Snow. None of this shit should have happened. Not to Anthony, not to any of you."

Caroline jabbed away tears with a talon-tipped thumb while Deena did her best to breathe. What was all this? Why was she stirring this vortex?

"That was Dean's baby that dog murdered. My brother, dammit. He would have killed for anybody in this room. He would have killed for anybody that was his, and his family was his. And he didn't give no damn about what they looked like."

Caroline shot a withering look at Grandma Emma, who had slumped into silence. Interesting, Deena thought, the way coherence came and went. If it truly went at all.

"I used to see what I wanted to see with Snow," Caroline said. "Make myself believe what was easy. Everybody knew what he was. Just because he smiled smiles and mouthed the right words, didn't mean that you couldn't see no soul stood behind it all. But that didn't suit me, especially once Keisha had his baby. I should have had a spine. I should have spoke up. There ain't a day I don't think about what I could have stopped by putting my foot down, by opening my mouth and meaning it, back when she first started bringing him around."

Tariq cleared his throat.

"I think I knew he killed Anthony."

The room shifted, a sea of incredulous faces all in one direction.

"But saying it made it real," Caroline's oldest son said, eyes on the floor. "Saying it meant you had to act on it. Be ready, for what it brought. I never…" He struggled, as if defending against a barrage of insults. "I did say something. Once. About the way he treated Keisha. He put a gun to my head for it. Cocked it. Told me to let my family be my lesson. He could have meant Keisha or Lizzie. But we both knew he meant Anthony."

Silence swelled the room.

"Well, since we're all confessing," Ken said brightly, his arm in a navy cast, "I'm having another child. With Karina."

He turned a smile on his wife. Asami slapped him. It was a ringing sound that brought delight to a room full of faces. Ken gripped his cheek belatedly with a glare of incredulity, incredulity that melted into red-faced rage.

"You're brand new with all this family around you," he spat. "You're all sister girl and bold. We'll see how you are in Atlanta, though, when it's just me and you though. Something tells me, you'll find humility."

Daichi stood.

"Outside, Ken."

He strode for the door.

"I'm not a Tanaka," Ken called after him. "I don't come when the great Daichi summons me."

Except he did, because Tak and John were up and dragging him into the hall.

At their backs was Uncle Yoshi, on his feet and howling.

"'That low down dog! Didn't I tell you he was trash?" he shouted at his sister. "Didn't I warn you he was nothing? You should have let me lay him low years ago! He never fooled me. I say we toss him to the hurricane."

Grandma Yukiko hushed him so they could hear in the hall.

"I think you know that I am not a kind man," Daichi said from just beyond their door. "That I'm known neither for my generosity nor my ability to forgive."

Despite his careful tone, not even the hurricane rivaled the chill he brought in that moment.

"You are an enemy of mine, Ken Wantanabe, and you are ignorant enough to mistake the gravity of this. I am ruthless in revenge, and you may yet learn how much. When the house you own with your whore has the entire sum called in by First National Bank. When her employers at the Children's Trust take a surprisingly conservative view of her lifestyle, a view encouraged by their biggest backer. When you, yes you, are called before the CDC's Management Board for indiscretions on the job, and when your mother and father lose the house they raised you in because there is no record of mortgage payments for the last three years, you will understand how far I can go. I will unhinge you, Ken Watanabe, if you cross my sister again. I care not who or what gets dragged in the undertow."

Daichi returned to the room and sat, scowling under the weight of their stares.

Tak reappeared at Deena's side.

"He's always been scary," he said. "But that—" There was

a hint of awe in his voice. "That was like, look-back-and-become-a-pillar-of-salt frightening."

"Yeah, it was," Deena said.

She looked over to see Asami sitting in the corner, arms folded, smile smug, satisfied.

LAUREN LOOKED UP.

"I have a problem," she said. "I—I forgot my…vitamins."

The things that people worried about.

"You'll just have to go without, Lauren. In a few days you can get more," Deena said.

"These are really important." She pulled up to full height "I'll go get them myself. They're nondescript things, in there with some of the supplies."

John stood. "I'll get it."

"But you nearly drowned last time," Tak said. "Let me go. I'm a better swimmer. You know, if swimming's necessary."

"And you have three children. All I have are divorce papers. Let me go," John said.

Tyson got up.

"Tell me where it is and what it's called."

He stared straight at Lauren, body stiff, insistent. Interestingly enough, she looked just as rigid as him.

"A small bottle. Called PharmaCare," Lauren muttered.

Tyson disappeared without a word, leaving Deena to grin at her husband.

"You're going to pop if you turn any redder," she said.

Tak turned so that his lips brushed her ear. "I just keep feeling like he's…"

"In love with you?" Deena guessed. She couldn't help the smile of amusement on her lips.

It died when Tyson screamed.

Tak bolted.

Deena knew it would be him, with his constant need for responsibility, with his guilt simmering the moment Tyson went down instead of him.

"Tak!" Deena hollered, but it made no difference, of course. By the time she made it to the door, he was at the bottom of the stairs, wading through waist-deep water.

"Do you see him?" she said and started downward, only to have her father-in-law grip her by the wrist.

"No," Tak said and grabbed the stair railing as a gush of water flashed by onward in its rush elsewhere. "It's freezing." The lights flickered, on, then off, on, then off, plunging Deena's husband into darkness.

"Tak? Are you still holding the rail?"

She snatched from her father-in-law, hissed that he should go back, and took a few tentative steps, stopping when she splashed.

"Tak?" Panic eked into her voice.

"Yeah, Dee. I'm here and I have the rail again."

Again?

Never had he sounded further away.

"Come back," Deena said. "Just—come back."

Icy incisions of rain pricked her arm. Was it possible? Was it raining in the house? Deena knew the answer, but feared it.

She swiped a hand in the air, feeling around for her husband as the storm freight-trained through her head. They were in the thick of it now, in the thick of something massive and unforgiving in administering God's wrath.

Her fingers latched on to fabric.

"Tak?"

Her fingers twisted around cloth.

"Tak?"

"I—I think I found Tyson." He hesitated. "I need help pulling him up. Hold on to me tight; you'll feel some resistance. He's pinned some sort of weird way."

Deena roped the extra fabric of his t-shirt around her hand and grabbed on to the railing with the other. She listened to her husband curse and splash in the dark, biting back the mounting horror of what would emerge from the dark. Tak twisted under her grip and a reverberating thud sounded on the stairs, just near Deena's feet.

"Okay, let go. We're out of the water."

Like hell she'd let go. Deena backed up another stair to give him space and yanked forward as Tak bent low. She flailed and snatched in a moment of blind panic, before latching onto the banister and safety.

"Dee, let go. You're choking me. I'm trying to give the man CPR."

She clamped down tighter even as he lurched rhythmically in her grip, grunting from the exertion of his efforts. He counted out in the dark, jerked, counted out, jerked. Still, she clung to his shirt, not caring how twisted up he felt as he moved from one position to the other.

"Tak?"

Tyson should have coughed by now.

"Nothing's happening. It's hard to know if I'm doing it right in the dark."

His grunts of exertion resumed. Steady, steady, feverish, frantic.

Tak cursed and gave a wild thrust. Then nothing.

Stillness.

"He's dead, Dee."

"What? Of course he's not dead. Tak—"

"He's dead, Deena."

Tak was mistaken. There was no way that a man could drown retrieving a bottle of vitamins. There were on vacation, Christmas vacation, for Christ's sake. In Aruba. He couldn't possibly be—

"I'll put him in one of the rooms. I don't want the kids to see. Or your cousin. I think there's something wrong with his head."

They backed up, so Tak could lift him. Even in the dark, his exertion seemed enormous, with each thudding step, each groan sounding off every move.

"Tak, please. Let me help. It'll be easier if we—"

"No, Deena. Now move."

She did as he said, slipping her hand from what felt like the collar of his shirt down to the hem when they'd cleared the stairs.

"This way," Deena said, and felt around to fumble from surface to surface, blind on her wide-eyed trek to the end of the hall. There laid some semblance of privacy in the smallest guest rooms.

She couldn't shake the feeling that she led him to a tomb.

To a final resting place where they would fold his arms over his chest, whisper Amen and back out.

Dead.

It felt like a lie, a gross lie, soaring on the wings of obscurity.

That was it, she told herself. That was where the truth lay. With light and sound and the abating of this storm. There they would see that Tyson was alright, surely a little injured, but alright just the same.

She pawed her way into the guest room until a bed stretched out before them. Tak slumped and dropped Tyson onto it and a squeak of coils responded.

She felt his absence, before hearing another caustic spring of coils. A hand pressed flat to the small of her back, then found her arm to pull her down. She took a seat on the bed at her back. Ever familiar arms went around her. The lights flashed on.

Deena saw Tyson.

Face ashen, eyes open, staring. And there, above his brow, was a sunken hollow, an indentation the size of a baseball. Tyson's arms and legs sprawled out in four directions as water fled his body in gross streams. It seeped from his mouth, flooded from his clothes, and already pooled to the floor.

She couldn't look away. She didn't dare look away, making sure he burned into her retinas instead. He was a human being, the man her cousin loved, twisted to the point of grotesque. Deena took it in, took him all in, committing him to memory as a last act of decency.

The lights flickered out once again.

Deena sat there, aware of her husband's arms around her and aware of her own labored breathing, as images pressed in on her. She remembered her brother, gunned down, left to rot, and her having to identify his remains. She thought of Tyson, of who loved him, of whatever mother and father he'd left behind.

"I don't think we can say anything, yet," Tak said. "About Tyson. About the condition of the house." He looped his fingers through hers, kissed Deena's temple, and squeezed her hand. "We have to keep calm, no matter what happens. Calm is the only way."

His words were like a mantra, reminding him more than her.

"The water's rushing," she said in the voice of another woman.

"It has power behind it," Tak noted. "Like a current."

Deena wondered how much he'd figured out on his own. Judging by his words, the answer was all or nearly all. She decided to be candid with her husband.

"Our walls have been breached," she admitted. "Water rushes as it seeks a level surface. We are no longer a level surface."

Tak shifted. "Okay. Then…what is?

"The ocean," was what she wanted to say; they were practically on top of it as it was. There were other concerns, too. A wall had either been breached or removed. If that wall was load bearing, part or all of the house could crumble. They could drown in a rush of water as it rose, or they could crush beneath the roof itself. Either could happen at any moment.

Tak pulled her to him for a kiss.

He kissed her like the road to hell was through her mouth and he wanted in there first. He kissed her with desperate hardness, with despairing greed, in cloying pain, his embrace crushing as Deena rose to meet him. Tak kissed her as if it were the thing he wanted to die doing, mouth soldered to hers in unchecked need.

Except it was him who pulled away first.

They felt their way back to the linen room hand in hand, only to find it illuminated with two flickering candles.

"You didn't see him?" Crystal said.

"No," Tak said.

Crystal stumbled to her feet as if to seek him, when Tak gave a slow shake of the head.

He wouldn't permit her to go.

Deena thought she might scream and fling herself at him, but Crystal backed up until she hit the wall, slithered down and remained. She knew the truth, Deena realized, knew it but would make them say it just the same.

CHAPTER
fifty-Two

Tak's mother sat in one corner, eyes vacant and darting. Eyebrows slick. Silk near transparent. Every inch of her bathed in sweat, with her layered curls plastered to her skull. Her rich alabaster skin had dulled to chalkiness while her hands—wrinkled things—twisted each other as if bent on breaking them both. Her breaths came in steady pants.

"What's wrong with her?" Tak said to no one in particular. "Am I the only one that's alarmed?"

Indeed it seemed that while he stared straight at her, everyone else made a point of looking away.

"Can you people not hear me?" Tak shouted.

Daichi and Deena opened their mouths and shut them at the exact same time. Both seemed willing to let the other one explain. Tak looked from one to the other, face raging.

"You," he said, eyes on Deena. "How about my wife tells me something for a change?"

Deena wished the storm louder in that moment, loud enough to drown out her ability to speak.

Tak waited.

"Withdrawal," Deena said and felt her stomach fold inward. "I think your mother is going through withdrawal."

"Withdrawal."

That look was cold. Bottom-of-the-ocean cold. Abandoned-at-an-ice-cap cold.

I-hate-you cold.

"Tak—"

He turned to his father.

"How long? How long since she's last been sober?"

Daichi's lips parted, hovering over the question.

"Years."

Tak got up and strode for the door.

"Tell him about your mother," Daichi said and Deena couldn't hold back the gasp. "Tell him about the phone calls. Get it all out now."

Tak turned on them, eyes abandoning his head.

"You know about the phone calls?" He looked at Deena directly. "He knows?"

Daichi weathered his son's scorching stare and his daughter-in-law's forsaken one. He took it better than Deena, who shrunk under the weight of unspoken accusation.

You trust him with your heart, not me, is what that stare said. I'm your husband and you choose another as confidante.

Her bottom lip moved, as if coerced without her knowledge. Words jumbled in fragments, excuses ran alongside explanations, competing for first dibs out her mouth. She couldn't bring herself to speak another word. Some part of her knew there'd be no excuse. So, she stood there numb and not moving, withering from his hostile glare.

"Well!" Tak hollered. "You do everything he says. He just told you to tell me. So, of course, you'll tell me now."

"Tak—" Deena struggled to her feet and reached for him, only to lose courage in the face of his contempt.

"She's being released. She's been released. By the time we get back she'll be out."

Nothing.

No reaction to the news. Only the scald of fury, boiling malice in his eyes.

"She—" Deena weighed her words, pressing back on the urge to shield him, even then. "Wants to live with us. She... expects to live with us."

Gone.

A shove out the door had her husband gone, barreling on into darkness, not caring where he went.

"Tak!" Deena called, only to have John grab a candle and rush after.

"Tak!" John called into darkness. "Tak, where are you? Don't do this. It's dangerous."

"Do what? I'm standing right in front of you."

A whip of the candle brought him into stark relief.

"Do me a favor and go back inside," Tak said. "I'm not in the mood, okay?"

"In the mood for what? Truth? Reason?"

Tak shot him a blistering look.

"John."

It was a warning. He didn't care.

"You act like she's the only one with secrets. Like she's the only one hiding shit."

Tak turned a thunderous black.

"If you believe that crap about Aubree—"

"Mike. What he did to her. Why he's gone."

Tak stopped. He shot a look at the door they'd emerged from, then looked back to John.

"Are you crazy? Why would you even say that out loud?"

"How else would you like me to say it? In my head?"

"Preferably!"

Tak started a truncated pace. To and fro, to and fro, in steps clipped by a narrow walkway.

"Tak," John said gently. "She has a right to know."

He couldn't put a name to the sound Tak made.

"What she has a right to," Tak eventually spat, "is to not be hurt by her husband's family under her own goddamned roof. And don't tell me about what my wife needs. Worry about your own."

John watched him pace.

"Oh? Well, you're all self-righteous," he said. "Demanding truth, no matter what. Why don't you deliver some truth? Why don't you go tell her that Mike waited like a vulture for her to pass out, felt her up and—"

"What did you say?"

Deena.

Deena. Deena. Deena.

John cursed. Cursed the mouth that opened and said too much, cursed the brother that made this mess, then ran.

"Nothing," Tak said. "He—"

"Liar," she hissed and shoved her husband aside, taking off to disappear from their flicker of candlelight.

CHAPTER
fifty-three

OUTSIDE THE STORM RAGED, A BEAST of injustice hell bent on righting perceived wrongs. Deena listened in the dark, glad for the thing that gave voice to her feelings. When her bedroom door opened, she turned away from it, facing the boarded patio doors instead. The eternal darkness beyond it howled.

Tak stepped in, illuminated by the glow of a slim white candle.

"Deena." He said her name as if it pained him. "Deena, please don't—"

"How far did he go?" she said, jaw tight. "How much did your cousin do to me against my will?"

Her skin tried to flee her body at the thought.

"He touched you." Tak said. "He…kissed you. I swear, if he hadn't tried to kill—"

"You didn't tell me," she cried. "Why? To protect him?"

"What? No! Baby, I—"

His hand found her shoulder. She shrugged it off. No one could touch her just then.

Tak drew back, pain painted in bitter swipes across his face. Life drained from him like the color from a picture set to sepia.

"All this time," Deena said and felt the rage rise like high tide. "All this time, you've been giving me hell about every little thing. And you—you with your house from your lover, with your cousin you'll protect at my expense. To hell with you both."

"Deena—"

He reached for her and she gave him her hardest shove. He stumbled back a step and righted, more incredulous than anything.

"I've made my own way and forged my own life. I have never asked for anything from you. Yet, you stand here, stand here knowing what he did…" She shook. Shook with the rage of uncertainty, shook with the range of possibilities. She could have been violated in any number of ways.

"And what?" Tak whispered. "Say it."

"And you decide what he deserves? That he should just go? No input from me? It was me that he touched! Me that he hurt! Maybe I want vengeance. Maybe I want to see his pain. Ever thought of that?"

Tak looked weak just then, as if wrenched in a dozen different directions, and succumbing to the notion that he would be unable to keep his body intact.

"I kept things from you because I didn't want to burden

you or see you hurt," Deena said. "But you, you kept things from me because it was the neatest and most convenient of options. Or because you didn't want to see your grandmother, aunt, and uncle hurt."

There was the truth. Deena saw it in the pinch of his face, in the way he went inward, as if retreating from accusations he wanted no part of.

She realized it then as she thought back to Daichi's words. "Your question is not one of Aubree Daniels or not. It's of Deena Tanaka or not, isn't it?"

Or not. That was what he'd chosen when he took the only weapon she valued. Choice. Choices were what took her from the ghetto to where she stood. Choice was what made her her.

He'd delivered a final kick to an already crumbling marriage, a marriage heavy-laden with secrets.

A marriage, Deena realized, that had finally found its end.

The wild look in his eyes said he knew this. She side-stepped him amidst a clamor of protests.

CHAPTER
fifty—four

Tak told himself that she didn't mean it. That it was anger talking, an outrage that she had every right to feel. He had deceived her—about his one-time relationship with Aubree and about Mike. He'd wanted to protect her, to free her from the onslaught of pain that followed wherever she went. But all he'd done was wound her again.

His hands wouldn't stop shaking.

He wouldn't let her scorch the earth like this, or smite everything like some vengeful god. They had years together, flawless years and memories still to be made. If anything, she had to see—he'd make her see that innate protectiveness of each other was to blame for their downfall, not some purposeful malice.

Tak thought of God while he sat there alone in their room. God with a little 'g' and God with a big 'G.' Maybe the years had been too good for someone who could never conjure more than a disinterested nod in spiritual matters. The wooden butsudan at home saw only rote ministrations; unlike his father, he neither prayed to deceased family members nor expected their intervention. Tak envied his wife in that way; envied her unwavering faith and resolute belief that her murmurings to an unseen god would be answered. How she, of all people, managed that was but a testament to the fire within. Interesting, he thought, how the thing that should have divided them irretrievably was what drew him irretrievably. She had something to believe in, to draw strength in, to move mountains with…still. He saw strength in her when she didn't and knew that strength intimately. It was what led her to protect her husband instead of confide in him, to shield him instead of lean on him. His wife would have to change all that.

And yes, she still was his wife.

REMY FIDDLED WITH an old transistor radio recovered by the help when they were gathering supplies. Never-ending static met his every turn and at the moment he seemed to give up, a signal came through.

"Hurricane force winds in excess of 100 miles an hour have been clocked as far south as Martinique," droned a polished yet weary voice. "While torrential rains continue to devastate the ABC islands of Aruba, Bonnaire, and Curaçao, life-threatening flash floods and mud slides have been reported as far north as the Dominican Republic and as far south as in-land Venezuela."

Deena reached over and turned it off. Irritated, Lloyd extended a hand to power it back on, only to freeze at the sight of Crystal's silent tears.

"I went out into the hall," Crystal said, with arms around herself as if to ward off frigid conditions. "The water's climbing the stairs. Tyson's down there. Tyson was down there." She choked. "God—what am I going to tell his mother?"

An arm went around her. It was her brother Tariq's. But as soon as it landed, she shrank with a recoil of disgust, as surely as if a cockroach had attempted affection.

"Crys—" Tariq said.

"Don't touch me. You know I don't like it."

"Okay, fine. I only thought—"

He reined his arm back in.

"You see, this is why I didn't want to come. I don't want people trying to touch me. I can't stand people touching me."

Deena stared. Everyone stared.

If she knew the absurdity of her words, she didn't let on.

As the hour grew late, most everyone found some variation of awkward sleep. Blankets and pillows from the bedrooms were strewn about all over the floor. Makeshift pallets meant that they slept lined head to feet in a room not designed for so many. With a body pining for rest and a mind trucking on overdrive, Deena lay awake, fitful. Noah lay snug against her stomach and Mia at her back, with Tony flanking his sister's other end, then Tak on the other side of him. No words had passed between them since she'd said they were over.

"Can't sleep either?" Crystal said in the dark.

There was no way Deena wanted to have this conversation. No way she could be the sort of selfless comfort her cousin needed when her own life burned down around her. Deena wanted to feign fatigue, mimic sleep, but somehow that seemed cowardly and mean-spirited.

"I keep trying to imagine Tyson dead," Crystal said. Lying on her side, she walked fingers back and forth across the carpet, following them with her gaze as she did so. "But it feels impossible. He was so strong and tough."

Deena said nothing. She didn't trust herself to speak on the topic just yet.

"He had a...friend," Crystal said. "Named Ash. He died last year. I've been telling myself that they are somewhere, enjoying each other's company. And that, in a way, he must be happy now."

Deena swallowed. "They were close then."

Crystal nodded.

Deena opened her mouth and snapped it closed. There was something she wanted to say only it was the worst possible time for her to say it. Hence the dismissal of the words.

Except Crystal saw it and urged her to speak. It made Deena cringe.

"I thought that," she dropped her voice to a whisper. "I thought you and Tyson lived together."

"Yeah?"

"Okay. And his friend Ash, he lived with you, too?"

A nod.

"So, the three of you lived together," Deena said. "And there was never any...?"

She shut her mouth. Why did she care? She didn't care. It was only the disbelief in her that propelled her to speak.

Lovers did things without thinking—lingering stares, a touch of the hands, all told the tale of what they were to each other. How had Crystal never felt like the third wheel?

Crystal looked at her.

"What do you want me to say, Deena? That I dated a gay guy on purpose? I didn't."

"Yes, but in five years' time you didn't..." She caught herself. "Never mind. This is so insensitive of me to bring this up."

Crystal opened her mouth only to hesitate when Lauren hacked out a cough. Dragging minutes passed before she spoke again.

"He didn't like certain things. Things that it would seem a man should. But then, I didn't question it because... I had my own quirks."

"Well, you can't leave it at that," Deena said.

Crystal scanned her cousin as if trying to determine her allegiance.

"He was a neat freak." She frowned. "My God, I'm referring to him in the past tense."

Deena squeezed her hand. Crystal flinched but bore it. When Deena retracted, she remembered her earlier words. She remembered how it was before.

Crystal didn't like being touched.

Ever.

A thousand memories clamored for domination in Deena's mind. Her cousin melting from embraces, stiffening under the simplest of touches and feigning illness whenever relatives paid a visit. Why hadn't she seen it and questioned it sooner? What kept her from questioning it now?

"Why do you do that?" Deena said, and surprised herself with the sharpness in her voice.

"Do what?" Crystal said, though her hesitancy meant the question was unnecessary.

Deena slapped a hand on top of hers. Crystal jerked away.

"That."

"Deena—"

"No BS. Just tell me what—"

Clarity snapped into place and she gasped with the realization.

"You and Tyson," she whispered. "You've never had sex."

Crystal shot up like a dart. Her gaze swept the room in a single frightened motion. When she turned to Deena again, it was with a forbidding look.

And then the second revelation came down on top of the first, leaving Deena in staggered disbelief.

"You've never had sex, have you?"

Was that even possible? Crystal was her older cousin.

But color leaked into her cheeks, flooding it, meaning it was not only possible, but true.

"Deena, I don't want to—"

"Crystal, you can't be a virgin. You're gorgeous. You're—you're forty-two."

"This conversation is over."

Crystal collapsed onto her back.

"But you're forty-two!"

"Will you shut up? I'd talk to you if you'd only shut up."

Deena's mouth clamped shut, tucking away her latest protest.

Her cousin let out a gust of air.

"I've always been this way. Always straining just to tolerate what other people enjoyed. Grazes grate my teeth. Hugs churn my stomach. Anything more..." she shook her head. "I can't stand any more. I live in fear that someone will touch me and I won't be able to stop them."

"Has that ever happened before? Has someone ever—"

"No," Crystal said. "And I'm not a virgin either."

She wore a smile devoid of any humor.

"Can you remember Corey Rhodes? He was in my grade growing up."

A dark and rawboned boy came to mind. He had the face of a rodent. Not particularly handsome, of course, but warm enough that kindness shined in his smile.

"He was your best friend, wasn't he?" Deena said.

Crystal nodded.

"We tried to fix this thing that's wrong with me. This thing that...curdles my insides."

Deena knew what she would say, sensed it and wanted to cover her ears in anticipation.

"We figured that the person I cared about most would be the one whose touch I could bear the easiest. We thought that sex would cure me. So we tried it."

"In high school?"

"In college. He came to FAMU with me."

The story had the weight of bad news on its back; she sat in expectation of its fall.

"I let him do it. I let him do it because we were so convinced that it would fix me, that if I could get past my hang ups, I would actually enjoy it. Enjoy it with him. But I didn't. The second Corey climbed on me this wave of revulsion consumed me. At the end, I vomited. I knew I never could do it again."

Deena's magic bag had no words. No amount of bumbling and fumbling could turn up a response to that.

Crystal sighed. "I might as well tell you the rest of the story."

"There's more?" Wasn't the rest that Crystal made up her mind never to let another human being touch her again, thereby creating the ideal relationship for Mr. Tyson Down Low?

"We have a daughter."

"Who has a daughter?"

Crystal gave her a long look. It was a deciding one, with trust and distrust battling for domination on her face.

"Me and Corey. Her name is Hannah. She's twenty-two and goes to Duke."

Deena blinked.

"I'm sorry, what?"

"I said that—"

"I know what you said, damn you! But you can't have a child. I'd know. I'm your cousin. How could I not know?"

Except she wasn't listening. She was looking. Crystal was looking at Caroline, her mother, who stared right back at her.

Apparently, Deena wasn't the only one who'd just found out.

CHAPTER
fifty-five

No matter how Caroline baited her, Crystal refused to say another word. She lay there in the dark feigning sleep, until sobs racked her body and silenced her mother. Aruba had been a nightmare for Crystal. A dead gay boyfriend, a secret child, and a chance of dying before sunrise. The evening was rich, even by Hammond standards.

Deena stared blindly at the ceiling, heart like a brick in her chest. For the rest of the night she kept company with Crystal's tears, aware that with Tony, Noah, and Mia between her and Tak, they would lie no closer. Ever again.

Morning brought the ceasing of the rain.

Tak sat up. Black hair tousled, gray tee rumpled, he had the look of a man who'd just left a woman's bed. He had the look of never-ending desirability.

"Do you think…"

This question was meant for her. It was obvious, not because he looked at her, but because the uncertainty in his eyes was so clear.

She shoved back the desire to embrace him.

He hovered, searching her face, before his shoulders slumped, defeated.

"I'll check the water level," he said, and rose up on two sneakered feet.

Three strides had his lean physique in the door, with a hand on each side of the frame, muscles flexing in his back as he leaned out. Half a head separated him from the top, maybe less with his hair looking like that. With a cursory look Deena's way, Tak stepped out and started down the hall. Already she knew where he went.

"The house is a nightmare," Tak said on return. "The water's at the top stairs, half the windows are smashed out and there's hardly a place to walk without breaking something or getting tangled."

"At least our water worries are over," Crystal said.

"They're probably just beginning," Deena said. "It's not just the interior of the house that's brimming with water. Outside could look just as bad."

Tak waded through the tangled web of bodies, most still sleeping, until he found his way to the window.

"Yeah. Either we moved," Tak said, "or the sea did."

Deena slipped in beside him for a view and the bottom fell out of her belly. Ocean waves beneath her feet, lapping at the second floor window.

TAK STRODE FOR the corner of the room that held their meager supplies—bottled water purified with nine drops of bleach, a handful of candles, matches, a few plastic utensils, and a mountain of canned meats, vegetables and fruits.

Soon, he had the order he needed. John came to his side and they divvied up the food so that everyone had, at the very least, a bit of potted meat and fruit for breakfast.

It was disgusting. Vile cold sludge sloshed around in Deena's mouth until she swallowed it with the aid of held breath. Brandon refused to eat his, as did Noah, until Kenji admitted that such food was the secret to his performance on the field. Noah scoffed it down then, which made Brandon do the same, both clamoring for seconds.

"It's like Hurricane Katrina," Tariq said. "Trapped in a house with rising water, hoping somebody will rescue us. And we all know how that turned out."

"Right," Lauren snapped. "Why didn't we evacuate again?"

"Because we didn't know to," Deena said.

"Well, it's official. Worst vacation ever." Lauren hugged her legs to her chest, chin pressing knees. Her food sat uneaten.

"Next time try paying for your own," Deena said.

Lauren choked out a bitter laugh.

"You don't actually expect us to be grateful do you?"

"Quiet, Lauren," June warned.

"Do you?" she pressed.

Her eyes stood wide in expectation and challenge. Were Deena not in a broken relationship with Tak and facing the distinct possibility of death should the waters not recede, she might have been more tolerant of Lauren's frustrations. She might have even expressed some sympathy. But she'd had bullets of sorrow lodged in her heart. There was no room for other's pain.

"I expect you, Lauren Tanaka, to be as ungrateful, argumentative, obnoxious, and self-serving as you've always been," Deena said. "I expect you to continue masking self-loathing in an outward disdain for everyone and everything around you, including the parents that love and care for you even when you treat them poorly. And I expect you to keep pretending you're not pregnant."

Bull's-eye.

Lauren gasped. Every head snapped to face her.

"What are you talking about?" June whispered. "If my daughter were pregnant, I'd know."

"PharmaCare," Deena said, "is a prenatal vitamin. I took it with Noah. That's why she was so bent on having it. That's why she looks so plump."

"You bitch!" Lauren scrambled to her feet. "You had no right to open your mouth."

She strode for Deena, only to be cut off by Tak, arms spread wide.

"Shut your mouth, Lauren, and go have a seat."

"No! You sit here and let your—*kakujin*—"

"Careful now," Deena said, also on her feet. "People will think you mean it."

"What's a *kakujin*?" Tariq mused.

"It means a 'black,'" Mia spat, and shoved a Vienna sausage into her mouth, gray eyes narrowed on her cousin.

"Funny," Jayden said. "She wasn't minding *kakujins* last night."

"The consensus in this house is that she prefers 'em," Lloyd said.

Yoshi sat in the corner, weak as a wad of wet tissue, slumped like a man who'd bled too much.

June stared at her daughter.

"Is it true, Lauren? Are you really—"

Lauren threw up her arms. "Oh, don't look at me like that! Like you weren't practically a child when you had Michael."

June stood, green eyes wide and wild.

"So, you are pregnant?"

Lauren's dark eyes searched her mother's face, contempt spreading with each sweep of the gaze.

"I am so not having this conversation."

"Uh yeah," June said. "You are. It should be easy enough."

Anger held onto Lauren as she stood her ground, seeping out with each passing second that her mother did the same. Finally, the daughter exhaled.

"Yeah."

"And do you know whose it is?"

It should have been an insulting question. It should have earned all the fire and rancor Lauren had in her soul. Instead, the girl dropped her gaze.

"No," she said. "You know I don't."

"Lauren, I told you the last time—"

"The last time?" Yoshi echoed.

Deena wanted to burn the house to the ground. She

wanted whatever madness had crept in to be eviscerated, purged.

Yoshi rose and faced his wife, fever in his face.

"The last time, June?"

Yoshi Tanaka had half a head's height on his wife. Broad shouldered and potbellied, he dwarfed the slight yet wide-hipped woman. She looked up at him with the uncertainty of one handling damage control by wielding a single pistol in the face of a mob.

"Yoshiaki, you know how free spirited our daughter is."

"It's not the word I'd use," Yoshi muttered.

June nodded in the way people did when they were hurrying on to something else.

"It was a long time ago. And it was…handled."

"Handled?" Yoshi cried. "What the hell does that mean?"

"This conversation belongs in the hallway," Daichi said. He rose and placed a hand on the shoulder of his younger brother and another on his sister-in-law, before leading them and Lauren out.

Shouting exploded from the corridor. Yoshi blaming June for lax rules, June blaming Yoshi for the need to keep secrets, Lauren screaming that both of them needed to get out of her life. Daichi's attempts to referee and reprimand went so poorly that soon he was neck deep in the shouting, with June sobbing and accusing him of never thinking she was good enough for his brother. Meanwhile, Yoshi demanded to know what he'd done so wrong that Lauren had become a whore.

Deena sat, eyes wide, and eventually realized that John was staring. At her.

"Happy?" he snapped, and fixed her with a grim smile.

He stalked out of the room, only to fall headlong into the argument with his parents, sister and uncle.

CHAPTER
fifty-six

DEENA DISAPPEARED DOWN THE hall. Tak watched her go, watched her walk that same Deena walk, as doubt, determination, and want fought a bloodless battle to dominate him. How many times since she said she was leaving him had he opened his mouth only to choke on concern, clamp down on despair, bottle up the mounting need to touch her? She was there, always there with him, and yet so far away. Raw emotion ate at him, smothering from the inside out. He'd had enough. Never had he wanted out. He needed a way back to before. Misery scorched like the desert sun, taunting him with the mirage of the wife that wouldn't have him again.

Tak tried to imagine a life without Deena and found emptiness instead. There was nothing apart from her. No thing he wanted, no thing he wished for. She bore his name, his children. He couldn't see a way to him without them.

He stood without knowing it. Found her in their bedroom without knowing it. Went to her, without being able to help himself. She was busy doing nothing, staring out at a window she couldn't see through, thoughts so distant she didn't bother to blink.

Tak lifted his hand, hovered, and then touched her arm. Just fingers, fingers, brushing her shoulder and then tracing down.

So many years. So many years, and still, she inhaled at his touch. His own chest rose and fell, as everything he saw, felt and knew, came down to his skin on hers. He didn't know if they'd ever see home again. He didn't know if they'd perish there, marooned, dehydrated, dead. But what he did know was that if he died on that day or another, there was no way he could go in peace without knowing that she loved him still.

With her forehead pressed to the glass, her chest rose and fell in uneven bursts, as if forgetting how to breathe then remembering, only to forget again. He thought of the first time he made love to her. Back then, they called themselves friends, but it was the sort of friend that roused bitter jealousy, that sparked flashes of loneliness in their absence, and stabs of want in their presence. The sort of friend that was never really just a friend to begin with.

So they were those kinds of friends when she saw him with another woman. Their gazes met through the window of a New York restaurant and Tak couldn't figure out how to breathe anymore. Deena stared back at him, eyes glittering, a riot of emotion on her face. Tak toppled both his agent's lunch and his in his hurry to get to her. But she ran like she hoped never to be caught and he'd chased her down because he needed to. Chased her down and backed her into their bedroom, whispering all the little things he'd been too stupid and too cowardly to say. He wouldn't be stupid anymore.

"Deena—"

"Tak." She suffocated on his name. "Don't."

Thick lashes swept her cheeks once, twice, before she closed her eyes altogether.

Don't.

Don't think. Don't breathe. Don't be. Those commands were just as reasonable as what she asked of him, of what she wanted from him.

"I can't help it," was what he wanted to say.

"I need you," was what he should have said.

Tak wanted to argue with her. He wanted to scream. All the compromises in the world, all the promises were hers, if only she could let them be. Why was she doing this? Why was she wrenching a stake through them both even as tears tracked her cheeks?

"How do I fix this?" he said. "Tell me."

But it was the wrong thing to say.

She whirled on him, fury painting her face and darkening her features.

"There is no fixing life. There is no fixing what is. People are born, live miserably short lives, and die. Who are you to begrudge the amount of happiness you've been allowed? All things come to an end. You should have expected this. I did."

Words wouldn't come. Not for this…this confidence in

the worthlessness of their love, this certainty that their vows would eventually mean nothing.

He left. Left her to her tears or muted screams or whatever it was that people who expected the worst out of life did when they got it.

He made up his mind not to care about her or their worthless marriage.

CHAPTER
fifty-seven

THE RAIN CAME BACK IN a whirlwind.

It seeped in under the door, slow but persistent, until they stood, upright as the carpet grew irretrievably wet. Hours passed with nothing but anger to linger on and the dawning realization that no one knew where they were, that no one knew to come, and that the wind would peel back their roof and the water would swallow them before any rescue would happen.

In an odd twist of fate, Tak and Deena stood shoulder to shoulder without touching, while Allison contented herself with John's arms wrapped tight around her. Tak's mother, who had hardly uttered a word since the storm began, sat pasty and drenched in sweat, the rigors of withdrawal having set her to shaking.

Tak swept Noah up into his arms, soothing him with

soft tut tuts before rubbing his back in a circular motion. When his arms grew weary, he placed Noah on his shoulders. John did the same for little Elijah as Kenji's torn rotator cuff prevented him from holding him up with Brandon on his back.

Water sat at their ankles, then at the hind part of their calves, inching upward as the children whimpered. By candlelight, Deena studied the water that pooled at her legs and thought it too dark, too cloudy.

Pillows floated like ice floes before taking on so much weight they sunk. Plastic knives, forks, and spoons swarmed in a pooled vortex with trembling people at the center.

They were dying.

Every last one of them would drown.

When the water reached Deena's hips, she reached out for Tak, and their fingers laced.

CHAPTER
fifty-eight

Deena's pulse bled fear into her brain. Silence at last, after a barrage of cannon thunder, a Fourth of July's worth of lightening. Wind screamed its fury like a scorned Medusa, clawing at the house, tearing for the fools inside. She could think of nothing but the snatch of scripture she'd whispered when Tak flat-lined, when her world fell into a gaping black hole and knifed her for good measure.

Though he causes grief,
Yet He will show compassion,
According to the multitude of His mercies.

Tak, whose hand she clenched to numbness, began to whisper the scripture with her as they stood in the linen room, immersed in storm waters. At their feet, at their calves, at their thighs. The cries of children were all that pierced the fury of their hurricane. That and their prayers.

Though he causes grief,

Yet He will show compassion,

According to the multitude of His mercies.

No way out. Not through a too-high roof with no way to reach it. Not while the winds of the storm could hurl them into the ocean. Not when the ocean waited outside their door. Scratch that. Not when the ocean waited at their feet.

Tak and Deena's voices climbed, reaching for places the water couldn't go. She hadn't even known he knew that scripture. She didn't know that he knew any.

They fell still when the storm abated.

His eyes were on her. Those eyes that saw everything, right down to the swallow in her throat. He saw her thoughts: both those she was thinking and those she hadn't come up with yet. He saw through her. And knew her heart.

"Please God," Tony said. "Send someone."

His eyes were on his great grandmother, with her one hand clasped with Rhonda's, the other with Caroline's. Seated in her wheelchair, the waters met Grandma Emma's chest.

Deena handed her oldest son her candle and went into action.

"Open everything," she said. "Let as much water out of here as we can, now that the rain's stopped."

Grateful for something to do, virtually everyone dove into action. Prying open the French doors that led to the back patio took work. Once done, they saw what Deena already knew. Their property had been obliterated. They were surrounded by dark and ominous water. How high or how far this water stretched was impossible to know, but given their proximity to the sea, the worst seemed certain.

Tariq inched open the door to the hall and was rewarded with a great gust of water that knocked him on his ass. Sputtering and kicking and thrashing, he pulled up from the ink-like substance and gasped desperately for air.

"It's foul," he croaked and spat. "All of it's foul. I can't imagine what must be in the water."

"Feces," Daichi said. "Also Hepatitis, E. Coli, shingles, and an assortment of parasites are very likely."

Tariq stared at him, chest heaving.

They went back to work, more careful still. Wading through the house in pairs, rushing water out of every opening. When Lloyd and Remy went in the direction of where Tyson's remains laid, Tak cut their path off and said it was dangerous.

Their children ventured out to the patios, where already a deceptive sun peeked out from the clouds. How such an abomination was possible, Deena didn't know. Only, she felt the heat and steadiness of the sun, the glorious shine of a white too bright, and thought it mocked her.

They worked as that orb streaked the sky, burning from paleness to a brilliant furnace of fire.

Eventually, the whirr of a chopper sounded overhead. Those closest to the patio door rushed out, joining the handful of bodies already outdoors. Great blasts of wind and motor power whirred like the second coming of the storm. Deena looked up and saw the yellow belly of a great beast.

"Thank you, God," she whispered.

She knew neither how nor why, nor did she try to understand.

A man spoke through a megaphone directly into her skull.

"How many of you are there?" he chimed.

"Maybe forty!" Deena yelled back.

"What?"

"Maybe forty!"

A ladder descended from the aircraft.

"We can only transport fifteen at a time," he said.

"Then send a second helicopter!" Daichi yelled.

He received no response.

Fifteen. Fine. She'd send her sister, the elderly, the sick, and as many children as she could manage on the first round.

Deena held it together with wet glue resolve, as Yukiko went up, then Lauren and Lizzie, before a co-pilot came down and strapped up with first Noah, then Brandon, then Brandon's younger brother Jacob, each child held in a harness as they winded up to safety.

Helicopter propellers whisked Deena's hair and whipped it into wild knots. As her youngest child disappeared, as other children disappeared, she told herself that they were all safe, that they would all go home—all except Tyson.

A few of Tariq's grandchildren went next and the knot in Deena's chest grew tighter. It came undone when she insisted that Tony go up and he refused, giving the seat to a smaller cousin instead. When she pushed for Daichi to go up, he too ignored her.

Deena knew they were right. Knew that the smallest and the frailest of them were to go, but in the secret chambers of her heart, in her secret selfishness, she had those she couldn't do without. She needed her children, her sister and brother-in-law, she needed certain people safe even if she wasn't. She needed Tak safe even if she couldn't be.

So, she didn't watch the helicopter ascend, slicing through the air on retreat. But once they were gone, she found herself grateful that Daichi had given up his seat.

"Where did they go?" she asked.

Daichi stood on the patio, face turned to the heavens.

"Probably the consulate in Curaçao. It would be ideal. Especially since I have a friend there."

Of course he did.

They measured the seconds in heartbeats. They measured minutes in stares. Too many went by before the whirlwind of choppers returned.

A second helicopter arrived, smaller than the first and able to transport only ten. More Hammond children piled into this one, alongside Tony, who Deena forced, Kenji, who she also forced, Crystal, Rhonda, and Mary Ann. Their group had dwindled quickly. Those who remained clustered together, desperate for a once too-hot sun. Night approached, heavy handed and ominous. Before the last of dusk abated, the first helicopter returned and carried off another fifteen. Among them were Tak's parents, his aunts and uncles, Tariq, and the help.

When night arrived, there was only Tak and Deena.

CHAPTER
fifty—nine

STANDING OUT ON THE PATIO, HUSBAND and wife stared out at the water because it was a great deal easier than looking at each other. With family gone and their property in ruins, it seemed only poetic justice that their marriage had not escaped this storm. Far be it for Deena to begrudge what joy she'd been given only to have it melt away; she knew all things of this life were fleeting.

A decade and a half of marriage meant that she could always feel Tak's presence, could sense the displacement of air when he shifted, and knew the ins and outs of his breathing as subtly as she knew her own. His hesitancy fell like a cloak around her.

Why wasn't he defying the verdict she'd handed down? Begging her to reconsider? She'd been bracing for the full gauntlet of his determination.

It never came.

Deena decided that he didn't care about their marriage and that she didn't care either.

She decided that she absolutely wasn't close to tears and blinked them away.

"Deena?"

She looked up at him with strength and defiance. She had survived so much. She could survive him.

"I'll notify authorities about Tyson," Tak said. "Just as soon as we're somewhere safe. I'm not sure how they'd want to handle it."

It wasn't the conversation she wanted to have. Not when she felt half dead and wholly ruined. Not when every joyous second of her life seemed like a set-up for the proverbial yanking of her carpet. In those instances, she always fell face down, in the hardest possible way.

But it didn't mean she no longer loved him. In fact, her loving him was why she needed to leave. She couldn't bear to watch them spiral down to nothingness, to the hatred of bitter divorced couples. Not when he'd once been her everything. Not when he was still her best friend.

Tak stood with his back to the patio railing, hands jammed into the jeans of his pockets, openly staring at her. Black wisps of hair danced in the wind, brushing the contours of his face. Ruggedness battled the faint hint of humor incessantly playing at his lips. Gorgeous. Born to laugh, born to smile, born for joy. He was all of that, though none of it was apparent at the moment.

A distant rumble, like thunder, made them both cock their heads.

Silence. Then the two looked at each other. It was Deena who dropped her gaze first.

Tak laughed bitterly.

"You know," he said. "I don't even know how to feel right now. Half of me wants to tell you that I can't be without you. That I can't be me without you. That there's a part of me so yours, that if you take it, if you take it and leave, I'm afraid of what I'll become."

"And the other half of you?"

Tak looked at her.

"The other half says to let you go. That you came into this marriage expecting failure. Then you made sure you got it."

"I made sure? You're putting all this on me?"

Tak reared on her, a bull ready for battle.

"You're damned right I am. When I said my vows, I meant every word."

"So did I!"

"Yet, you give 'em an expiration date. Amazing, the determination you have when it comes to the things you believe in. Your sister, our kids, your career. Yet a bad week has you deciding that we aren't worth saving. So, yeah. The blame is yours. Own it. Be proud of it."

There it was. The rumbling again. A thousand hooves in the distance, a thousand quakes en masse in their direction. Deena cocked her head.

"Tak—"

"I promised to cherish you, Deena. To be your truest friend, your unfailing confidante, the strength when you had none of your own. I promised to never put another before you, even when that other could have been me. That's what I said and that's what I meant. It's what I thought you meant too."

"I did!"

Words battled on her tongue for domination. Denials and explanations waged a fight to the death.

A deafening roar grew in size and sheer obnoxiousness, louder even than the chopper, and happening in her head, it seemed.

Tak started for the door. She followed him inside.

"Did you even believe any of this Aubree Daniels crap?" he shouted, whirling on her. "Or was it that convenient out your paranoia's been looking for all these years?"

He careened around, searching left then right, irritation painted on his face. He heard the sound, the rollercoaster roar that came from nothing and everywhere.

"Tak," Deena said and found her pulse strangely steady. "I don't want an out. I've never wanted an out."

"You—"

Tak opened his mouth and the house fell away around them.

CHAPTER
sixty

DEENA PLUMMETED INTO THE FOUL blackness of the first floor. Sinking, sinking, pitching wild as water filled her nose and mouth. An undercurrent suctioned her deeper. Eyes wide, she caught glimpses of plastic soda bottles and a red toy truck in her submersion, a Styrofoam cooler and a dead cat bobbing in the murky waters. Bits of wood drifted up, where she imagined the second floor used to be, while glass petered down, settling on her floor. The west rotunda, she thought on sighting the Corinthian pillars. They were in the west rotunda.

Her lungs felt filled with gasoline, and in a minute she would light the match. Deena jerked wildly as the panic set in. She needed oxygen. She needed it now.

Deena thrashed arms and legs, swirling, pivoting in her search for a way out. She fought upward, as the weight of water pushed her down, before realizing the sinking debris meant there was no second floor to go to. Large swaths of the area around her were filled with chunks of wood, plaster and roof tiles. The whole house, she knew, had come down on their heads.

Air.

Deena kicked wild, heart pounding in skull, lungs set to burst, before the sight of a bolder sticking into her house stopped her.

Moonlight streamed in.

Deena swam, making a strong pitch for the wood before yanking herself up to safety. She sucked on the oxygen in barbaric fierceness, inhaling more than she needed and coughing up the rest.

It wouldn't come fast enough. The air couldn't come fast enough.

Deena halted, then whipped around with a realization.

She was alone.

No.

Deena dove into the water.

It was darker now, thicker, with more debris to wade through than before. Frantically, she swam back and forth knowing that he had to be near—they were right next to each other when they fell. He had to be—

There.

Under a giant slab of metal.

Not moving. Eyes closed.

Deena vaulted through the water, seized the metal and heaved. Two great yanks wedged it back enough that she could siphon him out. Feverish prayers filled a blunted mind pressing in its need for oxygen. She needed back to air, back to her rock. A little further. A little further. When she found it, Deena climbed on and dragged Tak atop. Water coursed off him in great streams.

Deena swept his mouth with fingers—fingers that tangled in damp seaweed. Gunk followed, trailed quickly by a vat of dark water purged from his body.

She waited.

There was only stillness.

"Don't do this. Please don't do this to me."

She raked at his mouth, blew into it, watched, and repeated. Then again. Then again.

No.

"Tak?" Deena whispered. "Tak!"

She came down like a freight with both hands, slamming into the V of his ribs. Again and again, with tears streaming her face, she blew into his mouth, then beat the hell out of him.

Nothing.

Nothing. Nothing. Nothing.

She threw back her head and screamed. A maniacal, throat-stripping shriek that grew wings and flew. With her fists clenched and her on her knees, Deena heaved a thousand curse words at the heavens. She brought down a sledgehammer of a fist on Tak.

He vomited.

Bile, seaweed, and a gallon's worth of water.

Right in Deena's lap.

She tackled him in an embrace.

CHAPTER
sixty—one

"STOP DYING ON ME, YOU BASTARD."
Deena squeezed Tak fierce as a Heimlich, only to
have him shove her away, rough.

Hurt flooded in as surely as if he'd hit her. Then he
vomited into the flood waters.

More liquid, more bile, until he did nothing but gag.
Deena beat him on the back, then rubbed, waiting for the
moment he'd calm.

She looked up at the sky. Would the chopper even
recognize their property anymore? It sat like pins in a
bowling alley, shards here and there after a hit in the dark.

Which made her think of something else.

"What happened?" Tak said. "One minute I was standing
there giving you hell, the next..."

"The rumbling," Deena said. "It was a landslide coming

for us. No doubt, it had been traveling for miles, picking up boulders, all manner of cars and parts of homes en route."

"But Aruba's flat," Tak said. "Flat as our house."

He fed her a weak smile. Leave it to him to already find this funny.

"Slopes can be subtle," Deena said, deciding she wasn't ready for his humor just yet. "And with so much rain saturation, anything remotely unstable unhinges once the soil or foundation is compromised. Sustained winds of—"

"Alright, Daichi. Tell me if it's done. Or if we're going to be swept into the sea in a few seconds."

Deena took in the decimated ruins on either side of her. Initially, she believed herself to be in what once were their gardens, but on realizing there were roof tops of homes she knew behind her, she guesstimated that they were on the side of the house.

"I don't want to get back in the water. But we need higher ground. If you can swim at all—"

"I can't."

Deena looked down and saw—really saw—the condition he was in. Black hair painted to his skull, face the color of wash-worn parchment. Blotches of red at his cheek. His teeth clamped down into a careful grimace. He didn't want her to see the extent of his injuries. Even after all that had happened, he still tried to protect her.

"Tak—"

Then she heard it. Wild winds that sent her hair airborne, slicing a roaring vortex.

The helicopter was back.

They were saved.

CHAPTER
sixty-Two

ONCE THE SUSPENDED LADDER DROPPED, it became apparent that Tak couldn't climb. In fact, he couldn't even stand. The realization sent ice through her veins. The same co-pilot that strapped up with Noah descended again, this time to fit Tak with a bright orange vest adorned with an assortment of black straps and buttons. As he worked, Deena informed him of old injuries sustained by Tak's car accident years ago and the possibility of aggravating them. When Tak was secured, she peppered the co-pilot with questions during the lift about weight capacity of the vest and load capacity for the pulley system. When those ran dry, she moved on to his trainings and certifications, when they were up for renewal and how many such rescues he'd completed. A congenial if alarmingly slim man, he admitted to her that his work in the US Army trained him for the task just fine.

Then his mouth spread wide for Deena.

"But that doesn't ease your worries, does it?" he said, pleasure apparent in his voice.

She wanted something snarky to say, but could conjure no anger for the man who'd rescued them.

"No," she admitted.

"Love's funny that way, I reckon," and only then did Deena hear the yawn of a warm Texas drawl.

After Deena and the co-pilot boarded, they airlifted with chopper blades slashing, blasting out all sounds and thought.

Tak sat still and whitened; white as a harvest moon with teeth baring, slick with the filth of polluted waters.

"Tell me where it hurts," Deena said and slid her hand into her husband's.

He bore down on it. Faintly, she registered pain.

"My leg. Lift my pants leg for me."

His dark blue jeans ran black, swathed in grime and dripping a grease-like substance. But when she drew up his jeans as far as they could go, stopping at the knee, blood gushed from a crosswise slash.

"Give me something," she said. "To staunch it."

"First aid kit behind my seat," the co-pilot said. Strapped in and at the side of a stern captain, both men focused on the endless panel of controls. Their ascent had them cutting a sharp turn east. Deena sucked in a wave of nausea, bit down on resolve, and concentrated on an immediate series of tasks.

"Dee—"

She snatched the white box with its oversized red cross and threw it open, before dropping it altogether. Trembling fingers fumbled with the metal latch. She scolded them to steadying and opened the box. Tourniquet in hand, she lifted it, dropped it, picked it up, then set it aside to search for a cleaning agent.

"Deena."

Not a question. He'd said her name with certainty, with the utmost of familiarity. She'd answer to a thousand different pet names, so long as he said them like that.

What was it that Shakespeare said about names?

That which we call a rose by any other name would smell as sweet.

She shoved the thought aside and found the peroxide before scouring a third of the bottle onto his wound. She tied the tourniquet tight enough to earn a hiss. She went for the other leg, found a similar cut, though shallow in comparison, and repeated her treatment. He said her name again. She shushed him, buried her smile, and yanked up his shirt for a view of his torso. Carved, filth strewn-muscles were all that met her.

Tak grabbed her by the wrist.

"What about you?"

"I'm fine."

"Good. Let's see."

So, she found her seat and proceeded to reveal first one leg, then the other, before rolling up her shirt. The gash running down her side surprised her.

"My turn," Tak said and set about dressing her wound.

He worked in silence. When the cleaning and bandaging were done, he looked up at her, bleary-eyed.

"We need to talk," he said.

Her eyes shot wide in disbelief. Surely, he could think of nothing but the fact that he'd nearly lost his life…again.

"Whatever you have to say can wait. You practically died," she said. "You could have drowned. That metal could have severed an artery. You would have bled out in minutes."

The truth of it collided with her, colossal in its strength. She struggled it down in a thousand swallows, fought it back with a billion eye blinks. With a sigh, Tak's hand on her wrist relaxed to run up the length of her arm.

"But it didn't, Dee."

"Yes, I know. But you could have!"

She snatched away, remembering her maniacal rage, her torment, and the hateful, spit-laden words she'd shrieked at God. She'd been an animal in grief, knowing and understanding nothing but her own agony.

And still, Tak was given back to her.

Again the tears wanted out, hot violent tears that shoved at her. Deena shoved back and went to work cleaning the first aid mess she'd made.

"It's not enough to love me," Tak said to her bowed head. "You have to believe in me, you have to believe that I can be the things you need. That I can be as strong or as there as you need me to be. That I can handle whatever comes as it comes."

He could. She knew he could. But to relinquish that part, to freefall in that way… She'd loved her parents, needed them, and knew what it was to lose them nonetheless. That part of her, folded tight as origami, couldn't bear to be opened, to be revealed for the flower it was meant to be.

"I love you so much," she said. "And I was so afraid of ruining what we had. I thought leaving you…separating from you, was the best way to preserve it."

She'd feared losing him completely. Like the false mother in the bible, subject to King Solomon's rule, bitterness meant she'd take him piecemeal and under her own terms, rather than lose him altogether to another.

Bitterness and a need to control had made her the fool.

Tak pulled her to him and wrapped an arm around her, before burying his face in the filth that was her hair.

"Baby? That's the stupidest thing I've ever heard."

Deena couldn't help but laugh.

CHAPTER
sixty-three

Tak traced lazy circles on the back of Deena's hand, looping script that only he knew the meaning of. Partially upright in the hospital bed, white bedding draped his legs and tucked underneath the mattress. Outside was a view of the sea.

"I've been thinking," Tak said and ceased his hypnotic drawing to lace fingers through his wife's. "About everything that happened in Aruba."

"Tak, you don't have to—"

They had gushed their apologies on the helicopter, desperate rambling words meant to capture every regret and every emotion ever felt. Still, it had somehow fallen short. But what more could be said?

Infection had him hospitalized for two weeks. Muscle melted from his frame as he lived off the offerings of his IV.

Stitches knitted both his legs, and he'd spent his every day wading through a mountain of painkillers to form thoughts. Clarity had found him at last.

"I miss you," Tak said. "Sometimes when you're right beside me. A part of you detaches and you're distant. It's how I know you're keeping something from me."

She'd done away with her foolhardy plans to protect him through secrecy; done away with them for good. What could he possibly mean with this latest accusation?

"Your mother," he said. "When is she released?"

She blinked in surprise. He had a way of slicing to the bone without trying, of sifting through the junk to find treasure in an instant.

"She's already out," Deena said. It wasn't that she'd kept the secret from him. It was only that he'd been so preoccupied by his condition that the right time to discuss it hadn't come up.

"Did you tell her that she could stay with us?"

Stay with them.

Deena released him and went to the window. His private suite in St. Elizabeth Hospital afforded lush views of shimmering blue waters and a sky that, for the moment, dulled to a bleeding rose on the sun's exit from it. Thin white clouds pockmarked the heavens.

Each of them had spent some time at the hospital, first for routine exams and tetanus shots after the exposure to polluted waters, and second, for various treatments as needed. Deena and a few others had suffered from mild dehydration and a low grade infection or two. But only Tak's condition and Grandma Emma's had required extended treatment. She had been flown back to Miami for that, where pneumonia had set in. Respiratory failure soon followed. Eventually, the family would have to take her off the ventilator. When Tak and Deena returned to Florida and life settled down, they would make the final arrangements.

"Come here," Tak said, "and tell me what you want. What you think you want, if you're not sure."

She crossed the room and he took both her hands in his.

There was warmth there, but something else: a purposefully blank expression, slack and unreadable. He was leaving it up to her. He was leaving the decision of her mother absolutely up to her.

Deena snatched away from him and collapsed into a chair.

"Don't do that to me," she said. "Don't make it all mine. Am I really supposed to know the right thing? Automatically?"

He studied her in that way that had once been all Daichi's, but had become his as age crept up. Astute, deliberate, studious.

Tak exhaled.

"You're right. She's our mother. So, let's figure this out."

Our mother.

She had never heard the phrase. Not from Anthony. Not from Lizzie. No one took on the enormity of that burden; it had always been hers in a single, solitary world.

And here he was to join her.

Deena came to him and cupped his face with both hands.

"Tell me what you want," she said and ran a hand

through his hair. It could have been her own; that hair was so familiar.

Tak scooted over, away from the IV and monitoring machines strapped to his torso, and created a tenuous tangle of cords.

"Get in."

"In the bed with you?"

He looked at her.

"Fine," Deena grunted. But then she stared at the sliver of spot he'd provided. White sheets pulled back to reveal white fabric on a thin stretch of mattress.

"I'm sure there are rules about this, sweetheart."

Tak twisted his lips into a heavy veil of scorn.

"Oh, tell me what you want, Takumi," he mocked in a high pitched whine. "I almost lost you and—"

Deena kicked off her loafers, twisted enough to keep an eye on the machine cords and slid in delicately beside them. Her jeans rustled against his bare skin. He felt smaller, frailer. She bit back the fright.

"I should drown more often, genie."

Tak smiled at her and pinched the bridge of her nose.

Deena exhaled. His constant flood of jokes when his health was poorest always hit her wrong. Unlike Kenji, she didn't lash out at him or chastise him for ignoring her feelings. If quips about a debilitated condition somehow empowered him, then she was all for anything that led to healing.

"I don't think I could take you drowning again," was all she said on the matter.

"Me either," he said and kissed her.

His lips were chapped but insistent, parting her as his hands roamed. A clear cord streamed across the side of their faces, while another rested on her chest. Still, she inched closer to him as he reached underneath her simple black blouse, cupped her breast and ran a hand down the ridges of her spine.

"Tak…" she protested. It was all she could think of to say.

"Don't make me waste my second wish, genie." He muttered it into her mouth as her bra snapped open.

"Why?" Deena said. "What were you saving it for?"

He dipped again for her lips, claiming with a fierceness that said he resented interruptions.

"For us," he said. "To renew our vows. Now that you know how un-leaveable I am."

CHAPTER
sixty-four

Mᴵᴷᴱ'ˢ ꜰᴵᴿˢᴛ ᴡᴱᴇᴋ ᴵɴ Bᴜᴇɴᴏˢ Aᴵᴿᴇˢ was spent holed up in a Sheraton, where he penned vicious letters to Tak, passionate ones to Deena, and hateful ones to himself before tearing them all to shreds. His request for a transfer from Seattle to Buenos Aires had startled his supervisor, but it had, nevertheless, been granted. They gave him a six to eight week window, however, before the position he required would be available.

In order to save money, he moved to an apartment in the city. A simple place by Seattle standards, it was in an impressive barrio, according to Carmen. The lush greenery of Las Cañitas was incomparable, the land seemingly infinite, but the need to stretch his meager savings meant that his apartment could have doubled as a dorm room. But Carmen didn't seem to mind.

He wouldn't let her clean, no matter how much she insisted on it, and he only sometimes let her cook. But even that was because he had a limited repertoire and she turned her nose up at his American dishes. Mike bought creams and lotions for her scars whenever he went grocery shopping and listened to stories of life growing up in Bolivia while she stuffed him with *pique macho*, *salteñas*, or *locro*—a stew that she loved but he didn't particularly care for. It turned out that she could get him to eat just about anything, including the *aka cuy* that turned out to be guinea-pig.

She was beautiful. Not in that obvious, erection-inducing way, but in subtle, less dramatic variations. He saw it in her smile and heard it in her laugh. Anyone who smiled like that when they spoke of family had to be good, had to be all heart. Which was all the more reason for him to keep his distance.

Mike continued to write angry letters, expanding his audience, going deep for complaints. Angry, stupid things to a father who preferred his younger son, to a mother who always thought of John as handsome, but never him. He said snake-like things to a grandmother who had nothing but disappointment for him, vitriol for a sister who thought him slime. But when Mike turned the page to give his Uncle Daichi a piece of the act, he found he had to grapple for something to say. Here was a man who had paid his tuition, room and board, leaving him to bartend only when he needed spending money. Here was a man who was slicing and curt, but in equal turns to his sons and nephew. He had dealt him an even hand, his whole life, without Mike ever realizing it. Still, Mike raised his pen, concentrated, but ran dry on words to say.

He set the pen aside and sighed.

"What is it?" Carmen said.

On turning, he found her folding a stack of his t-shirts so sharply she creased them. Mike rose and took them from her.

"You're not my maid," he said, and hurled the clothes into a cheap dresser drawer.

She slammed both wrinkled hands into her lap, like a child deprived of some toy.

"I have to earn my keep, Michael. You cannot pay me what you do and require nothing of me."

"I require plenty of you," he said and tore up his letters. "Your company, for instance."

"And if I tell my father that, he'll think I'm a whore. Already, he thinks you are a wealthy American who has secured me my own accommodations. Constantly, I am asked to accept visitors."

He swiveled to face her. "Is that what you want? Your own place?"

Carmen rolled her eyes as if he were an idiot, before rising and venturing to the window.

"You can't afford it, Michael. And I haven't earned it."

He studied the tenseness that held her taut as a stretched coil.

"You're unhappy," he said. He wished she'd just tell him how to fix that.

"Why do you write?" she said. "You write to people who never read the letters. You maintain a cell phone but never make a call. Why do you run from your American life? Why do you no longer want a woman? Who has hurt you so?"

He sighed. It wasn't as if he never expected her to ask. He supposed he'd been lucky she delayed so long.

"I hurt myself," he said. "By falling in love with the wrong woman." He shook his head, needing to get the story right. "I fell in love with the idea of this woman, not her. She was my cousin's wife."

Carmen gasped.

"The two of you did not…"

Mike laughed bitterly. "No, although I would have. She loves my cousin very much. Me? Not so much."

"You are not hers to love," Carmen said, drawing up indignant. "Nor is she yours to love that way."

Mike turned from her, scalded. This had been his confession, delivered too soon. He hadn't told her in order to earn a lecture. He didn't even know why he'd told her, but whatever the reason, it wasn't for the look of superiority she gave him.

"You said you loved…the idea of her. What does this mean?"

"Nothing. Forget it. Go fold something."

Seconds passed where the weight of conviction bore down on him.

"Carmen, I'm sorry," he said.

She went in the drawer and retrieved his t-shirts robotically, folding them with twice the force and twice the amount of creases.

FOR A WEEK they said nothing to each other, beyond the pleasantries necessary to get through a day in close proximity. She went out to see her family when he had no tasks for her and she attended mass every day. He imagined the services at the glorious cathedral to which she walked to be as tedious as the Methodist ones he remembered growing up. The erratic times she returned must have meant that her priest rambled the way his used to about the second coming of the Lord. Christ was on his way during every commercial break if you let some people tell it.

They spent a week not speaking to each other before he asked her out to dinner. She accepted as if it wasn't in her powers to reject. They walked to a nearby steakhouse where they gorged on Argentinean beef and drained a bottle and a half bottle of local vintage wine before strolling the streets for fresh air. When she slipped her arm into the crook of his, Mike looked down in surprise but said nothing. They hadn't spoken all evening.

She was beauty itself. A simple, South American beauty who'd spent her life in the sun. Her skin blazed with bronze life and the smile she deprived him of spoke of happiness. Her full figure did more for him each day.

So, he wasn't surprised when he stopped her beneath an acacia and brought his lips to hers. Mike only found surprise when she responded, wrapping her arms around his neck and pressing soft to hard against him.

One kiss. One indulgence. It was all he would permit.

Still, he thought with a meteoric grin, it was a start.

A start to a life all his own.

CHAPTER
sixty-five

TAK AND DEENA FLEW HOME at the end of their second week in Curaçao. The next day, they were to pick up her mother, lodged in a hotel on the beach until they moved her to what would be her new home. Lizzie, who had no interest in seeing the woman ever, refused to even discuss picking her up. She could "climb into a dumpster," as far as her youngest daughter was concerned. Likewise, Gloria Hammond's grandchildren elected not to see her, leaving just Tak, Deena, and a few thousand contradictory emotions for the journey.

Morning came. When it did, Deena recognized its arrival, not through the usual presence of sun rays insistent on their beam into her room, but with the shrill of an alarm clock on the nightstand. Bleary eyed, she nudged Tak, who shot an arm out from beneath bedding to paw blindly at the offending object. Only when he upended it, did he manage a peek through one eye.

"Time," he demanded.

"Morning. Time for dear old mother."

He sat up. Looked her over.

"Baby, if you don't want to go, I'll pick her up. I'll explain the apartment to her. When you're ready—if you're ready—then you can go see her. No pressure."

He meant it. That tender, protective gaze said he did, as did that little way he rubbed her hand, as if he didn't even know he was doing it.

"No," Deena said. "I need to do this. We should do this."

It was a milestone for her, for them. They would conquer it, whatever the hell that meant.

Tak dressed in a pale blue button up and dark, close fitting jeans. Both emphasized the ropy sinew of a lean body. Deena decided on a teal, pleated sundress and strappy sandals, and was halfway through her makeup regimen before the likeness to her mother in the mirror made her pause. Eyes, nose, mouth, chin, all compact and exacting in their replication.

But she was okay with that.

"Ready?" Tak prompted from behind her.

"Ready or not," Deena said and stepped away from the mirror.

They took the Range Rover to her mother's hotel. Once there, Deena sat, hands in her lap for the drive, mind a myriad of thoughts, mouth dry and useless.

Vestiges of the sun peeked out from behind silver-lined clouds just as Tak parked in one of the designated slots.

Deena closed her eyes and tried to remember something about her mother besides murder, hatred, hurt.

Meatballs came to mind.

"Deena, not so large. Your father'll choke on them, for sure."

Deena's mother grabbed the half dozen chunks of ground beef gathered in the massive plastic bowl next to her daughter. Deftly, she broke off small portions, marrying a few to create another half dozen.

"But I like them large," Deena insisted.

"You like to have your way," her mother said. "But I've already told you how it'll be."

Deena's lip touted out. She refused to mold another ball.

"Sing for me, pumpkin," her mother said brightly.

Deena shook her head, knowing it to be her attempt at a truce. Everyone knew how she loved singing.

Her mother shrugged as if it made no difference to her, before hurling herself into a tuneless, rhythmless, and hip rocking number of her own creation. Fingers covered in threads of raw meat mixture, she threatened to smear it on Deena's face as she sang her horrible tune. Deena jerked and bobbed and swatted, laughter choking her as she dived. On recognizing the old reggae tune her mother made an unintentional mockery of—it was one of her father's favorites—Deena chimed in, mock accent absurd, annoyance with her mother forgotten.

She remembered joy. Joy buffeting on the winds of time, joy that felt timelessly shrouded in hugs, kisses, comfort. She remembered a mother who sung horribly, danced worse, and promised to love her eternally.

That was the woman they went to get.

"I'm terrified of saying something stupid," Tak said. "But I—I want to say something meaningful."

Deena slipped her hand into his.

"You just did," she said and kissed his cheek.

Her mother emerged from the hotel.

She stood taller without her shackles, lighter, thinner. Yet, she was somehow not Deena's mother without them and absolutely her at the same time. Clad in a simple white t-shirt and plain blue Wranglers, she crossed the parking lot in wide, sweeping strides, as if afraid to look back, to go back.

Deena climbed from the vehicle.

Her mother's face transformed at the sight of her, a cloud of doubt disappearing in the place of unfettered hopefulness, before she checked it, burying it deep.

"Nice car," she said instead. When Deena didn't answer, her mother squinted up at the sun. "I'm still getting used to it. I can't remember that thing being so bright."

"Have you not been…out?" Deena said. The woman had a South Beach room with an oceanfront view.

Her mother shook her head. "Television and room service. It hasn't got old."

Deena stared at her, willing her mouth to produce words.

"We should go," she said. "I have…things to do."

She had nothing to do, except stop her hands from shaking and get her mother to the apartment in her name that she knew nothing about.

The two women headed for the car. Tak bounded out and opened the doors. Gloria blinked her surprise.

"Takumi," he announced breathlessly. "Your son-in-law. Your...son."

Her mother's face split wide in a grin. "I know who you are. You're stunningly handsome, too."

Tak stood up straighter at the compliment, noted Deena's smirk and deflated.

He held his mother-in-law's hand to help her with the climb.

"It's high," he warned. "Be careful."

Deena caught his wrist after he slammed her door.

"You're...interesting," she said.

Tak studied her face.

"I'd like to know the woman responsible for giving me my wife and my brother his. So much traces back to her, you know? I guess I'm just...grateful."

He hesitated on the verge of more, before tucking words away with a kiss to her forehead.

Grateful. She turned the word around and examined it.

Once they were all in, they took off—not toward home, but toward the apartment they'd secured for Deena's mother.

They would have her in a place of her own, close enough that they could drive and see her with ease, but not so close that an unexpected bus ride would bring her to them. They would give her a living allowance and cover all her expenditures. They explained this on the ride over and fell into silence when she didn't respond.

"The grandchildren," she said. "Lizzie."

Deena's hand, nestled under Tak's as he drove, shifted into a fist. Her exhale came out as a shudder. She took her time responding.

"They don't want to see you now. When that changes, one of us will let you know."

Again, silence filled the cabin.

"And you?" she said. "Do you want to see me again?"

That wasn't the question she wanted to answer.

So, she didn't.

Deena owed her life to this woman. Not just because she had nursed her in her womb and given birth to her, but because she had traded her freedom for her daughter's safety. Some might say it was something that any mother would have done, but Deena knew better. People sold their children for drugs, for money, or turned their backs on them in cowardice. Her mother had killed the man she loved to protect her children, knowing they would hate her for it.

Long ago, Deena stopped tormenting herself with the question of whether she could do the same. No answer she came up with left her anywhere close to sane. When she rode the endless merry-go-round of torment that question gave her, Tak would remind her that she shouldn't even ask it, that it was unfair. That question was born of a life filled with deliberate choices and expected consequences. Her mother chose to marry and stay married to a drug dealer.

Life, Deena knew, came down to choices not circumstances.

Her mother's life, her brother's, Tony's life, and hers. All of it had been dictated by the choices they'd made.

A fitting thought, Deena realized, as they prepared to renew their vows.

A fitting thought, Deena realized, for the moment Tak's hand slipped into hers.

Forever.

That was the choice she'd made.

To spend forever with him.

ABOUT THE AUTHOR

Shewanda Pugh's a tomboy who's been writing romance since an inappropriate age. While she's been shortlisted for a few awards and snagged a bestsellers list or two, there's nothing she enjoys more than hearing from her readers.

In another life, she earned a BA from Alabama A&M University and an MA in Writing from Nova Southeastern University. Though a hardcore native of Boston, MA, she now lives in Miami, FL, where she sulks in the sunshine, guzzles coffee, and puzzles over her next novel.

BOOKS BY SHEWANDA PUGH

Love Edy
Bittersweet (Love Edy Book Two)
Wrecked (Love Edy Book Three)
Love Edy Four (Forthcoming)

Crimson Footprints
Crimson Footprints II: New Beginnings
Crimson Footprints III: The Finale

Sign up at
http://ShewandaPugh.blogspot.com
for email updates on new releases.

If you enjoyed this book, please consider leaving a review.
This author appreciates even a few words.

www.ingramcontent.com/pod-product-compliance
Lightning Source LLC
Chambersburg PA
CBHW050905250626
47155CB00001B/109